BOUND

ALSO BY SALLY GUNNING

The Widow's War

BOUND

SALLY GUNNING

WILLIAM MORROW

An Imprint of HarperCollins*Publishers*

This book is a work of fiction. The characters, incidents, and dialogue are drawn from the author's imagination and are not to be construed as real. Any resemblance to actual events or persons, living or dead, is entirely coincidental.

FIRST EDITION

Designed by Cassandra J. Pappas

Library of Congress Cataloging-in-Publication Data

Gunning, Sally.
   Bound : a novel / Sally Gunning. — 1st ed.
     p. cm.
    ISBN 978-0-06-124025-6
    1. Massachusetts—History—Colonial period, ca. 1600–1775—Fiction.
2. Indentured servants—Fiction.   3. Cape Cod (Mass.)—Fiction. I. Title.
PS3607. U548B68 2008
813'. 6—dc22

                    2007029785

08 09 10 11 12 WBC/RRD 10 9 8 7 6 5 4 3 2 1

For Tom. What Abigail said.

Humanity obliges us to be affected with the distresses and Miserys of our fellow creatures. Friendship is a band yet stronger, which causes us to feel with greater tenderness the afflictions of our Friends.

And there is a tye more binding than Humanity, and stronger than Friendship, which makes us anxious for the happiness and welfare of those to whom it binds us. It makes their Misfortunes, Sorrows and afflictions, our own. Unite these, and there is a threefold cord—by this cord I am not ashamed to own myself bound.

—Abigail Adams, 1763

ACKNOWLEDGMENTS

The historical references needed for this book came my way through the gracious help of Kathleen Remillard and Nina Gregson at Brewster Ladies Library, Suzanne Foster and Teresa Lamperti at Brewster Historical Society, Lucy Loomis at Sturgis Library, Mary Sicchio at Cape Cod Community College, Elizabeth Bouvier at the Massachusetts Supreme Judicial Court, Jennifer Fauxsmith at the Massachusetts Archives, and Stephen Farrar, archival consultant for *History Preserved,* who donated his time on behalf of Barnstable Historical Society.

My brother David Carlson reminded me about the "white slaves." Susan Carrick sent a valuable article from *The Highlander* on the "Scottish Slaves." Author Evan J. Albright shared some useful resources on colonial crimes and misdemeanors. Captain Steven Brown and Rusty Rice answered any number of annoying questions during a thrilling sail on the Revolutionary-era sloop *Providence.* Maureen Leavenworth taught me to cook over an eighteenth-century open hearth at the 1772 Caleb Nickerson House in Chatham. Heather Mangelinkx of Kristal Sunnyside Wools in Brewster shared her sheep as well as her spinning skills and threw in some extra-yard research in response to the question "how many bags full?" Susan Kelley took time out of her duties at the 1736 Josiah Dennis Manse in Dennis to demonstrate the great wheel. Jennifer Leaning and Ruth Barron assisted with the medical issues. Ellen Davies helped me sort out seating arrangements in an eighteenth-century church. Arlyn Whitelaw went above and beyond and then kept on going, unraveling the legal knots over a span of three centuries.

My agent, Andrea Cirillo, saw everything I didn't and was, as usual, always there when I needed her. My editor, Jennifer Brehl, simply put, made it better. Associate editor Kate Nintzel made it happen. Publicists Dee Dee DeBartlo and Seale Ballenger fueled me with their enthusiasm. My family of readers, Jan Carlson, Nancy Carlson, John Leaning, and Carol Appleton, provided the ever-important early insight and encouragement. My husband, Tom, did all of the above and everything else, many times over.

My heartfelt thanks to all.

BOUND

ONE

March 1756

For a time Alice remembered the good and forgot the bad, but after a while she remembered the bad and then had to forget everything to get rid of it; when it came back it came back in bits, like the pieces in a month-old stew—all the same gray color and smelling like sick, not one thing whole in the entire kettle.

First was the ship. Alice had lived her first seven years of life in London before she got aboard the ship, and if she hadn't got aboard she imagined she might have remembered better those early years of her life, but the ship and what came after it took away all but a few brown heaps of London ash and dirt. She remembered helping her mother to hang the wash on the fence; she remembered learning to pump the foot wheel to twist fine linen fibers into thread; she remembered constantly sweeping lint and bark and wood chips from under her father's bootheels as he sat and smoked and talked about the ship.

It seemed to Alice that her father talked about the ship a long time before they ever got on it. Alice's two older brothers joined in with excited jabber about great stiff sails, sturdy beams, and wide, salted oceans, but Alice watched her mother's face and stayed quiet. Her mother's face had clouded at the word *ship* and stayed so through all her father's and brothers' happy clamor; Alice saw the face but didn't understand it. As her father described it, leaving two rooms full of smoke and damp for a fine house new-made by his own hand in a place called Philadelphia seemed to promise a life as big as the word. But after a time Alice stopped looking at her mother when her father and brothers began their talk of the ship, and when the cart finally came to collect them she was hanging on the windowsill in the same eagerness as her brothers.

Alice's mother held her tight on her lap through the whole cart ride; when they drew up onto the wharf and saw the ship looming in front of them, Alice's mother said, "Don't be afraid, Alice," but Alice wasn't. She squirmed out of her mother's quivering fingers and chased after her brothers up the gangway. The deck of the ship seemed nothing but a large, fenced yard covered with boards, except that it groaned and creaked and swayed back and forth like the pendulum on a clock she had once seen at the magistrate's.

A man wearing both hat and kerchief on his head led them down a narrow, laddered passage into what he called the "'tween decks"; there Alice entertained herself looking at strange faces and listening to strange tongues as her mother hung a curtain around a row of bunks no wider than a set of dough trays. Alice had only just sorted the people around her into families when the tramp of feet overhead grew louder and the creaking and groaning of the ship grew stronger. The deck below her feet began to slant, a little and then a little more, and a collection of cries sprung up around them: "We're away! We sail!"

A small child wailed. A woman. Another. Alice looked at her mother and saw her eyes brim. Alice returned to her study of the oddly dressed, strangely gabbling people around her and felt herself well entertained until they began losing their stomachs.

Alice's mother was the first in their family to turn the color of paste and go up to the rail; by the time she returned, half a dozen small children had already washed the 'tween deck with their vomit. Alice's brothers went next, and last Alice, too sick to notice anything around her; when she returned below, the boards beneath her feet had already turned slick, the air sour and rancid, and the strange families that had amused Alice not long before now seemed too close, too loud, too familiar.

After a time Alice's mother couldn't raise herself to climb the companionway to the deck, and Alice, who had stopped getting sick first, was assigned to run up and down with the bucket. Her first trip above in health amazed her. She could look around her now and saw the sails were indeed great and stiff as her brothers had said, the beams indeed sturdy, the ocean indeed wider than anything Alice had ever seen or imagined. The air off the deck felt like a cool, damp hand on Alice's hot forehead; she breathed it in as far as it would go and held on to it through her return below as long as she was able.

With each trip above Alice noticed that the wind blew harder, which Alice's father told her was a good thing because it would push them faster to Philadelphia, but Alice thought it good because it built white-topped mountains out of flat seawater and crashed them on deck in great snow showers. But after a time Alice's father took the bucket from her and wouldn't let her go on the deck anymore; she heard him whisper to her mother of a young boy who had been swept overboard, to which Alice's mother replied, "Lucky boy," a remark Alice didn't understand and which her father wouldn't explain to her.

At last Alice's mother's stomach settled, but she began to run as if from a physic, and the brothers too, the stink of their running worse than the stink of the vomit. Alice begged to go out on the deck and cried, which only caused her father to slap her and tell her to go clean up her brothers, so she gave up crying. By now Alice felt well enough to be quite hungry, but the meat they gave her to eat was so salted that she was in great thirst every minute and the water so black and thick she didn't like to drink it.

There came a row of days of much the same grayness, where it seemed that everyone but Alice and her father lay sick and moaning, but after a time a few of the men began to raise themselves, and the talk began, at first in a low rumble and then in something louder, with shouting in it. Alice strayed close enough to listen and learned that the wind had come around from the wrong direction, blowing so hard that the captain had ordered the crew to take down sail, which made them drift far off their course for Philadelphia. Some of the men wanted to turn back to London but some didn't, and Alice's father finally shouted at them that they might as well stop jawing because the captain wasn't going to turn around on account of a few days' short rations. It was true that the salt meat had run out, but Alice didn't mind because her tongue and lips had begun to blister from it and even though the biscuit they gave her had bugs in it that she had to pick out and snap between her fingers.

Alice's mother was the first to get fevered; she moaned and called out whenever the waves smashed the ship and knocked her about. One of the men yelled at Alice's father to shut her up, and Alice's father hit the man in the face, so other men had to push Alice's father to the ground until he quieted. The brothers' fevers came on next, one fast upon the other, but they made no noise at all, which disturbed Alice as much as her mother's cries.

After a time a surgeon traveling in one of the above cabins came down into the 'tween decks with some bottles of medicine; Alice's father took out his money pouch and bought a bottle of it; the next day he bought another, but it didn't help them. The following day he paid the surgeon to bleed Alice's mother and brothers, but that didn't help them, either.

Alice's mother died first. Alice's father carried her up the companionway, telling Alice to stay with her brothers, but Alice followed her father and watched from the hatchway as a sailor with a missing finger and one with a broken tooth took her mother out of her father's arms and threw her overboard into the water.

After that Alice's father grew quiet; Alice had to tell him when her brothers died, near together, two days after. Alice watched them go over the side too, imagining her mother catching them and calling them lucky boys as she'd called the boy who'd been swept overboard near the start of the voyage.

Another long, gray period dropped down until a morning when a great disturbance woke her from sleep; she opened her eyes to see people sick and well laughing and shouting and pushing for the companionway. "'Tis land!" "Land sighted!"

Alice and her father went up on deck with all the others; after a time Alice saw a flat, brown crescent dotted with low hills and a smattering of little steeples, but everyone cried with joy at the sight of it, except her father, who cried but did not look joyful in it. Alice didn't feel like crying, but neither did she feel joyful, so she stood silent and clung to the rail, peering over at what she had thought was Philadelphia but soon learned was someplace else called Boston.

The ship sailed past many little islands into the harbor, toward the brown crescent, which Alice could now see was rimmed by buildings, little dots of things, nothing like the walls of brick and stone that framed the river at London. A smaller boat rowed out to meet them, and the ship was towed until it could be tied up snug against a long wharf that stuck out deep into the water. The captain shouted the sailors into lines to fold the sails while Alice busied herself watching the carts and carriages and people moving along the wharf, trying to find out if these people were different from the ones in London.

After a time Alice's father took her hand and led her back to the companionway. Down below, one of the ship's men walked among the passengers too sick to go on deck and wrote things in a log; quite often someone would shout weakly at him but he never shouted back, only answering in a flat voice before moving to the next person. Alice's father stood for some time in silence, watching the man, and then dropped Alice's hand. "I must go talk with that fellow. Put our things together, Alice."

Alice changed her dirty shift for one that was a little cleaner; she put on the least worn of her two dresses and packed the other things in the trunk on top of her mother's shoes and stockings and shawl, which her father had removed before he'd seen her into the water. She added the pair of pewter mugs and plates, the three blankets, her father's tobacco pouch, and some papers he'd been looking at before land had been sighted. She watched her father as he talked to the man; she could hear her father's voice well enough, but not the man's quiet answers. She moved closer.

"Like I told you," the man said. "Dead after half the voyage still means full fare."

"The girl's but seven."

"Seven's still half fare."

"Then I'd like you to tell me what surgeon charges ten shillings for a bloody bottle of piss and a bleeding I'd have done better with a marlin spike!"

"That you take up with the surgeon."

The man walked off. Alice's father returned to Alice. He looked at the air above her a long time, but after a time he drew his eyes down and took her in from top to bottom, as if he weren't sure how

6

she'd happened to come along on the ship with him. He said, "Wash your face. Comb your hair. Brush up that dress and stay here till I collect you." He disappeared up the companionway.

Alice did as her father said; as she waited for him to return she looked around and noticed others doing much as her father had told her to do. A mother spit on the corner of her skirt and rubbed her wasted children's faces; a near-grown girl yanked a comb through a smaller girl's hair; a girl Alice's age picked at a crust on the seat of her brother's breeches.

Alice's father came back and kicked the trunk. Alice remembered that—he kicked the trunk—but she couldn't remember that he said any words to her. Later she thought there were some words she'd forgotten; later again she thought there were no words whatever. He took her hand, led her up on deck to a line of worn-down, bleached-out passengers, and pushed her onto the end of it. After a time a stream of finely dressed men and ladies walked up the gangway and down the line of passengers, looking them over with what seemed to Alice an odd amount of interest. One lady stopped at Alice and felt her arm. A gentleman told her to open her mouth. Another lifted her skirt. One man with a locked knee asked Alice's age and then moved off, so Alice didn't think of him any more than another, but after a time he came back and asked if Alice's father was her father, and when her father said he was, the man asked him a lot of questions, which Alice's father answered in a high, tight voice Alice hadn't heard in him before. *She's the healthiest on the whole ship, as you can see for yourself, sir. She's quick and she's good behaved, and she can spin and use a tape loom, if someone sets the web for her. She'll not give you a sorry day, I promise you that, sir.*

The man with the locked knee waved Alice's father out of the line, and they disappeared into the after cabin. When they returned, Alice's father had a paper in his hand, which he folded and pushed into his money pouch. He tied the pouch around Alice's neck. "You're to live with Mr. Morton now. Do as he tells you. Remember God. And keep hold of that paper."

Mr. Morton took Alice's hand and led her to the gangway. "Grab onto the rope, child. Watch your feet." Alice grabbed onto the rope and watched her feet, but once she landed on the dock she twisted around, looking for her father. Mr. Morton pulled her along, but she continued to twist, looking over the feeble string of passengers stumbling onto the wharf, not finding her father in them. Mr. Morton led her to a dusty carriage and boosted her into the seat; from there Alice had a better view and after a time she spied her father pushing their trunk into the back of a rough wagon. He climbed in after the trunk; three other men Alice recognized from the ship climbed in after him; the wagon clattered into the road heading into the sun so that the wagon and the men became nothing but a sharp black lump against the sky. Mr. Morton moved his carriage into the road and moved off with the sun behind him.

TWO

The paper Alice's father hung around her neck read:

This indenture made the twentieth day of May one thousand seven hundred fifty-six between John Morton of Dedham in the County of Suffolk on the one part and Simeon Cole of London in the County of Middlesex on the other part that the said Simeon Cole has bound and does hereby bind minor child Alice Cole his daughter to any lawful work for and to reside with the said John Morton until the twenty-first day of March one thousand seven hundred and sixty-seven at which time said minor child will have reached the age of eighteen years during which time said John Morton covenants to use all means in his power to provide for said Alice Cole suitable boarding lodging clothing and such attendance as necessary to her comfortable support in sickness and in health and further shall cause her to be taught to read her Bible as she is capable and the said John Morton shall furnish her with two good sets of clothes at such time as her term of indenture shall be canceled.

The paper had been signed by John Morton and Simeon Cole. John Morton began his name with a wavering, feathery spiral. Simeon Cole began his with a thick, sideways wave. When Alice first took the paper out to look at it, the spiral and the wave were all she could make of it, although she ran her fingers over the rest of the letters many times.

At first the Morton household contained Mr. Morton and Mrs. Morton, a son nearing manhood named Elisha, and one daughter three years older than Alice named Abigail whom they called Nabby. Mr. Morton was the one with the locked knee, but Mrs. Morton was the one always in bed with an ail, which she put sometimes to her lungs and sometimes to her stomach. A tall, bony Negro named Jerubah tended Mrs. Morton and ordered the kitchen, working her tasks in dark silence, but the girl Nabby chattered and bounced from one piece of work to another without a care for what was left to Alice to finish. Alice didn't mind the girl's chatter—in fact she took great interest in it—and Alice didn't mind the work, as it was much the same as the work she had done alongside her mother back in London: beating, bleaching and boiling clothes, sanding floors, oiling woodwork, spinning, weeding, and picking the garden; but now Alice worked under a new kind of sky that might shed bright sun and thick snow in a single day, or remain all sun or all snow for weeks together. And space! So much space! The land ran like the ocean, wave after wave of it, and off into a distance nothing but more waves, until it faded into a soft green haze.

Alice hadn't been very long at the Mortons when Mrs. Morton died of something to do with neither her lungs nor her stomach, and the son, Elisha, married and left to settle in the westward part of the colony. With each change in the household the work changed, perhaps less washing but more spinning, or less cleaning and more weeding, but it didn't matter to Alice what kind of work it was—it took up all the daylight hours no matter what it was made of.

Mr. Morton saw to it that Alice was fed, clothed, and attended in illness as her paper demanded, and himself taught her to read, remarking many times on her quickness. By her eighth birthday Alice could read the paper that still hung around her neck, and she had stopped going to the window to look for her father in any of the wagons that rumbled along the road. By Alice's ninth birthday she was reading to Mr. Morton out of Pope and Dryden and had come to understand her life as made up of two parts, divided by the paper. Taken together she didn't think of the second part as greatly worse than the other. Mr. Morton called her his "sweet, good girl," sat her next to Nabby at table, and quizzed them out of the Bible together. He smiled at her and patted her cheek each time he passed her in the house or yard and only struck her when she dropped an onion soup in his lap or tipped his pipe into the fire or scorched his stock with the iron.

Nabby Morton in her turn treated Alice as one might treat a younger sister, or a younger sister as Alice had been taught it by her brothers, which meant she was to follow around when allowed and keep away when she wasn't, yet with Nabby it also meant that when she wanted someone to share a stolen pie or run bare-legged in the creek in the heat of summer it was Alice she called, and when she needed to cry over her mother, she did it into Alice's apron.

That didn't mean that Alice forgot her old family altogether. After the day of the spilled soup Alice curled up in the bed she shared with Jerubah, closed her eyes, and conjured up a big, new house in Philadelphia, with her mother in a blue dress trimmed with lace just like a favorite dress of Mrs. Morton's. She dreamed her father came in from work to smile at her and pat her cheek and give her an orange.

On Alice's arrival at Mr. Morton's he had offered to keep her indenture paper safe for her in a drawer in a desk in his study, but as Alice's father had told her to keep hold of it, she'd been loath to give it over. As time went on, however, and as repeated reading of the paper told her nothing more of her father's whereabouts, and as she remembered nothing more of her mother than a pair of limp feet dangling from sharp-boned ankles as she went over the ship's rail into the water, the cord around her neck began to chafe more than it comforted.

At Alice's tenth birthday Mr. Morton called her into his study and gave her a twopence; Alice put it in her father's money pouch and at the same time took out the indenture paper, giving it to Mr. Morton to lock up in his drawer.

Alice didn't see the paper again until the year she turned fifteen and Mr. Morton gave her to Nabby on the occasion of Nabby's marriage to Emery Verley of Medfield.

THREE

April 1764

A lice carried her workbasket to the cart, stepped wide of the cow already tied behind, and attempted to wedge the basket between the linen trunk and the washtub, but she felt no great confidence in its purchase. The workbasket had been given to her by Mrs. Morton, already filled with her own scissors and pins and needles, and Alice didn't wish to lose it in the road or dislodge any of its contents. She took the basket out, climbed onto the cart beside Verley's Negro, George, clutched it tight in her lap, and waited. Nabby Morton, or Nabby Verley since the night before, wouldn't get in the carriage ahead; her new husband had to get down out of his seat to collect her.

"Come, Nabby, before you kiss all the hair off your father's head. Mr. Morton, sir, you must shoo her away or we'll not get to Medfield by sunset."

Nabby rubbed at her eyes and ran her thumbs over her father's wet cheeks to dry them. The father's and daughter's tears caused a bad effect in Alice; she dashed at her own eyes, and the movement brought Mr. Morton's attention, causing him to untangle himself from his daughter and approach the cart.

"My sweet, good girl. My pretty girl. You'll sit in my heart always, next to my daughter's place there. God bless you, child." He turned to his daughter. "Nabby, you see the example you set for Alice? Stop your tears and obey your husband. Get into the carriage."

Nabby went to the carriage and climbed in; Mr. Morton began a lock-kneed step toward his daughter for one final word, but Verley had already flicked his horse into motion, and the carriage pulled away. The cart lurched after, full of the washtubs, churns, cheese molds, iron kettles, and trunks of linens that, including Alice and the cow, were all part of Nabby's marriage portion from her father. Mr. Morton didn't attempt a final word for Alice, which Alice was glad of, because she still found herself in a state of some disturbance.

Alice had been in a state of disturbance for the fortnight past, ever since she'd been handed the new paper that transferred her remaining time from the father to the daughter. The disturbance came from the fact that she couldn't feel the same way two minutes in a row about her change in circumstance; one minute she felt the wrench of leaving Mr. Morton and what she knew of home, the next minute she found herself caught up in the excitement of Nabby's prospects.

When Alice had first seen Emery Verley's well-formed features and the fine set of his coat she had thought there was little to be done in the way of physically improving him; he had turned away from Mr. Morton's hearth, spied Alice, and given her a little bow—a bow, to Alice—and from there she'd found little to fault in him altogether. A fortnight after the intentions had been published Alice had lifted a carelessly set latch and walked into the supposed empty front room to find Nabby spread-legged under Verley's dropped breeches, but when

Alice carried Nabby's water to her chamber later that night and found the girl in a cascade of giggles over the adventure, Alice had decided it cast no great mark against the suitor. Add to it that Verley was already set up with a sawmill and good-size farm in Medfield, and Alice could only look ahead with her own share of enthusiasm toward the venture.

Their arrival at Medfield added no discouragement to Alice's outlook. True, her first look at the village included a black swamp and ugly potash works, but the cart and carriage took them safely beyond, turning along a pretty stretch of river that ended at a well-kept orchard and a pasture speckled with livestock. The house sat back handsomely on a gentle rise of land, the front door boasting its prosperity with both paint and knocker; a fresh-turned garden framed the back door, and the hens charged fat and thick around Alice's feet as she stepped down from the cart, still holding firm to her workbasket.

The keeping room looked bare compared to Mr. Morton's, but of course it sat in wait for Nabby's collection of goods, still piled outside in the cart. The other rooms were more fully fitted, and Alice liked the weight of the furnishings, as if promising they wouldn't soon be shifted. She especially liked the little room in the lean-to at the back that was to be hers alone, a thing she hadn't had at Mr. Morton's. She also liked it that she was included at the supper table, just as she had been at Mr. Morton's; she further liked it that supper wasn't just bread and cheese and beer but apple tart and candied plums and seedcake. Above it all, she liked it that Verley lifted his glass to Nabby and then to Alice and said, "To my new family!"

Alice went to bed that night with only one brief, low thought for Mr. Morton, and fell into the restless sleep that excess excitement often caused in her, coming half awake at the sound of the lifting latch, coming fully awake at the sight of Verley's gold hair glinting above his candle.

He came to the bed and stood over her, wearing nothing but his shirt, hanging loose to his knees. He held the candle high. He said, "Well, now, my pretty Alice, let me see just what we've got here," and before Alice could understand his presence or his words he set the candle on the floor, pulled down her blanket, pulled her shift over her head, and pressed himself on top of her. When Alice cried out his hand came across her throat, cutting off air with sound, and that soon became the worst of it—not the pain below but the suffocation above. After a time Verley made a sound like a log falling off a fire and pulled himself away. He stood up, reached down, and picked up the candle. He said, "Not a word of this to my wife, Alice; if you try it I'll simply counter that I came to your room because I heard a noise and caught you bedding young Sherbourne, the smith's apprentice. You might imagine who she'll believe. Then, of course, I'll be forced to add a year to your time for fornication. Or I might have to sell you to Old Peters at the tar pit. He has one eye and the breath of a corpse and he likes to puncture you in odd places. Boys or girls, it makes no matter to him. Should you like to go to Old Peters, Alice?"

Alice shook her head.

"Good girl, then." He raised the candle, swept it over her. He said, "Oh, you are a lovely thing, aren't you, Alice?"

FOUR

lice would have said she never slept if the sound of the crow hadn't so startled her. She opened her eyes and saw the first graying of the sky; with it came the first gray uncertainty. Had she dreamed it? As she eased her feet to the floor she felt the burn between her legs and thought no, it had been no dream, but even as she thought it she began to search for other reasons for the soreness. The long, rough cart ride. An early onset of her courses. Irritation from the stiff, new linens. Yes, a nightmare, surely. But how real it seemed! And how could she know such a thing in order to dream it? Was it from seeing Nabby and Verley in the front room at Morton's? Might she have gone to bed full of thoughts of the reenactment going at that moment, and at no great distance? Might she, indeed, have imagined herself in Nabby's place, and from such a sinful thought the nightmare had descended?

Such half-belief-half-disbelief allowed Alice's feet and hands to move, to take her skirt from the hook and collect her shoes and stockings from the floor, to dress herself and enter the keeping room to begin the morning ritual. The sight of the keeping room table reminded her of the comfortable supper the three of them had shared the night before, and gave even more weight to the idea of a nightmare. She removed the ashes from the fire, blew up the coals, fed in enough wood to get a blaze for the kettle, unwrapped and sliced the bread, and set the first slice on the toaster.

Nabby appeared from her brand-new marriage bed in such wide-mouthed cheer that Alice felt even more sure of her imaginings. But the minute Verley appeared she knew it had all been as real as he was, standing there smiling at her.

"Good morning, Alice," he said. "And how did you enjoy your first night in your new bed?"

Alice blushed and made no answer.

"Now look how you embarrass her!" Nabby said. "Don't tease my Alice."

Verley bowed an apology, and Alice marveled that only now could she see how the gesture mocked her. She marveled too that he could continue to smile at her. Alice felt the lock of that smile as she'd felt the lock of his hand at her throat, forcing her to draw breath as if through a cheesecloth; only when he'd finished his gill of cider and left for the sawmill did her breath come clear.

THE FIRST DAY at the Verley home was spent as many at Mr. Morton's had been, working side by side with Nabby to order the household. They shifted and unpacked trunks, brushed and aired clothes, set up her iron spiders and kettles. On this day, however, Alice's thoughts weighed as heavy as the work, and the only thing that kept her hands and feet in rhythm was her fear of drawing Nabby's suspicions. She didn't want a year added to her time. She didn't want to be sold to Old Peters at the tar pit.

Oddly, when Verley returned for supper that night, he seemed to take no notice of her, and Alice's spirits lifted. He made a fine fuss over Nabby, reading to her from the almanac after supper as she hemmed a curtain, getting up twice for no purpose but to drop a kiss on her hair or draw a finger across her sleeve. This last appeared to be the signal that he wished to retire; Nabby leaped up, all smiles and giggles, and followed him to the bedroom.

Alice finished the curtain hem, banked the fire, and went to her own room in some good hope that Verley had done with her, but she hadn't yet managed sleep when the latch lifted and he came exactly as he had the night before, standing over her in his shirt, holding his candle. Alice crabbed backward into the corner of her bed, against the wall.

"What's this, now?" Verley said. "You can't mean you're not glad to see me."

"I am not, sir!"

His hand snaked out, clipped her throat, and pushed her back against the wall she'd foolishly thought might be some help to her. "Now, Alice, why do you beat those lovely bird-wing lashes at me? Could it be you've not understood me? Or could it be you don't like your breath stopped? Very well, then, here's where we strike our bargain. I take my hand away and you lie quiet. You may nod your assent when you wish to breathe."

Alice nodded. The hand came away. Whether she wished to make noise or not, the sucking of air was all she could manage.

"So," he said. "You keep quiet. 'Tis a wise child you are, Alice," and he yanked her away from the wall by the ankles, pulled off her shift, and beat himself into her.

Afterward, as before, he held the candle high and looked her over. He said, "It would be a shame, indeed, to let Old Peters have you. Or did I mention the hot tar? It would do bad things to such a skin as yours. Very bad things, Alice."

OVER THE YEARS Alice's daydream of the house in Philadelphia had grown and expanded. Her mother had acquired more fine dresses; her father had brought her dolls as well as oranges; every night he pulled her onto his lap and held her tight while he listened to her recite her Bible passage. Even her brothers had grown kinder, sharing their books with her, showing her the pictures and even teaching her some of the words. That night Alice's dream changed again, the house changed; it sported a room just for Alice on the second floor, the window too high for anyone to climb up from out of doors, and the door locked with a big gold key that Alice kept on a cord around her neck. The house itself was surrounded by a high fence and a gate barred with a long, iron bolt; she and her mother spent their days behind the fence planting tall lilac bushes that twined together with long-thorned roses.

AT FIRST ALICE'S daytime hours appeared safe, as she and Nabby worked so often side by side there was little space for Verley to fit between them. Alice bore his nighttime intrusions buoyed by the hope that after a time he must surely grow tired of his little game with her, but instead of growing tired he grew bolder in the daytime, as if testing her will to keep silent: he grabbed her buttocks as she left the room just behind Nabby or thrust his fingers beneath her skirt as she leaned over him at table; once, with Nabby absorbed in cutting out a pattern in the front room, he followed Alice out to the barn and pushed her facedown across the feed bin. The rough head of a nail in the lid of the bin cut into Alice's cheek, and when Alice came inside Nabby said, "Good heaven, Alice! What have you done to yourself? You're bleeding all down your face!"

Now, Alice thought, now is the time to tell her, with the smith's apprentice hard at work at the forge, with Verley just taking his horse from the barn behind her. She said, "'Twasn't I did it," and readied to say more, but Nabby's eye had fallen to the damp stain on her skirt and come back up to her cheek, and there looked away.

It seemed to Alice that Nabby looked away from her many times more, but then came the day of the escaped mare. Verley was at the mill, and Nabby was first to see the horse through the keeping room window. "Alice!" she shrieked. "Come! The mare's got loose!" And she leaped out the door. Alice ran after her and they divided, Alice down the road behind the horse, Nabby striking out across the field to cut the horse off farther along the way. Nabby reached the fence, picked her skirt up to her waist, and flung herself over. She ran into the road, flapping her arms and shouting to turn the horse; it pivoted on its hind legs and ran straight at Alice, who in her surprise leaped back and turned the horse again, this time away from them both and into the neighbor's meadow. Alice and Nabby took after it, by now gasping like a pair of bellows, finally cornering the horse up against the neighbor's stone wall. Nabby whipped off her apron and tied one end around the horse's neck to lead it home, but there they collapsed together against the wall to collect their breath, and they began to laugh.

Oh, how good it felt—the laughing, the damp grass, the cool stones against her sweating back! And oh, how silly the horse looked in its apron! The laughter rose and rose, and burst, and turned wet, and dried away. They fell silent. Now, thought Alice, now I'll tell her, and she began to form up the words, thinking out which ones might work best to show Nabby who her husband was and that she must take them back to her father. She had the first words ready, but she felt she needed to give Nabby some kind of warning; she reached out and touched Nabby's arm.

Nabby leaped up and began pulling at the apron to start the horse back toward the barn. In a tight, fast run of words that left no room for Alice, Nabby began to talk of her husband. Her husband had bought her the mare. Her husband had just that week bought her a pair of silver hair combs. Her husband had declined to go to Boston for a lucrative trade because he couldn't bear to part from his bride so soon. She could not have asked for a finer husband.

Alice stayed silent.

Nabby said three other things to Alice in the course of that day: she'd oversugared the pudding; she'd put out the wrong plates; she'd raised too much dust with her broom.

THAT NIGHT ALICE heard husband and wife arguing in the study; when her own name rose up out of the noise, she made her way closer to the door to listen.

"Your father?" Verley said. "What the devil do you want to give her back to your father for?"

"I told you last week after my visit to him. He misses her terribly."

"No doubt. But he's missed his chance now."

"He would give us Jerubah instead. He wished to in the first place, but I begged for Alice. I now see the mistake I made."

"And what should I want with old Jerubah?"

"Why, she's not yet thirty. In three years Alice will have served her time and be gone; Jerubah we'd have forever. In truth, Emery, I'm not happy with Alice. Not happy at all. She's lazy and careless, and today she spoke to me most rudely."

"You would take one wrong word as an attempt on your life? I'll speak with the girl."

"I don't wish you to speak to her; I've already spoken to her and misliked her answers. Indeed, I fault my father for making such a fuss over her, sitting her at table and teaching her out of his books as if she were my sister. She's grown so bigheaded only he can manage her."

"Leave the girl to me. I'll set her right."

"I don't wish her set right, I wish her gone! She must go back to my father or be sold. I've decided."

The next words were said softer but pierced the air all the harder for it. "Perhaps you forget, my love, that what was yours became mine by law at the time of our marriage. 'Tis I who'll decide what's to be done with Alice."

Alice waited for Nabby's answer but heard none.

AFTER THE ARGUMENT in the study Verley changed the game. He stopped troubling to close the door. He spoke loud, laughed loud, grunted louder. One night he said, "You don't make a sound no matter what I do to you, do you, Alice?" And he picked up her hand and thrust it palm down into the flame of the candle.

That night Alice stopped dreaming of a house in Philadelphia and began dreaming of a high-walled ship sailing across a wild but sunlit ocean. Her father sailed the ship, pulling Alice between his knees and holding her warm and close as he steered; her mother and her brothers had become odd, finned creatures, half human, half dolphin, who swam around in the water and leaped out of the wake to smile at her.

TWO DAYS LATER, with Nabby not ten paces away setting candles in the front room, Verley pulled Alice onto his marriage bed and drove himself into her. No matter how quiet Alice chose to be Verley made his own kind of noise, too much noise, or so it seemed until footsteps approached the door and Alice saw—no, felt—the surge of excitement in Verley; there Alice understood it. Verley wanted Nabby to hear. He wanted her to see. He had grown bored with his quiet wife and his quiet Alice; he would test them each against the length of her separate chain, forged by her separate contract. But good, thought Alice. *Good.* Because Nabby had now seen for herself what her husband was; now she would take them away from there.

ALL THE WAY through supper Alice watched Nabby for a sign. They must wait for the right time, of course: after Verley had paid his visit to Alice, after he had returned to his room and fallen asleep. That was how Alice would do it. But after supper Verley went off to his study with his bottle of Madeira, and Nabby declared illness and went to her bed. Was the illness a ruse? Alice couldn't determine. She cleared away the supper and put the beans to soak for morning, listening for sounds of Nabby stirring, perhaps secretly packing, but she heard only Verley, leaving the study and going outside; soon after she heard the horse pounding out of the yard and down the road. *Now*, Alice thought. *Now.* And yes, she'd barely drawn up the thought in full when Nabby appeared in the kitchen.

"Where's he gone?"

"I don't know."

"You don't know? *You don't know?* Is that how you talk to me? What of 'I don't know, *madam?*' Do you think yourself the equal of me? Is that what you think, Alice?"

"No, madam."

Nabby lifted her hand, drew it back, and slapped Alice hard across her face. She dashed to the fire and grabbed up the poker; Alice twisted away as the poker came down, and it glanced off her shoulder, clattering to the floor.

Nabby leaned over, clutching her stomach. She straightened and caught Alice gaping at her. "What do you stare at? Why do you stand there? Get away from me! Be gone!"

Alice backed toward her bedroom door, whirled around, and dashed through it.

FIVE

Verley returned from wherever he'd gone and came into Alice's room, reeking of spirit, as drunk as she'd seen him. He dropped on top of her but seemed to have some trouble bringing his part to attention. He closed his hands around her throat until she thrashed wildly under him, near to passing out, but it didn't aid him; he flung her onto her stomach and there managed to enter— a new place, a new pain, a new kind of shout from him. *He likes to puncture you in odd places.* He pulled himself off her, stood up, and picked up the candle, but he didn't hold it over her. He stumbled out.

Alice lay breathing in and out, pressing her hand against her chest to try to push her heart back into calmness. After a time it quieted enough so that she could hear Verley's progress through the house: a chair knocking against the wall, the outer door banging open, piss hitting stone, the outer door banging shut, and finally, the door to his bedroom. Nabby's blow had reopened the old cut in Alice's cheek; she could feel the sting of it along with the throb in her shoulder where the poker had struck as well as the burn of the torn flesh between her buttocks, but she didn't know who had frightened her more, Verley or Nabby.

Get away from me! Be gone! With those words Nabby had settled it once and for all—she wouldn't help Alice—and yet those words *had* helped Alice. She knew what to do now. She must be gone from there, alone. Now.

Alice waited a time longer, but no one stirred. She slid her feet to the floor, crept to the pegs, put on her workday skirt and bodice, took down her winter petticoat, her shawl, her one spare shift and skirt, her extra stockings. She emptied her workbasket of Nabby's mending and stuffed her clothes in, then reached under the bed tick where she'd tucked her father's old money pouch that again held her indenture paper, as well as most of the birthday coins Mr. Morton had given her. She lifted the tick and thrust her hand deeper; she could feel nothing but the straw pad and the rope web it lay upon. She pulled the tick right off the bed frame and onto the floor; she ran her hands over every square of rope and over the floor beneath; the pouch wasn't there.

Only when Mr. Morton had made out the new indenture that bound Alice to his daughter had Alice understood the exact meaning of the paper she'd carried around her neck for so long: two copies written out, one set atop the other, the edges of the papers cut into a matching set of indentations. Alice's father had told her to keep hold of her paper because as long as she kept it she held proof against any change made in the copy held by the owner. Now Verley had both copies and could make any new kind of paper he liked; he could write Alice as bound for five years, or eight, or ten or twelve, instead of the three years that lawfully remained on her contract. Yes, Verley could do as he wished with the paper, but what did it matter if he didn't have Alice?

Alice left her room for the keeping room and stood still, listening again. Still quiet. She opened the back door, eased into the half moonlight, stepped around the wet stones in the dooryard, and into the Dedham road.

THE TEN MILES to Dedham took Alice near dawn but not into it, which left her with a problem. If she walked across the Morton's dooryard the geese would start awake, raising the household, and Alice didn't want to speak with Mr. Morton on the heels of so rude an entrance. She found a damp patch of soft June grass by the woodpile, shielded from both house and road, and dropped down onto it. She had an idea that she might sleep until Jerubah came out to empty her night jar, waking the geese herself, which would in turn wake Alice, but her hand and cheek and shoulder pulsed too much for sleeping. She lay in the grass until she heard the geese, lay some more until the sun streaked the woodpile, then stood up, shook off her skirt, and crossed into the dooryard.

Jerubah had left the door open to the June air and Alice stepped through it. Jerubah lifted her head from the eggs she was beating and stared at Alice; her eyes could go either soft or hard at will, but she seemed unable to decide how to fix them until she fixed them on Alice's neck, no doubt speckled by now with the plum-colored marks of Verley's fingers.

"I've come to speak to Mr. Morton," Alice said.

Jerubah's eye slid from Alice's neck up to her cheek, and down again to the hand, which had closed on itself in an awkward claw. She raised a finger and pointed to Mr. Morton's study.

Alice walked up to Mr. Morton's door, attempting to lift her good hand to knock, but discovered that the injured shoulder was less agreeable to movement than the burned hand. She switched sides, and tapped the wood with her knuckles. Mr. Morton called out, "Come along, come along!" with an impatience Alice hadn't remembered in him.

Alice opened the door and stepped in. Mr. Morton lifted his head from his papers and pushed his chair back. "Alice!" he cried. "Alice, my pretty girl! My sweet, good girl! Come here, child, and let me feast my eyes on you!"

Alice drew closer to Mr. Morton's chair. The low morning sun cut across her, causing odd patterns and shadows; Mr. Morton peered at Alice until he'd sorted shadow from skin, skin from bruise, bruise from blood, and with his daughter's eyes, looked away from her. After a time he returned his eye to a spot just beyond her and asked, "Are you visiting with my daughter?"

"No, sir."

"She sends you to do her errands? Some business here in Dedham?"

"I've come to speak with you, sir. To ask if you would take me back from the Verleys. I've not been treated well there."

"Not been treated well! If you mean they don't spoil you as I used to do—"

"They've hurt me, sir. First him and then her. The both together."

"Now, Alice, you don't expect me to believe such a fib as that about my daughter. Not unless you've grown rude and lazy since you went there."

"I've grown nothing like it, sir. I only wish to come back here and go on as we did before."

"Now you know we can't do that. You know that Mr. Verley owns your time now," and there he jerked around in his chair to peer out the window. "What's that noise? Is it the fox again? Pray tell Jerubah to come in here."

Alice had held it in her mind all the way from Medfield that when Mr. Morton saw what had been done to her he would take her back and keep her safe, as he would have kept his own daughter safe, but now she wondered what had dulled her brain so. She wasn't his daughter. She wasn't even his servant anymore. She turned away and walked to the door, but there she looked back. Mr. Morton seemed happy enough to look at her more directly from afar, but even so, he began to blink as he looked. Alice might have pretended he blinked out a tear, but in the slashing light the only thing she felt sure of was the look of fixedness that grew on him the longer she stood there. Why should he disrupt his family's life over a servant he had liked to call his "sweet, good girl," but who wasn't so sweet and good anymore?

Alice returned to the keeping room and let Jerubah stare at her again, longer this time, as if reading the wounds on Alice's skin the way someone not a slave might read words on a paper. Alice said good-bye to her without passing on any order from Mr. Morton; she wasn't his servant anymore. She stepped out into the yard and looked first left, then right. The road ahead of her had long been called two different things, depending which way one turned into it—the Medfield road if one headed for Medfield, the Boston road if one headed for Boston. Alice knew well enough what lay in one direction and little enough what lay in the other, but the one was enough for her to make her choice. She stepped into the Boston road.

SIX

lice clutched her basket in the fingertips of her burned hand and pulled down a few wisps of hair to attempt to conceal her cheek and neck; she didn't want to attract any kind of attention whatever. She walked at the steady pace of a servant on an errand, crossing the road as if to enter one of the shops if someone appeared ahead, and as she walked she counted off each familiar establishment as she passed: Courtenay the smith, Hatch the cobbler, Shaw the weaver. As she left the village cluster she counted off the familiar farms as she'd counted the shops in town: Houghton, Young, Wood, Walker, Sexton, until the road stretched empty on either side and she had nothing to count but the crows, or the clouds, or her own footsteps. She began to feel more and more like a drifting ship with each place she left behind. She couldn't imagine herself in front of any of these places again, but neither could she imagine herself against any other horizon. At times Alice slowed to ease the discomfort in her shoulder and hand, both of which pulsed whenever her heel hit the ground, but in the main she kept to a steady pace, feeling Verley behind her like a great tidal wave, ready to roll over her and suck her back to Medfield.

After Alice had walked a fair way she stopped alongside a horse trough to plunge her hand into the coolness—a rust-red star now flamed out around the central wound—and the cold felt so good she dipped her face as well, the black bottom of the trough reminding her of the water on the ship, but as she'd drunk that and survived she decided to drink again there. She wiped her face on her skirt and noted the pink stain left behind on the cloth; she attempted to scrub it out against the trough, and when she finished she was wet in more places than she was dry, but she didn't let it trouble her. The day was as fine as any she could have wished, the sun just hot enough to dry her clothes but not hot enough to overheat her, the road smooth and hard, as it wouldn't have been in the rainy months before. As Alice moved into her stride again she thought of the day, the road, that portion of luck that had set her loose in such a season instead of another, and wondered if she should take it as a sign. Alice trusted in God, but she also trusted in signs; in truth, she'd never got quite clear in her head where one took up from the other. She'd walked the Dedham road toward Mr. Morton as she might have walked any road that contained no turning, that route being the only one she knew, and so, in a way, had it been with the Boston road, but from now on all would be different. Alice had formed no great plan for when she arrived in town beyond hoping to hide in its crowds; once she got there she would need some sort of sign to guide her future turnings.

Alice calculated by the sun that she'd walked nearly three hours when the traffic began to thicken. Farmers drove pigs and sheep and cows ahead of them along the road; carts rolled by loaded with poultry crates, barrel staves, and shingles; women shouldered past carrying baskets of new greens, dried herbs, and great, round cheeses.

Alice stooped to fuss with her shoe every time another walker drew too close, afraid the next pair of eyes to fix on her would belong to a Medfield neighbor who would report to the Verleys the minute he got home—*saw your girl on the Boston road*—but no one appeared to take any great notice of her.

At length Alice came to a narrow, marshy spit that she remembered from her childhood trip out of the town, the gallows marking the entry gates hanging empty but still full of warning. Alice passed through the gates, following the market crowd. The way grew more congested, the houses tall and close, the crossroads more frequent; a gentleman on a fine horse wearing a fine coat swerved in front of Alice, and she caught her breath, thinking it was Verley; she decided the gentleman was a sign that she should leave the main road for a side one. She glanced down each narrow lane as she passed, not knowing what she looked for, until she caught a flash of gold light gleaming on purple water like the jewels on a king's robe.

Over the years Alice had held varying ideas about the water. She remembered her mother's early fears, but she also remembered her own excitement at the sight of it; she remembered the terrible knocking of the ship, but she also remembered the beautiful towering mountains of spray crashing on deck; she remembered the boy being swept overboard, but she also remembered her mother calling him a lucky boy. On a particularly black day during Alice's first year at Mr. Morton's she had thought she might better understand what her mother had meant by that remark—that her mother had wanted to be done with the ship, that she had wanted to go in the water—and as Alice thought about her mother afterward she took some comfort in the fact that she *had* gone into the water. Perhaps that was why her daydream of the ship had come to her, and the vague, green, syrupy place where her mother flew about like a finned bird, safe and happy with her brothers. Of course, Alice understood better now what the water was and wasn't, and where her mother was and wasn't, but understanding was one thing, and believing was another.

Alice walked toward the water.

THE WATERFRONT SEEMED different from what Alice remembered, the sheer mass of sights and sounds and smells battering her senses. A row of small wharves stretched left and right, nothing like the great long wharf she remembered from her first landing, but behind her rose a familiar handful of steeples, similar shops and stalls. The air smelled of bread baking, fish drying, tar, sewage, seaweed, and spices; bells rang, dogs barked, hawkers cried out over their fresh fish and oysters, men stood everywhere in twos and threes or more, sometimes talking and sometimes arguing, the same odd words flicking through all the conversations like a flame: sugar, taxes, and an expression Alice had never heard before: non-importation. She also heard much mention of a man named Otis. She found herself standing and turning in a dizzying circle, following a voice from one crowd as it got picked up in answer from another: *Otis says Parliament can't tax us without our being represented in that body . . . Parliament can do as they bloody well please . . . Otis calls it tyranny . . . I call it treason and so will the king when he hangs him!*

Alice stood looking and listening, too struck by the greater scene around her to notice the nearer, until a cart swung too wide around the turn and knocked her to her knees, dislodging her basket. A man and woman who had been walking arm in arm across the road were forced to jump back as well, but once the cart had gone they hurried to Alice, the gentleman helping her to her feet.

"Are you all right, miss?"

"Yes," Alice said, before she had any idea if she was or she wasn't.

The man took out a handkerchief and handed it to Alice, for what purpose she wasn't sure, until he pointed at her cheek. Alice pressed it to her skin and it came away red; she handed it back with great embarrassment, but he took it with little fuss and tucked it back in his pocket.

In the meantime the woman had retrieved Alice's basket and rejoined them at the side of the road. She held out the basket, and as Alice reached for it she stopped and stared; the woman's hand was burn-scarred. Alice lifted her eyes and found the woman's eyes fixed on Alice's hand in like manner; the eyes lifted from hand to neck, from neck to cheek, and there Alice looked away from her.

"Are you quite sure you're all right?" the man asked again.

"Indeed, sir. Thank you."

"We've a friend at no great distance who would be quite delighted to offer you a cup while you recover."

"I'm quite fine, sir, thank you."

"Very well." The man turned to the woman, who had continued to study Alice. "We'd best get along or they'll sail without us." He offered the woman his arm, and they continued across the street. What else could a matching pair of burned hands be but a sign? Alice followed them. The couple wasn't young, past forty by the look of them, but the man was greatly tall with loose-hinged limbs, the woman of good height herself and possessed of her own healthy gait; Alice had to skip to keep up with them. And keeping up with them became of greater interest to Alice once she caught the woman's first sentence.

"Did you see the girl's hand?"

The man's answer was lost in the noise of the street, beyond a head shake in the negative. The woman pointed to her own body to demonstrate the rest of her observations. Neck. Cheek. Shoulder. She'd missed none of it. At the conjunction with a busy wharf the couple paused and Alice picked up the talk again.

"A worse fall than it looked."

"Are you blind? She didn't get those wounds from that fall."

The man looked at the woman. "And such a lovely thing."

"Well, I'm glad to see you noticed something."

They exchanged a look between them, and Alice caught a better view of their faces, the man's well creased but with the kind of creases that came from smiling as well as frowning, the woman's softened some with age, but not enough to hide the clear line of a jaw clamped tight in agitation. Alice looked again at the woman's hands and saw that both were burned, back as well as the front, the scars old and white and thickly ridged, perhaps to the point of being crippling. Perhaps to the point of requiring a girl's help in managing her household.

The couple resumed walking and turned onto the wharf, Alice making the turn with them. A full breeze off the water lifted her hair, reminding her of the joy of her first visit to the ship's deck after the sick days below, and she filled her lungs with it. The couple moved toward a pretty little ship tied at the end of the wharf, not half the size of the one that had brought Alice across the ocean but with the trim freshly painted, the deck better ordered.

"What say you of this wind?" the woman asked.

"I say we should have a fast run," the man answered. "Perhaps land tomorrow evening."

No long trip, then.

A half-dozen carts pulled onto the wharf and up to the ship. A stringy crew of different shapes and ages dropped off the deck and began to pile crates and barrels in a great heap near the forward hatchway. A square-built man with white hair came down the gangway and walked up to the man from the street; the two began to pore over some kind of ledger together. The woman moved off toward a vendor cart bursting with oranges, raisins, and lemons, and began to pick through them. Alice moved closer to the ship to read its name: the *Betsey*. Alice's middle name was Elizabeth. So many signs! The name. The burned hands. The short voyage. The empty, unwatched gangway. What more could she wish for? Her mother's voice, calling to her from the water? Verley's voice, shouting from behind her?

The thought of Verley set Alice's feet in the direction of the gangway. She looked at the distracted crew again, the two men bent over the ledger, the woman fumbling among the fruit; still not a single eye following. She could go back unseen as well as forward unseen, of course, but how much easier to go forward, up the gangway, across the deck . . .

Alice wouldn't have said she had indeed decided to do it, and yet the next thing she knew, there she stood, at the top of the companionway. She pulled her skirt tight, hooked her basket in her elbow, and gripped the ropes on either side, the hemp stinging her burned palm like nettles, but as her palm had hurt before, she didn't count it as a sign against her. She dropped one foot to the lower rung and eased the other after. She took another step, and another, listening for sounds from above and hearing nothing. At the bottom of the companionway Alice found lockers, bunks, benches, and beyond, another locker. She moved forward again, pulled open the door to the forward locker, and found herself in a kind of storage space crammed with boxes, rope, sails. How simple it was to shift a few boxes until she'd formed a small space, how effortless to curl up in her new nest, how easy to reach out and pull a piece of sail over her! And oh, how safe she felt, for the first time since she'd climbed into the cart that had carried her to Medfield!

ALICE COULD MAKE no calculation of how long she lay among the smells of pitch, hemp, salt, fish, and mold before the feet began to pound overhead and the deck began to rise and fall beneath her. After a time her stomach griped, her flesh dampened, and she vomited into the sail. The rise and fall grew rougher, as if the deck beneath her had been picked up and slammed down from a great height; she collected new bruises on hips, knees, and elbows. There came a time when she was forced to pull up her skirt and empty her aching bladder where she lay; she grew so hungry she swallowed air, so thirsty she sucked the sweat from her fingers, so tired her eyes burned even against the dark.

After a time the pounding beneath Alice fell off, the bootheels and voices above quickened, and the only motion became a gentle rolling side to side, but that gentle rolling proved harder on her stomach. She vomited the last of her bile and lay waiting for the voices and bootheels to stop, for the ship to empty so she could sneak off as she'd snuck on, but instead of the noises growing quieter one pair of bootheels grew louder. Closer. The hatch to her hiding place blasted open.

"Ho! What the devil! Look-y here, will you?"

Alice blinked against the dim cabin light and made out a sunbrowned face, then another similar, and another; at length a paler face appeared, more familiar, but she couldn't think why it should be so familiar to her. He peered at her in the same kind of shock as the others until the shock melted into recognition, a recognition so complete that in her confused state Alice thought for a minute that perhaps it was her father come to get her, until she recognized the man from the street in Boston. First he pushed aside the other men, and then the boxes and sails; he took careful grip of her arms, eased her out of her nest and back through the vessel to the table and benches. He set her down on the bench. He peered at her, not smiling, but neither would she have said he frowned.

She said, "Will you tell me where we are, sir?"

"Robbin's Landing."

38

"In what town, sir?"

"In no town. 'Tis the village of Satucket, on Cape Cod."

Cape Cod. Alice had heard Verley speak of it, of a trip he'd been forced to make to it; he'd called the place "all sand and wind and contrary opinions." Because Verley hadn't liked it, Alice at once felt safer there.

"Perhaps now is the time for you to tell me something," the man said. "Such as who you are and where you come from and what you're doing in my sail locker."

"I'm Alice—" she began but at once saw her mistake. She looked down at the table and spied the remains of a loaf wrapped incompletely in a cloth. She put her hands under the table so she wouldn't grab it. She said, "Baker. Alice Baker."

The man peered at her some more. "And where do you come from, Miss Baker?"

"I got on at Boston, sir."

"And here I thought you'd flown aboard somewhere along the way on the back of a seagull. I mean to say, Miss Baker, where do you live?"

Alice thought. She must make no trail back to Verley. This man knew her at Boston, but nowhere other. She said, "I live at Boston, sir."

"I see. And what urged you to secrete yourself aboard this vessel?"

"I'd not the fare, sir."

He peered again. "I suspect you to be a clever girl, Alice, if I may judge by the wit behind your answers, and I suspect you've no plan to be any less witty in the future. 'Tis of course the shipmaster's task to handle such things as stowaways; I only thought to do him the favor, considering my position as partner in the vessel, but once he finishes shouting at his men he'll certainly come down here and settle the matter. I assure you he's a plain-speaking man, uncluttered with such useless things as humor; no doubt you'll get on with him better."

The man stood up. From the deck above them Alice could indeed hear the shipmaster shouting at his men with gusto. *Stand by to furl mainsail! Furl mainsail! Stand by to take in headsail! Haul away!*

Alice looked up at the loose frame before her, the face atop it all long, still angles, the eyes as calm as well water. She said, "I've just finished out my time at Boston. I've come here to look for work."

"In Satucket?"

"Yes, sir."

"I see. And you are how old, Miss Baker?"

That was easier. "Eighteen, sir."

The man said nothing. He stood up, pushed the loaf three inches closer to her, and retreated up the companionway.

SEVEN

She knelt at the foot of the companionway, the last crust of bread tight in her fingers, ready to leap back at the first sound of boots approaching, and listened to the three people talking above her. The woman called the man who had picked Alice out of street and locker Mr. Freeman; she called the shipmaster Cousin Shubael; Freeman called the shipmaster Brother Shubael and the woman Widow Berry. Not his wife, then. Beyond that Alice couldn't determine the relation.

> FREEMAN: "She says she's eighteen, a servant just out of her time and looking for work."
>
> WIDOW: "In Satucket?"
>
> FREEMAN: "I promise you, she's not a day over sixteen. I also promise you she's got a master someplace yet."
>
> WIDOW: "If she's got a master he's sore abused her, I'll promise you that, Mr. Freeman."

FREEMAN: "So we return her to Boston and let the justices sort it out."

SHIPMASTER: "We can't return her to Boston tonight, nor tomorrow, nor the next day. Not till the vessel's unladed and we've got the herring from the mill creek and the clams off Namskaket."

FREEMAN: "Well, then, we give her over to the constable."

WIDOW: "The constable! I'd like to know what this girl's done to deserve the constable!"

FREEMAN: "She's stolen a passage, for one. And for another, the amount of truth in her story is smaller than your smallest fingernail. Mark me, she's run off from someone, which leaves Brother Shubael with the crime of transporting without papers."

WIDOW: "I should like to know how a simple case of finding a poor, abused girl inside a sail locker becomes a crime."

FREEMAN: "Look at her. Listen to that tale she tells. I'd be a simple case indeed if I took that girl for anything other than a servant run off from her master."

WIDOW: "So you would send her back to the person who's abused her."

FREEMAN: "You make some grave assumptions, Widow Berry, both of a stranger and of a man you should know better. I wish to do what's best for the girl. As will the justices who hear her. To set her loose without protection would be an abuse greater than any she's met thus far."

WIDOW: "And when did I ever speak of setting her loose? I speak of taking her home and giving her food and a bed and some care for her wounds. That hand, for one, needs quick attention."

FREEMAN: "My dear Widow—"

WIDOW: "'Tis no more than you would do for your horse,
    sir."

FREEMAN: "May I remind you that the law—"

WIDOW: "Oh, how neat you plead the law when it serves your
    purpose! I heard no such scruple when you and Mr. Otis
    sat plotting to shut down all trade with England!"

FREEMAN: "Mr. Otis and I scheme at nothing that doesn't lie
    within the law."

SHIPMASTER: "Here now, we get off the subject altogether.
    The girl may leave this vessel in any direction she chooses
    for all it matters to me, but leave it she must—I've a hold
    needs unlading."

FREEMAN: "This ship is in your command, Brother Shubael,
    and I naught but partner in the venture. Your home is
    likewise in your command, Widow Berry, and I naught
    but boarder there. My role as a man of law is solely to
    point out where the legality sits in the matter. You may do
    as you like, of course."

They did so, with a speed that hinted they must have heard a like speech before, the shipmaster calling for the lowering of the dory, the widow musing aloud over the preferred salve for blisters. Footsteps approached the companionway; Alice leaped back to the bench where the man Freeman had first put her, and watched his careful descent down the companionway, the effect of silver shoe buckles and silk stockings reduced by the hatless, wigless, wind-roughed hair. He motioned to Alice, and she climbed after him onto the deck, her first gulp of fresh air tasting as good as a first swig out of a new beer barrel.

Alice shielded her eyes against the brightness and looked around her. To one side of her lay the furrowed surface of the water she'd just crossed, to the other lay a high, white swath of sand fringed at one end by bright green marsh grass and at the other by sedge and pitch pine.

The widow stepped up to her. Her clothes were not the fineness of Freeman's, and the wind had done an even more thorough job of disrupting her hair, but she looked handsomer in the light of Satucket than she had in the light of Boston. Or perhaps it was the words she said to her.

"I live no great distance from here," she said. "I can offer you nothing but a cold supper and a tight bed, but this I do offer."

No wonder the woman looked so fair! But Alice had to look next at the man Freeman. His mouth had canted sideways in either a half-grimace or half-smile, she couldn't determine which, and as he appeared to live in the widow's house, she thought it might be wise to know the difference. She should know the risk in him, not only as a man of law but as a man who found her a "lovely thing"—she'd heard those words before. She knew she must do a better job of reading this man's face than she'd done reading Verley's.

Alice stared fixedly at Freeman but could make out nothing. Or could she? Perhaps the very blankness of his gaze told her something, for surely if he planned to accost her he would attempt to conceal it here, as Verley had, with a better effort at smiling. But such a flimsy thing to count on, a man's not smiling! Better perhaps to attempt to read the man's words instead of his face and hunt out the deception in them. But where had he deceived? The man of law had made his case and stepped aside, allowing the widow to make her offer; as to the man who found her a lovely thing, Alice could only count it a good sign that he seemed unanxious to keep her near him.

The widow stepped closer, picked up Alice's burned hand, and leaned down for a better look at it. "Come," she said. "I know something of burns. This must be poulticed."

Alice followed her.

THE WIDOW'S HOUSE sat not far from the landing, the walls low and the roof steep, the central door and two windows on each side giving it a solid, stable look, the silvered shingles melding with its surroundings as if it had always been there. Just behind the house Alice spied a neatly boxed garden, a tight barn and necessary house, a healthy stand of pine and oak. As they entered the yard a young Indian girl in an English checked skirt came out of the barn and began to speak with the widow in rapid, short sentences. *Cow milked. Hens egged. Horse watered.* The widow took some coins from her pocket and counted them into the Indian girl's hand; the girl dropped the coins into her pocket and ran into the road.

The widow led Alice inside. As Alice looked around she saw more plaster than paneling, more earthenware than silver, more iron than brass, but the plaster had been freshly whitewashed, the earthenware gleamed, the iron showed no rust. A proud house, if not a rich one. The widow picked up a pail near the door and pointed Alice to the well and the necessary house. Alice went to the necessary first and, once comfortable, crossed the yard to the well. The bucket came up sweet and cold; she put her mouth in it, thinking of Freeman's horse, and drank herself full. She refilled the bucket and returned to the house, where the widow stood waiting to lead her up the stairs.

The chamber at the top of the stairs was nothing more than an unfinished attics divided by a thick chimney, but the gabled ends were peppered with odd-size windows that caught the breeze as well as the light. A dusty loom sat tucked under the eaves on the east end, but a neat pair of beds, a washstand, and a small case of drawers sufficiently furnished the west end. Alice's spirits lifted.

The widow left Alice with few words, for which Alice was grateful. She stripped off her soiled skirt and shift and washed herself out of the bucket. She removed her best skirt and shift from her basket and put them on. She brushed and retied her hair in the same old soiled ribbon, returned to the stairs, and paused at the top to listen. She heard the door open below, boots cross the floor, and a brief, indistinguishable question and answer, followed by silence.

Alice descended. She found the widow moving about laying out the supper she'd promised, and Freeman standing with his back to the window, making an intense study of a newspaper. Alice went to the table to assist the widow, but instead the widow sat her down and picked up her hand with the sureness of someone acquainted with the art of medicine. The hand hadn't improved during its sea voyage, the red star having stretched its tentacles the full width of the palm, and the widow frowned over it. The promised poultice appeared, smelling of sorrel, rum, and something woody, like bark; the widow slapped it into Alice's palm and wrapped the hand with a long strip of clean linen. She next smoothed some kind of minty salve on Alice's cheek, felt her shoulder, said, "Not displaced, then," and as if it were part of the same sentence, "come, Mr. Freeman."

Freeman folded away his newspaper and came to the table. Alice took a first happy bite of moist bread and purple-black preserve, but she hadn't yet swallowed when Freeman addressed her.

"Tell me, Alice, just whereabouts in Boston did you live with your master?"

"Can we not leave the girl to eat in peace?" the widow said.

Freeman dipped his head in surrender, and they resumed eating in such utter silence that Alice found it as uncomfortable as the previous question had been. She drew her eyes down and struggled to swallow the pasty lump of bread in her mouth, but it wouldn't slide as she wished it.

After a time Freeman said, "I ran into Cobb at the landing. He reports the last of the whale men have left for Labrador."

"Indeed," the widow answered.

"He tells me also that Josiah Snow and Sarah Clarke are published and will be married a fortnight Saturday." He went on. Ned Winslow had had triplets, all in health; the herring men had run out of salt; Seth Cobb had bought a chaise; Bangs and Winslow were both late to planting due to a common distemper run through their households. None of it meant anything to Alice, but the gentle up-and-down of Freeman's speech began to relax her, and the much-needed bread and beer began to move down her throat with less trouble. Once Alice had filled her stomach, however, her second great need overcame her; her limbs and eyelids felt so weighted she thought they must fall to the floor ahead of her. She attempted to rise to clear away her plate, but the widow reached across and took it from her, scarred fingers gripping the crockery at an odd, claw-like angle. Perhaps she did need a girl's help, but just then she must have seen how little use Alice would be to her.

She said, "Go to your bed, child. We'll talk on the morrow."

Alice climbed the stairs with the last of her will, crossed the attics to the bed nearest the window, dropped her shoes, stockings, and skirt on the floor, drew back the coverlet and stretched out between the wash-worn linens. Daylight hadn't quite finished with the room; Alice lay on her back, staring up at the silvered rafters, thinking sleep would find her even with her eyes open, but when it didn't come she closed her eyes, and still it escaped her. She could feel the spot where Nabby's poker had come down; she could feel the sting of the widow's salve on her cheek and the continued throbbing in her hand; under it all ran the soreness in the new place Verley had entered. Oh, for a new body! A new Alice! She imagined the old bruised shell of herself lying behind in the sail locker, the man Freeman lifting a new, untarnished girl into the fresh, clean air of Satucket. She breathed in and out, tasting the unfamiliar bold salt air. She wondered how far she'd come, how far she'd left Verley behind her.

At the thought of Verley Alice began to tremble. She tried to push him away and start over, but he was like a fallen horse that had pinned her underneath him. She tried to cast herself back to the ship's locker—the old body left behind, the new one gentled into life by Freeman—but then what? Oddly, the next image Alice drew was one of her lying in a meadow of soft young grass, next to a glistening ocean, the meadow spotted all over with shining new chaises, laughing brides, smiling babies that all looked alike, and most odd of all, herring, flipping like green and silver waves all over the grass. One of the brides drew near and Alice saw that it was Nabby. She said, "Why haven't you spitted these fish for our dinner?" And there a horse broke loose from one of the chaises, charged over the grass, trampled the fish, and turned into Verley.

EIGHT

Alice woke with the first sense of light against her eyelids, but she didn't open her eyes. She felt worn out, as if she'd spent the night slogging through a marsh full of soft peat and spiky grasses, but the only dream that she remembered in all its shape and form was the dream—or nightmare—of the meadow. Alice could trace the path of the dream, of course, piecing it together from Freeman's talk of chaises, triplets, herring. Alice could make sense as well of how the presence of a Verley had turned dream to nightmare. As Alice lay, however, she realized that such a nightmare wasn't her worst fear; her worst fear was that this was the dream, this supposed waking in the widow's attics. This was why she couldn't bear to open her eyes; what if she opened them and saw not the widow's arching, sunlit rafters, but Verley's flat, plastered ceiling? Alice opened her eyes. Rafters. Her heart swelled inside her chest as if someone else's blood pumped through it, but still she didn't dare believe. She jumped out of bed and ran to the window.

The sky hung low and gray and sunless, the road below it empty and still, but beyond the road, even without the sun to decorate it or the wind to rile it, the surface of the sea expanded and shrank as if it breathed. Alice couldn't look away from it. After a time she forced herself to turn to the washstand and splash water on her cut cheek, taking care to keep her poulticed hand dry; both wounds felt better, she decided. She dressed herself and believed her shoulder too had loosened. She sat on the bed and waited. For what? A sound. A sign.

Footsteps. The rise and fall of a latch. More footsteps. Another rattle of latch and a pair of voices, followed by the clatter of a pot, or plate, or bowl. Alice was famished. She got up and went to the back-facing set of stairs that she'd climbed from the keeping room the night before, but at the top she halted; voices rose up the steep, narrow stairs like smoke up a chimney.

"And what if you'd woken this morning to find the girl gone, along with the contents of that money jar you leave so unwisely atop your cupboard?"

"I'd have asked you for your next month's keep in advance. But as the jar's still there, I'll ask instead for something a little more trusting in your nature."

"Mark me, I've nothing to say against the girl—"

"Other than to call her a thief."

"I don't call her a thief. I only call your attention to a certain possibility, in the hope that you might take a little more care when gathering in your boarders."

"You're quite right, Mr. Freeman. I've taken poor care in gathering in my boarders and paid a fine price for it too."

Freeman gave out a sharp snort that might or might not have been a laugh. Again, it seemed important that Alice know. She worked her way down the stairs and stumbled on the last step, bringing the man and woman around with a start as her shoes hit the floor. They collected their features into smiles together, the widow's coming easier than Freeman's. Alice had planned to scour the room for some kind of sign, but when she saw the widow's ready greeting she decided she needed no other. She knew well enough that she wanted to stay here with her. Oh, how she wanted to stay here! But how to make it come true? Alice stepped up to the table and began to slice the bread; she must show the widow that despite her wounds she could work yet and work well. She wrestled the toaster into place in front of the fire and laid in the first slices, then straightened up and stepped closer to the widow so there could be no mistaking where she placed her offer.

She said, "I should like to work for you, madam, if you'd have me. I'll do any task you wish to give me. I can spin and plant and weed; I can do the dairying and all the usual chores of a household. I know you should require a reference; I'm sorry to say my letter from my old master was lost in travel, but I'll write at once for another. While you wait on it you need pay me only my meals and one of those spare beds in your attics."

It had come out in a rush and used up all Alice's air. She stopped talking and took a breath, waiting for the widow to speak, but as she waited Alice saw that she had indeed learned something about reading faces. Before the widow even began speaking, Alice saw that all was plainly lost.

"Let me tell you how I live, child," the widow began, and went on to explain what she needn't, what Alice had to struggle to hear through the great, thick blanket of fear that had encased her. The widow lived by keeping boarders. Freeman was one, but she had recently lost three others, an old woman who had died, and two stranded sailors who had since found a ship; until the widow filled the empty beds that Alice called "spare," she couldn't afford to keep a girl to help with work she could manage well enough alone.

The widow stopped her speech there, but then she startled Alice by stepping forward and catching Alice's face between her scarred hands. She turned it sideways to examine Alice's neck. She said, "Who did this to you, your master?"

Alice began to tremble, much as she had the night before. She felt an odd pain in her chest, and her breathing wouldn't draw clear. The widow put an arm behind Alice's back and led her to a chair. She took the kettle off the fire and filled the teapot, leaving it on the table to steep. She returned to Alice and sat down opposite her. She picked up Alice's good hand in both of hers and began to speak in a tone that Alice remembered from nowhere.

"I want you to tell me, Alice, how you come to be here in our village. I want you to tell me what's made you run off. Tell me your story, child."

Her story. Oh, that it was a story, and someone else's, or if hers, one that could be turned to another ending! Or had Alice already had her chance to turn her story and taken the wrong turning? Should she have passed by the sparkling ocean, the burned hands, the white handkerchief, the pretty ship, and found some kind of work in Boston? No, not Boston. Boston sat too close to Verley. What, then? Should she have set out toward Philadelphia and looked for her father there? Oh what, then?

The widow still held Alice's hand, her own scarred palm rough and lumpy against it. She sat in patience, waiting for Alice to speak. Alice couldn't see Freeman from where she sat, but she could feel him, the man of law, standing tall and upright, somewhere behind her, waiting too to return her to Boston, to return her to Verley. Alice pulled her hand from the widow's and tucked it into the folds of her skirt. She said, "I finished out my time at Boston. I came to Satucket to look for work. There is all my story, madam."

The widow dropped Alice's hand, got up, and poured out the tea into three thick, earthenware mugs. She picked one up and carried it to Alice, but Alice had some trouble collecting it, because of her trembling.

The widow said, "You may stay here as long as I've a bed free, while you look for work in the village. You may work at what chores I give you to pay for your keep. You may start with the chickens. The egg basket is on the peg by the door. The coop is behind the barn. Keep your eye on the one-legged one; she'll pick off your shoe bindings if you don't keep ahead of her."

NINE

The door Alice passed through on her way to the chickens was thick, and she didn't expect to hear as well as she'd heard on the stairwell, but as she bent to the latch she could hear Freeman's courtroom voice well enough to burn her ear.

"I'd like to know what possible hope that child has of finding work in this village without a single piece of paper to recommend her."

"She said she would write—"

"Please."

"All right, then."

"I can't say how strongly I disagree with your decision to keep her here. I can't say enough what a grave disservice you do her. If you think perhaps of recommending her yourself—"

"You needn't remind me how far my recommendation might take her in this village. To be of any use to the girl it must come from another."

"If you mean to say it must come from me—"

"You're well trusted in this village."

"And how long do you imagine I should be trusted when she slits one of our neighbors' throat, as she might well have done her master's?"

"I don't understand how a man of your sensibility could look at that girl and think her a murderer. Why, if she were a murderer you would help her! But as a runaway servant you turn your back on her."

"I should like very much to help her. I should like to offer her free passage back to Boston and fair adjudication in a court of law."

"Then offer it to her. She already has my offer. We'll see which one suits her better."

"Against yours I imagine I might save my breath."

"Then save it, sir. I've a cow needs milking."

Alice scrambled away from the door and around the barn to the chickens. The widow's bandage gave her little trouble; in fact, it gave her freer use of the hand now she knew it was protected. Once she'd filled the egg basket she helped the widow with the milk pail; she rationed the milk between the jug for drinking and the pans for cheese making, laid the cheesecloth over the pans, and carried the jug to the cellar. She worked with just as much speed as she could manage with care, and she believed the widow looked pleased with her effort. As to Freeman, he had gone away into his room, one of the two below-stairs; Alice could see him through the door at work at his desk on some kind of ledger. At one point in Alice's back-and-forth he looked up and caught her eye; he rose and came into the keeping room.

"Tell me, Widow Berry," he said. "Do your plans for Alice leave her time to run a small errand to Sears's store?"

The widow looked up from where she leaned over the fire, stirring it up for the kettle. She peered at Freeman. "I could allow of an errand."

"Very well." Freeman led Alice out the door and into the yard. He reached into his pocket and pulled out a paper bill, one pound old tenor, worth about three shillings in silver. "I'm in need of a tin of tobacco." He pointed. "To get to Sears's store you take this landing road all the way to the King's road and turn right along it. Beyond the mills you take a right at the fork and soon beyond the fork you'll see the sign for the store—a red and black barrel. Don't go beyond or you'll end at Yarmouth."

Alice closed her fingers around the note and ran into the road.

THE LANDING ROAD dipped and jogged with sun-dried spring ruts, and Alice stumbled more than once, too busy looking around her to mind her feet. She passed few houses on the landing road, more when she took the turning onto the King's road as Freeman had directed, but most of the houses looked simple and tight, nested low to the ground like the widow's. Nearer the mills Alice found some grander houses of two full stories, even saw a door and knocker that reminded her of Verley's; her steps stuttered, then strengthened, as a small flame of anger found her. Why should every fine house have a Verley in it? Why not a Morton? But the thought of Morton did nothing to cool her. He should not have given her to the Verleys. He should have taken her back when she asked him.

Alice worked her way past the first grand house and came to a long, broad tavern building hugging the road. Behind the tavern the millpond shimmered in a slice of newfound sun, its waters somersaulting down the hill into the millstream below. The mill wheel spun under the force of the spring flood waters, churning gobs of spray into the air that the sun turned to minute snowflakes, reminding Alice of the spray on her first ocean voyage. How far she'd come! And how fine a day! How fine a village! Alice walked, and looked, and the anger that had leaked out dissolved into the clean salt air of Satucket.

The road near the mills grew busier, but not with the kind of busyness Alice had been used to at Dedham, or even Medfield. She passed an Indian in English clothes, a red-haired man driving a cart full of barrels, a pair of women in silk dresses, and a tumbling, noisy, mismatched group of children. None spoke to Alice, but they all took note of her, as she might have taken note of any stranger in her own village. Alice passed them all with her eyes fixed on the road ahead, keeping tight hold of Freeman's bill.

At the fork she turned right and almost at once saw the sign with the red and black barrel. The house looked little different from the widow's except for the sign, but the door stood open, and Alice stepped inside it. Shelves stacked with crocks and sacks and bolts of cloth lined the walls; several crates littered the floor. A man knelt over the crates calling out the contents while a woman stood behind him marking each item in a ledger: five reams writing paper, two dozen cakes soap, one dozen horn buttons. They both left off work and looked up as Alice entered.

Alice told them her made-up name, and where she was staying. She told them of her errand for Freeman.

The man said, "So he's back, then?"

The woman said, "The widow too?"

Alice nodded. The man and woman exchanged a look. The man got the tobacco and set it down on the counter. Alice put Freeman's bill next to it. The man gave her back two shillings eight pence.

Alice curtseyed and left the store, holding the coins tight in one hand, the tobacco tin in the other. She retraced her steps along the road, making note of each landmark as she passed to ease her way on future trips to the village, then caught herself at the foolishness of as-suming a future here. Even so, she continued to study each rock and

57

tree and stone wall as she passed it. She came to the landing road and turned down, thrilling at the sense of the already familiar, and found Freeman standing in the yard, wearing the look of an idler.

"Well now, Alice, you've managed that errand in short time. Did you have any trouble?"

"None, sir." She handed over the coins. Freeman dropped them into his pocket, where they jangled against some others. With the jangling of the coins something jangled in Alice's head; she knew in an instant what Freeman had been after. He'd given her a pound note where almost any coin might do; he'd told her how to get to the next town. If she'd been dishonest, as he believed her to be, she would have headed straight for Yarmouth, leaving him nothing but an I-told-you-so for the widow. All this Alice understood in the time it took Freeman to pocket the coins; what she didn't understand was whether Freeman was pleased or displeased that she'd returned them to him.

TEN

Freeman rode off for Namskaket to oversee the loading of the clams, and Alice and the widow spent the day at the various chores that the widow bemoaned had got out of hand while she'd been at Boston.

First they tied up their skirts and weeded the flax, barefooted so as not to damage the tender plants; as they each exposed their white flesh Alice saw that the widow's legs had suffered from burns along with her hands and arms. Alice looked as she could at the widow's scars and wondered about them; she wondered too about the widow's dead husband; she wondered if her husband had died in the fire and how long ago it had happened. She imagined the widow's husband carrying her to safety and then returning to the house for something else, perhaps his money, perhaps some papers, something important, but not as important as his wife had been to him.

The flax took till noon, after which they ate a quick dinner of cold duck and early greens, then collected the hoe and spade from the barn and began planting the bean, turnip, cabbage, onion, cucumber, and squash sets in the dooryard garden. The soil was loose and sandy in places and hard and claylike in others; they made uneven progress as they worked their way around. By the time they reached the last raised box of earth by the door the widow said, "Best get supper on." Alice looked at the sky and saw that her first full day in Satucket had run down.

The widow ordered her to take down the mugs from the cupboard, but after Alice had set out three and stopped, the widow said, "We'll need them all down. And both those platters."

Alice looked at her in surprise.

"They all come," the widow explained. "The first evening he arrives from town. Hot after the latest news, the latest talk, the latest predictions."

And so they did come. Freeman brought the first two with him, but the others came in fast behind; some Alice already knew, like shipmaster Shubael Hopkins and storekeeper Sears, but others she didn't, men greeted as Cobb, Winslow, Myrick, and a late arrival named Thacher who complained as he came in about how hard it had been to break away from his custom at the tavern. As each man entered the room his eye went first to Alice, who stood at the cupboard filling platters; the shipmaster looked once and away, but the others showed no such qualm at staring.

The widow moved around the table, pouring mugs of cider, and soon the air filled with the pungent odor of fermented fruit, yeasty bread, smoking pipes, and fresh-cut cheeses. The talk began light— crops, weather, ships in, ships out, prices—and then Freeman said, "Well, gentlemen." The table quieted. Freeman began to speak the same words Alice had heard in the streets at Boston—sugar, taxes, non-importation—and again Otis, who was well known to those present as a native of Barnstable, a town that Alice gathered lay somewhere to the west of Yarmouth.

Alice listened to the pieces of talk, and after a time she found she could make something of it almost whole. A thing called the Sugar Act had upset all the colony, and although it was called the Sugar Act it seemed that rum was at the back of it, because one of the things the act would tax was the molasses used to make rum. James Otis came into the talk so often not only because he had once been neighbor to them but also because he had recently stood up at Boston town meeting and proposed non-importation of all unessential English goods in answer to the Act; this non-importation agreement seemed to be the focus of the present meeting. That much was easily gathered; the rest came more slowly, especially the sorting of the various opinions of Otis and the non-importation agreement. Alice heard one man's "devil" answered with another's "savior," the words *genius* and *mad* out of a single mouth, mugs banged down and voices raised, as loud in agreement as in disagreement.

"It'll mean ruin," Sears said.

"It'll mean tight times," Thacher countered. "The ruin'll come if we let them get away with it."

"I'm with Sears," Myrick said. "I see naught but starvation in it."

"Over coffee and tea and a bit of sugar?" Winslow asked. "Come now, Myrick."

Hopkins said, "Now, now, we're all Englishmen here. I think if we but make our position clear—"

Cobb picked up the *Boston Gazette*, which Freeman had placed before them on the table, and slapped it down again. "Read our own legislature's instructions for our agent to the Crown, right here in this paper; 'tis Otis's work if I ever saw it. He says we admit to no right of Parliament to impose duties and taxes upon a people who are not represented in the House of Commons. He says if we are not represented we are slaves. How much clearer can we make it? And yet they pay no attention to our words. Full half of England's trade is done with these colonies; if we shut that down, I promise you, they'll pay attention."

"Perhaps a more peaceable means—" Hopkins ventured.

"Peaceable! What's not peaceable? I'm not asking for the king's head on a block. But if you'd rather bend over and kiss their arse while they rifle your pockets—"

"Well, no—"

Alice took count: Cobb, Thacher, Winslow, and Freeman for, Sears and Myrick against, Hopkins to be persuaded any moment. If the table represented the whole, the non-importation agreement would go, but whether it went or not meant little to Alice. Yet she couldn't help listen to the men's urgent pleadings, and though some of the phrases were strung together fine enough, she felt in the other men the same thing she felt in herself—they waited for Freeman.

Not until the jabber began to repeat itself did he speak. "Gentlemen, I take the measure of this room and I take heart. You all see the importance of this moment. You all speak to the necessary points. You all speak with reason. And I have no doubt, once we've garnered their attention with this non-importation agreement, reason will prevail in England. I need not tell a man in this room that I love my king as I love my father; nor do I doubt every man in this room feels as I do toward his sovereign. Now, as we all understand one another, the next step is to marshal our forces. Our *peaceful* forces. And one thing that became clear this past week in my discussion with Otis and some of the others at Boston is that our forces must include the women."

The table broke out again.

"Women!"

"What the devil?"

"What women?"

"Yours, gentlemen. All of them. If we can't buy English tea or coffee it will be up to the women to brew up a substitution. If we can't buy sugar the women must work the hives. And most important, if we can't buy West India cotton or English wool or Irish linen the spinning wheels our women have sent to the attics must come down and be put back into motion. We must marshal the women to the cause, gentlemen. And once we do, I have every faith they will quickly turn homespun into high fashion."

Some more general noise went around.

Then, from Cobb: "I'd take a wife in homespun if it would serve our purpose."

"Yes, but would your wife?" Thacher asked.

The men laughed. "A fair point," Cobb said. "I admit I'm in some doubt of it."

"You think she'd prefer to pay a king's ransom for a bit of cambric?"

Alice looked up from cutting the rind off a new cheese. The widow. It was the widow who had spoken. Hopkins, whose mug the widow had just filled, straightened out his smile of thanks and looked away in embarrassment. Someone else coughed. A pair of boots scraped the floor. The widow continued to move around the table, filling mugs, the clink of earthenware and the swish of her skirt the only sound.

It didn't surprise Alice that it should be Freeman who would break the silence, as she had already observed him to be uncommonly unruffled at the widow's forwardness. "The widow makes a fair point, gentlemen," he said. "If the wheels don't come down now, this tax they put on cambric and other goods will continue, and you may be sure of it, if we let this one slip by another will follow. What slave, once broken, is then offered his freedom? And make no mistake, this is what we shall be—slaves—our English blood and sweat going straight into another Englishman's pocket, an Englishman who thinks he's earned it for no other reason than that he lives on the other side of the ocean. So there you have it, gentlemen: 'tis a choice you make now between slavery and freedom. And what's the price of that freedom? A little sugar and tea and coffee and cloth. Leave it on the shelf now, and you may cast away your chains forever."

Storekeeper Sears clapped his mug onto the table and stood up. "You mean leave it on *my* shelf. How the devil do you expect me to eat, Freeman?"

"The same as we all will," Freeman answered. "Your shelves, our ships, Thacher's straitened custom, all will suffer for a time, but if we don't suffer a short time now, we'll suffer the rest of our lives. Otis reports they've received commitment from most of the merchants in Boston to cease import of all English luxuries come August; he's proposed our leading citizens to correspond with merchants throughout the other colonies; he's asked that we all go home and organize our villages in support of the leaders at Boston and see that they stand behind the non-importation agreement. So, what say you, gentlemen? Will you leave here committed? Will you go home and enlist your women?"

Thacher said, "My wife should make up for the foodstuffs well enough, but I don't know about the cloth."

The table rumbled. Hopkins had grave doubts of his wife agreeing to chain herself anew to a spindle. Winslow, who raised sheep but sold off most of his wool now that his daughters were married away and his wife not well, couldn't promise any great change in his household. Cobb declared confidence in bringing his wife to the cause. Thacher began to think better of his own wife. Hopkins allowed that if indeed homespun became the thing, his wife would be sure to follow along, although as to taking up the wheel again. . . . Seth Cobb admitted some doubt of his wife turning out any great yardage. Winslow spoke of working his fulling mill up to the old rate of production, and where Sears took loud note of one man's making his hay while another's out licking the bottom of the barrel, it appeared to Alice that the general mood around the table began to lighten.

The talk of non-importation ran down. Someone made comment on the fine run of herring. Someone else reported on the successful repair of the mill wheel. Someone else noted how behind his Indian corn was. Mugs were drained and refilled, and Alice was sent to the cellar for another jug. As Alice stepped through the buttery door she heard Thacher drop his voice a token register. "So who's the girl?"

"She came with us from Boston where she'd just finished out her time," the widow answered. "She takes a room here while she looks for work in the village."

A pause, into which Freeman spoke. "I might say a word on the girl's behalf—"

"Might you," someone said, and the rest laughed.

"She's a hard worker."

"Oh, I could work her."

Another laugh.

"Here now, without any joke, I could use such a girl at the tavern."

"I could use her there too."

Again, the men laughed. Alice listened for Freeman's rich tones in it and didn't hear them. She lifted the cellar hatch, climbed down the ladder, and collected the cider jug. When she returned to the room, Freeman had just risen to his feet. "All right, gentlemen, I'd say our work this evening is completed." He raised his mug. "To the king!"

The mugs came up.

"To the king!"

"To the king!"

"To the king!"

ELEVEN

A lice woke to the sight of dawn just touching up the rafters, and an unreasonable joy washed through her. She'd made it to a second waking in Satucket. She leaped out of her bed and went to the window, eager to get to know the look of the place, but already it had changed: rusty white plum blossoms sprang up like clouds over the scrub along the shore, the water pulsed more lavender than blue, a sudden breeze caught at the nearby pines, knocking clouds of chalky, yellow dust into the air. She breathed in and felt the grit in her lungs. Satucket. In her. She left the window and dressed herself with as much speed as neatness would allow, hoping to be first to the keeping room.

She was. She'd unbanked the fire, set up the kettle, and sliced the bread when the widow and Freeman appeared, sharing a matching somber expression that immediately damped Alice's spirits. She remembered, oh, how could she have forgotten! The man Thacher and his talk of hiring her to work at the tavern. Was this the grim news the widow bore on her features, that she was sending Alice to the tavern that morning? The little Alice knew of taverns had come from walking by Fisher's Tavern in Dedham on her various errands for Mr. Morton; it had spilled out a constant stream of hooting men, with an occasional girl not dressed as she should be answering back from an upstairs window.

Alice did not wish to work at the tavern. She kept her eyes down throughout breakfast in the hope that it would keep the talk away from her, and it seemed to do so; the widow and Freeman laid out their plans for the day, yet as the plans didn't seem to include her, she began to think their talk as bad as the actual announcement she dreaded.

But once the breakfast was cleared away, the widow's first concern appeared to be Alice's poultice. She sat Alice down, unwrapped her hand, examined it without change in expression, and went to the cupboard for the salve jar and a clean strip of linen. After she had swabbed and wrapped she said, "You must keep it dry. Fetch me the clothes you came in so I may wash them."

Alice went to the stairs, her face in flame over the state of her clothes, and over the fact that the widow had noticed them, but as her face flamed the thoughts underneath tumbled as hotly. Why should the widow care about Alice's clothes if she only wished to send her to Thacher? Or did she only care about sending her to Thacher in clean linen? In either case, of course, the clothes must be washed and laid out to dry; a thick haze hung damp in the air, and until the sun did something better Alice couldn't be sent anywhere. Or would the widow send Alice ahead and the clothes after?

Alice found her dirty clothes as she'd left them, wrapped in a tight ball and pushed as far back under the eaves as she'd been able to push them. She shook them out; they smelled of piss and puke yet; she balled them up again and returned to the stairs.

If the widow sent Alice away she needn't go to the tavern; she could empty the widow's money jar as Freeman had suggested and set out for Yarmouth, as Freeman had also suggested. But at Yarmouth, what then? She might find another widow. Or another Verley. Or another tavern.

Alice returned to the keeping room. Freeman had disappeared. The widow took her clothes from her without fuss and said, as if it had been the subject all along, "You claim some skill at spinning?"

"Yes, madam."

The widow held up her scarred hands. "I manage the loom, but not the wheel. For a time my granddaughter Bethiah spun for me—" Her voice trailed off.

Alice looked again at the widow. Yesterday Alice wouldn't have thought her old enough to have a granddaughter able to spin, but now something seemed to have aged her, troubled her. Had the granddaughter Bethiah died? The widow collected herself, went on. "And then, of course, foreign cloth came in so cheap, but now—" She stopped again, no doubt reminded of the men's talk of the night before. Was this what had been on her mind all along? She had hoped to do her part to aid the non-importation plan, but as she couldn't spin . . .

Alice turned to the wheel that stood pushed back in the corner of the keeping room, a walking wheel, for turning fleece into woolen yarn, not the smaller foot wheel that was used to spin flax into linen. Alice had begun to use the walking wheel at Mr. Morton's as soon as she'd come into her height, but at Medfield, Nabby Verley had put both her wheels away in favor of purchasing the more fashionable imported fabrics.

Alice said, "Where is your wool, madam?"

The widow turned and climbed the stairs. She returned with a dusty basket half full of combed and carded rolls of fleece, as if the spinner had been forced to leave off abruptly. Alice picked out a roll and pulled the end into a thin snake; she wound the snake onto the spindle with her bandaged hand, pleased to see she could work the fingers as she needed above the bandage. She tested the wheel, rock-ing it back and forth to take its motion, and began. It took her some time to recapture the rhythm: three steps back and spin the wheel clockwise to twist the fleece into yarn, three steps forward and spin the wheel the other way to wind the yarn off the spindle; three steps back again to wind the yarn onto the bobbin. Backward, forward, backward. Backward, forward, backward. Alice's fingers needed some time to adapt to the restriction in the palm, her aching shoulder wouldn't rotate as fast as she'd have liked, and she walked many un-needed steps, but soon enough the roll of fleece began to draw down and the yarn to build up on the bobbin.

The widow observed Alice for a time but then left her to her task and returned to her own. The wheel hummed like a steady wind, isolating Alice in her corner, and her attention was so fixed on her task that by the time she looked around she was amazed to see how much the widow had accomplished. The laundry tub had been set up in the dooryard, the water lugged, the washing already done and spread out on the shrubs to dry.

ALICE FINISHED OFF the basket of fleece that afternoon; that night she and the widow sat with the hand reel, winding the yarn off the bobbin and knotting it into skeins. Four of them, all told. Even Free-man, sitting nearby tilting a thick book toward a candle, looked at the finished skeins and lifted an eyebrow. Did Alice's small success disap-point or please him? The one arched brow didn't tell.

That night, as Alice climbed the stairs, she heard the widow's voice rising up behind her. "She's a good spinner. You might mention that in the village."

"I shall. Although you might recall my efforts last evening didn't end well."

"And these our better citizens. If she were to end up at that tavern—"

"This is why I so strongly urged returning her to Boston."

"So she might end up in some Boston tavern?"

"So she might take her case before a court, which will place her somewhere in safety to work out her time."

"You have such blanket faith in this court."

"And you such blanket distrust."

"I have greater faith in you finding her somewhere safe to work right here in this village."

To that Freeman seemed to make no answer.

TWELVE

Next morning the widow's face looked something brighter, Freeman's much the same. He set off for Winslow's farm as soon as he'd breakfasted. A brief altercation took place where the widow attempted to hand him some money from her jar, he attempted to wave it off with talk of a loan, the widow thrust it at him again. Freeman took the money and went off.

He returned lugging a bag of wool, and again that thing leaped in Alice's chest. More wool to spin meant Alice there yet, in the widow's home. The widow laid an old blanket over the keeping room table, and she and Alice sat one to a side, picking the bits of pitch, dirt, and matting out of the fleece until they were both slick to the elbows in lanolin. They picked the whole day, rolling up the blanket only long enough to serve up a cold mutton dinner, throughout which Freeman sat uncommonly silent; after the dinner he disappeared and didn't return till supper, where again he had little to say.

Alice went to bed and listened to the wind combing the pines, the waves raking the beach. She thought she might possibly be lulled to sleep by the sounds until she heard a new one: the rise and fall of voices below. She crept to the stairs in time to catch a question from the widow.

"You told her Alice could spin?"

"I did so."

"Mr. Winslow said right here at this table they had no one to spin at home."

"He did say that, yes. But as I said before, she's got no paper, no reference—"

"And a halfhearted recommendation from you. You needn't deny it, sir; you're incapable of speaking other than you think."

"I might say to you, Widow Berry, that one often puts to others what one possesses in oneself. I might also say that we should be a very great pair of fools if we did not assume our friend Shubael had spread the tale of his stowaway across the whole village."

Silence, after which Freeman took a second turn. "I might also remind you, Widow Berry, of the very fair chance that Mr. Winslow himself said something to his wife about the girl."

"What might he have said that could possibly turn his wife against her? He sat right here and watched her work at her tasks all the evening without a misstep or a whimper."

"Perhaps he reported on the uncommon beauty of her face and form."

Another silence, after which Freeman again took double turn.

"You understand the wife's not well."

"Yes, I do. And I understand you men are a great lot of fools. I'm going to my bed. Good night, sir."

"Good night?"

"Good night."

"Well, good night, then."

. . .

THE WOMEN BEGAN carding the next day, pulling the handfuls of fleece through fine-toothed wire brushes over and over until the strands came straight and smooth; after the carding came the combing of the fleece into rolls for easy handling, like the ones Alice had pulled from the dusty basket. As they worked Alice looked often at their paired hands. Alice's burn had already eased under the widow's care, but the widow's scars put an awkwardness to almost any task she attempted, and Alice wondered often at the flames that had disfigured her.

As the women worked, Freeman came and went, his long shadow moving in and out of the house, his horse shuffling in and out of the yard, and although in his absence Alice sometimes worried that he would pop up and surprise her unaware, she felt easier with him gone.

The women worked at the carding and combing until they had prepared enough wool for Alice to move to the wheel again; from there the widow carded and combed alone as Alice spun. The next full day at the wheel Alice spun six skeins of wool, and as that meant a backward-forward walk of near twenty miles, she had no great trouble that night with her sleeping.

THE DAYS MOVED along: one, another, and another; Alice spent most of each day at the wheel. The nights developed a habit of their own: the widow and Freeman would wait for Alice to take the stairs and then settle into a discussion of the day's events below; Alice would take the stairs loudly to the top, then creep halfway back to listen. But in that listening Alice caught no further mention of Freeman's efforts to find her work in the village. She considered what this might mean and decided it meant that for now the widow needed her to spin down her bag of wool. She calculated it would take her eight days to complete the job and lulled herself to sleep that night by chanting it over and over: eight more days in the widow's home.

ONCE THE WIDOW had finished the carding and combing she returned to the other work the season demanded: slaughtering the calf, cooking up its offal and making mince and sausage, milking, weeding, egging, and always, cooking and washing. But even a weaver of the widow's reduced dexterity could fully occupy three or more spinners, and so Alice stayed at the wheel. After Alice had produced a quantity of yarn the widow also took on the next chore—dyeing—alone. She emptied the night jars into the blue dye tub to dissolve the indigo cakes with the chamber-lye, and went woods-walking to collect red oak fronds for the red dye and sassafras bark for the yellow. She soaked and dried and soaked and dried and soaked and dried the yarn, first filling the house and then the yard with the stink of it as she spread the wet yarn on the bushes to dry.

When Alice had spun her way halfway through the bag of wool the widow asked Freeman to pull the loom out from under the eaves in the attic and help her repair its tackling, which he did with an ease and agility that belied his hinged-together appearance. Aside from that single task he began to spend more daylight hours outside of the home, attending to whatever was his business, or perhaps just avoiding the stench by visiting the tavern, but he always came home by supper and sat with them in the evening. Alice and the widow would wind yarn or sew while Freeman read, either to himself out of a book by someone named Locke, or out loud from something like Pope or Shakespeare. From time to time Freeman asked Alice to mend a cuff for him, or remove a sauce stain from his shirt, or affix a button, and for each task he gave her twopence. At first Alice feared those coins, suspecting what else the man expected them to pay for, but as time went by and the coins continued to come but the man didn't, she began to accept them with greater comfort. She even began to look forward to the evenings. Freeman seemed pleased that Alice knew some of the works he read from, and that she listened with such grave attention; he sometimes asked her a question about a particular passage, and if she knew what he talked of he seemed more pleased than he did over a clean shirtfront.

The walking wheel sat in the northeast corner of the keeping room, and from there Alice could observe and take note of the occupants of her new household with freedom. In addition to observing, she listened. She had long ago made note that few masters or mistresses credited a servant with a working pair of ears, but she also imagined that the hum of the wheel caused the others to believe their speech better muffled than it was. Through her listening she discovered that both the widow and Freeman had been raised in Satucket and that Freeman had been a particular friend of the widow's husband, which perhaps went some way to explaining the loose way of speaking between them. She learned that Shipmaster Hopkins was the widow's husband's cousin, that he'd married Freeman's sister, and had eight grown children. She learned that the widow had one living child, a daughter named Mehitable, who had married a man named Clarke and lived in one of the big houses near the mill, with two babes of her own and several older stepchildren, which explained the age of the widow's spinning granddaughter Bethiah, but not what might have happened to her.

As the position of the wheel allowed Alice to face the window if she desired she also came to recognize the widow's nearest neighbors, the mismatched Deacon Smalley, a man so slightly built as to appear near Alice's size from the road, and an Indian called Sam Cowett, taller even than Freeman and half again as broad. Alice had several times heard the widow or Freeman give their good-days to either neighbor as they passed along the landing road, and heard the neighbors offer up their greetings in return. Yet with all these people connected to the widow by blood or proximity, except for Freeman's political gatherings, no one ever came to the widow's home at all. Alice was therefore greatly surprised one day when Freeman returned from the village with a young, pink-faced boy beside him.

If the boy surprised Alice he more greatly surprised the widow. She let a skein of yarn drop from her hands into the dye kettle, and rushed toward the boy in such a hurry she trailed blue dye all down her apron. She gave him a fierce hug, stood back from him, and said, "Well!" and then "Well!" again, before seeming to notice his eyes darting toward Alice's corner like a pair of hummingbirds. The widow introduced him: her grandson Nate Clarke, her daughter's oldest stepson. It seemed she would have said more if she could have thought of it before Freeman came up and laid a hand on the boy's shoulder.

Freeman said, "Your lad has news for you, Widow Berry," but the boy stood dumb. Freeman continued. "He's stood the examination of candidates and has been admitted to the fall term at Harvard College."

The widow hugged the boy again; Alice gave him a second look. The fine bones, fine hair, and fine features had deceived her; she wouldn't have thought him the age for college. Besides that, he seemed dim-witted. As the widow inquired after the particulars of the examination he answered with two disjointed words: English. Latin.

After a time Freeman disappeared into his room and returned with the book by Locke, which appeared to be the real purpose of the visit. Freeman handed the book to the boy as if he were handing him a basket of eggs; in truth, Alice was surprised he could bring himself to relinquish it. He said, "Take heed of him, my boy. Take heed. You'll find his faith in the goodness of man most inspiring."

"But how does he account for the not-good?"

Alice gave the boy a third look. Perhaps some wit in him.

"Read the book, lad," Freeman said. "Now don't be late for your tutor."

But the boy didn't move. He seemed to have shaken off his stupor. "Will you tell me first, sir, what you say of this non-importation plan?"

"Well, lad, you're fifteen now—"

"Nearer sixteen, sir."

"Nearer sixteen, then. You tell me what you think of it."

"My father's strong against it. He's against the new tax too, but he thinks—"

"I know what your father thinks, as does all the village. I ask what you think."

"I don't know. I have some trouble over it."

"What troubles you?"

"Well, 'tis the law, sir."

"Ah. The law. Very good. The law declares the tax must be paid, and so the tax must be paid. Is that how you make it?"

"I do, sir."

"Very good. Now suppose you ask yourself if this tax is indeed a lawful one. Suppose you ask yourself who made the tax and why, and by what right."

"I should say a law come out of Parliament to be a law of the highest order."

"Higher than the law of nature? Higher than the law of a man's own conscience?"

The boy stood silent.

"Suppose you next ask yourself who gains by this new tax and who loses. Suppose you ask yourself too who pays it, and whether those who pay it are allowed a say in its making. Ask yourself these things, and report to me what you make for answers. Now be gone or you'll be late for your tutor."

LATER THAT NIGHT Alice heard the widow and Freeman in argument below, their voices rising in counterpoint up the stairwell. Alice moved far enough down the stairs to catch such phrases as would identify their subject, and when she discovered they talked of the boy she thought to return to her bed but found herself caught by the next sentence.

"You pit the boy against his father," the widow said.

"I let him see another side," Freeman answered.

"You let him see your side."

"Not mine alone."

"Nor all the province's, as you'd let him think it."

"He's old enough to think for himself."

"But not old enough to survive by himself. You shouldn't have brought him here. If his father were to learn of it—"

"The boy knows enough to keep quiet."

"Nonetheless—"

Silence.

"Nonetheless?" Freeman prompted.

"Nonetheless, sir, I thank you for it."

"Pah! A happy accident. By the way, did Myrick send a boarder to you?"

"He did not."

"How now? I was almost sure of it; a large party come for the wedding—"

"Mine is a 'pagan house,' Mr. Freeman. I heard the Myrick sisters call it so two days ago at the mill, before they saw me approaching. I expect no recommendation from them or anyone else in the village."

"You might do something for yourself in that regard."

"What 'something,' sir?"

"You might appeal to the reverend, return to the church."

"For that I must be greater starved than I am at present. When you're next in the village would you be so kind as to fetch another bag of wool from Mr. Winslow? Alice has neared the bottom of this one."

Alice heard no more talk. Another bag of wool. Eight more days. Nine or ten if she slowed some. Already, the waking dreams of Philadelphia and the high-walled ship had been replaced by dreams of Satucket and her bed in the widow's attics.

Her sleep dreams remained the same.

THIRTEEN

Alice's eavesdropping prevented any great surprise when the Sabbath came and the widow stayed home. Alice walked to meeting with Freeman, who took advantage of the widow's absence to pepper Alice with questions he'd no doubt wished to ask her for some days now, and Alice answered in varying degrees of truth. *Where was her family? All dead, sir. Had she always lived at Boston? They'd come from London when she was a girl, sir. And just where at Boston did she live with her master? No great distance from the docks, sir.* As the docks fringed the length of the harbor Alice felt her answer safe there. Freeman might have caused more difficulty over the exact part of the docks if they hadn't just then come upon Shipmaster Cobb and his wife and four children, also on their way to meeting. Mrs. Cobb was a loose-fleshed, loose-mouthed woman who took Alice under her wing, rambling on about her children's ills all the way to the meetinghouse, then directing Alice to the women's gallery.

Alice took her seat and looked down, pleased to discover she knew so many faces now; the boy Nate's stuck out as it swung in her direction and fixed there. Alice attempted to fix her own attention on the reverend, but she couldn't manage to keep it there. A young boy pulled a louse out of a smaller boy's hair and cracked it between his fingernails. Two little girls pushed at each other until their mother cuffed the girl nearest her. The boy behind the lousy boy took a pin out of his coat pocket and stuck it in the lousy boy's arm. A woman in the black of mourning began to weep quietly. What had the reverend said to start her tears? Alice tried to attend the sermon. *Eternal wrath shall come to the soul who neglects the call of the church.* Perhaps the woman's husband hadn't done his duty toward meeting. Or perhaps the reverend spoke of the widow?

Whoever he spoke of, he spoke till the sun had moved out of the east window and into the south one. As they filed out of church Alice saw the boy Nate wait at the steps till the pin boy passed close by him; he gripped the boy by the shoulder, bent low, and spoke in his ear. The boy passed something to Nate—the pin, if Alice were to guess— and Nate held the boy another second before releasing him. The pin boy rolled his shoulder, as if it ached him, and dashed down the steps, from time to time looking behind him.

AT MR. MORTON's all the household members had fasted between morning and afternoon services; at the Verleys a full dinner was prepared, but for Mr. Verley alone, which often left him snoring in his pew during the afternoon sermon; at the widow's a cold platter was set down so that each could partake or not as it suited him. The widow ate heartily and well; Freeman took a chicken leg as he walked past the table; Alice tried a piece of bread and butter and found, contrary to Mr. Morton's teaching, that it did not fight with God's words and make her ill.

If Alice had been shocked when the widow stayed home from meeting, her eyes indeed popped when the widow sat down to wind yarn after her meal; Alice hadn't worked on the Sabbath since the day a storm had flooded Mr. Morton's front parlor and they'd been forced to mop the floor. She stood in great unease halfway between the fire and the wheel until the widow said, "Mr. Freeman, before you retire to your room to go over your accounts—or excuse me, as it is the Lord's Day you of course do naught but pray over them—would you be so kind as to fetch down the Bible so Alice may spend the Sabbath as she's no doubt accustomed?"

Freeman retrieved a dusty Bible from the top left-hand cupboard next to the fire, handed it to Alice, and retired to his room without a word. Alice sat at table and opened the Bible wherever it would fall, but the words wouldn't take up any kind of order, her mind too busy piecing together new evidence about the people whose roof she shared. She got so far: The widow did not attend church, or abstain from work on the Sabbath, or read the Bible. Freeman attended church and would have the widow so do, to the point of his prodding her about it the night before. The widow did not care for his prodding and now jabbed back at his working his accounts on the Sabbath with a poorly disguised sermon of her own—those who lived in glass houses should not throw stones—the widow thus driving the last word home.

Or so Alice thought until Freeman's courtroom voice boomed out of his bedroom: "Eight pounds ten and two. Amen."

THE NEXT MORNING Freeman fetched the widow her bag of wool and departed for Barnstable. When Alice inquired when he might return, the widow said, "When he can. He's a law practice to attend to."

"At Barnstable?"

"'Tis our court town, and the place Mr. Freeman lives in his own fine home, when he's not engaged in trading with his brother at Satucket."

Alice pondered that in wonder a time. "So you have a room to let now."

"I don't let Mr. Freeman's room. He pays me twelve pounds a month to keep it ready for him."

Twelve pounds a month, for a bed not slept in! Alice's wonder deepened. It seemed an extraordinary amount to pay, an extraordinary arrangement; but if the widow collected her money whether Freeman lived there or not, she no doubt wished him long at Barnstable. It likewise suited Alice. Freeman hadn't made the slightest attempt at her person, but he wished her gone, and so Alice could wish him to be so with untroubled conscience.

And yet the house seemed strangely flat without him, although it filled with a certain easiness that had heretofore been absent, the easiness not come from Alice alone. The widow made less fuss over dinner and didn't always trouble to sit for breakfast, nibbling at an end of bread and sipping tea as she worked a paste or turned her cheeses; neither did she always trouble to put on her shoes and stockings or lace up her bodice.

Alice continued to work the wheel as the widow moved to the loom to lay a web for some blanketing. The loom was situated in the eastern, cooler part of the attics, positioned so that the light would pass over the weaver's shoulder, and the widow worked almost every morning there, the heavy thump of the loom traveling down the stairs as easily as the voices below traveled up. With Freeman gone, of course, Alice had no one to eavesdrop on and so heard no further talk of her finding work in the village, but the idea began to fix in her mind that the scheme to be rid of her had disappeared with Freeman.

Left alone, the widow would be content to keep her as long as she could afford to feed her. Thinking this, Alice resolved to take a smaller share on her plate at each setting.

The boy Nate came looking for Freeman, and when Alice told him Freeman was at Barnstable the boy hung silent and awkward on the doorjamb until Alice said, "Shall I get the widow down? She's upstairs at the loom."

"No!" the boy answered in a kind of alarm. "That is to say no, please. That is to say, no thank you, miss. Good day to you." He bolted out of doors.

The next Sabbath came around, but without Freeman to mark the day Alice nearly lost track of it until the widow said to her, "Are you not getting late for meeting?"

Alice ran the length of the road and slipped in under the darkening eye of the deacon, but again the reverend's sermon escaped her attention, her eyes too busy taking in all the colors of the villagers before and beside her. She found Nate Clarke's pale hair in his family's pew, but she couldn't find the pin boy until a loud knocking of boot on wood drew her eye to a seat a good deal farther away from Nate than the pin boy had positioned himself the Sunday before.

After the sermon Alice left the church, keeping her eyes to herself until she heard someone behind her say "Oh!" as if he'd been stepped on. She turned around to find the boy Nate.

"I didn't think you here. That is to say, I was looking out for you to ask if Mr. Freeman were returned."

"He isn't."

"I see. Thank you. Good day, then, miss," but he hadn't managed to move either forward or back before a couple drew up to them. The woman was striking enough to fix Alice's eye; the man she wouldn't have noticed at all if he hadn't barked at Nate, "Come along, come along, you take a week to get your knees up, I've not seen the like of you," which was an odd remark, considering that the man barking was the shape of a short, stubby cask, and his own legs could make but half the boy's stride no matter how hard he pumped them. Two girls came after them, the younger a pale, jumpy sprite who caught up to her brother and hung on his elbow, chattering at him until her father shouted, "Quiet yourself, Bethiah! God's breath! Show some respect for the Sabbath." The other girl, perhaps a year or two older than Alice, walked at a pace that kept her halfway between the three in front and the woman behind; in fact, the woman behind seemed to linger until she fell back even with Alice.

The woman said, "You're the girl that keeps at my mother's."

Of course, thought Alice, the widow's daughter Mehitable, the boy's stepmother, and so close a print of the older woman as to allow no question of the relation, except for the way she'd pinched her features.

"What is your name?"

"Alice Baker, madam."

"And how do you find it there?"

"I couldn't have found a better situation, madam."

"Indeed! And all are in health there?"

"Most certainly."

That seemed all the woman wished to know. She hurried ahead to chastise the younger girl, who had now dropped back to pester her sister with a chant: "Jane! Jane! Fair or plain! *Fair* says Joseph! *Plain* says James!"

Jane, if such indeed was her name, was indeed fair, as fair as her brother, and either as poorly skilled at being sociable or put out of humor by her sister's teasing. She increased her stride just enough until she was again balanced in solitude between the two pairings of parent and child, her spine as straight as a mast, and continued so until Alice lost sight of them down the road.

THE WEATHER WARMED, and with it came new changes to the view
outside Alice's window: the yellow pine pollen no longer rimmed the
puddles, the plum blossoms faded, the seaward skyline became dotted
with masts, as the ships prepared to set off after fish or whales. The
smell of the house changed too: the must of the seaweed that packed
the foundation, the salt of the sand flats at low tide, the yeast of the
new-turned earth, all came unimpeded through the open windows to
replace the winter smells of smoke and grease and too-close bodies.

The boy Nate Clarke came by several more times to see if Freeman had returned, but neither time did he step within the threshold.
The shipmaster Hopkins came by to leave off some papers for Freeman, greeting Alice now as if he'd forgotten how she came there, but
those were their only visitors.

Alice's hand healed into three thick, red, intersecting lines, forming a near star shape that caused that hand to open and close a frac-
tion slower but otherwise didn't restrict its function. Her neck had
returned to its natural color. Her shoulder had stopped aching. The
cut on her cheek could only be seen if one strained to look for it, like
a fine, pale crescent moon in daylight. Alice could look at the widow's scars and feel lucky.

The widow finished her blanket and laid a second web for a piece
of jacketing, in a fine, deep crimson. When it was done she sent Alice
to the fulling mill to get the weave tightened and cleaned of lanolin.
The fulling mill sat across the stream from one of the fine, big houses
Alice had made note of on her first walk to the village; as she walked
past she saw a boy chopping kindling in a hail of flying wood chips;
his hair glinted gold like the boy Nate's, but he seemed less delicately
built, unless it was the wild fury of his swinging shoulders that gave

the look of heft to him. He looked up as Alice passed and stopped his work to stand dumb. The boy Nate, surely.

Alice left the cloth with the fuller, who shouted over the beating paddles for her to come back for it on Thursday, without giving Alice a first look, let alone a second. Oddly, that was the moment Alice began to feel at home in the village.

WHEN ALICE RETURNED for the fulled cloth and brought it home to the widow she surprised Alice by saying, "Take it to Sears. Ask him if he'd like a piece of homespun on his shelf to soothe the non-importers."

Alice carried the piece of cloth to Sears with no small pride over her part in its making, but at the store Sears pointed to three bolts of English wool and said, "I've jacketing aplenty."

The widow took back the cloth with nothing but a mild stiffening in the jaw and sent Alice back to her spinning.

AT NIGHT THE widow and Alice sat together, winding yarn or mending or knitting; it was that hour, and the quiet in it, that showed up Freeman's absence the greater. It wasn't that the widow and Alice didn't try to talk; it was that there seemed no safe thread of talk for them to follow. If the widow made a remark that suggested a past life including husband and children and more back-and-forth with the people of the village, it would prompt a question from Alice that the widow appeared disinclined to answer. She would divert to talk of the great number of shipwrecks over the winter, or the lateness of the growing season, or the health of the rhubarb. And as the widow had learned long ago not to push at Alice about her past, it greatly narrowed their communion. But perhaps it was the fact that the widow leaped so eagerly on any general remark that Alice managed, such as the great number of crows, or the chance of a rainstorm, or how best to make a sauce for turkeys, that taught Alice a new thing about the widow: she was lonely.

WHEN FREEMAN DID return, Alice wasn't present to witness it. She woke out of a deep sleep to the sound of voices in the keeping room and crept to her spot on the stairs.

"'Tis a late hour, Mr. Freeman, to charge in and wake a household."

"I apologize for waking you, but I've brought news I thought you'd wish to hear at the first possible instant."

"What news? The agreement?"

"The agreement? Well, of that I may tell you that the merchants are all up in arms; the papers are full of nothing but these new restrictions. They guard us more in peace than in war; their ships swarm the coast and stop anyone at the least excuse. I couldn't sell our alewives at any price; all trade is near killed."

"By trade you mean smuggling."

"I mean trade as we've known it these many years in this colony. We've no choice but to ban imports if we wish to continue to make a way for ourselves."

"I've been thinking of this ban. At the rate Alice spins—"

"I'd not count too far on Alice."

"How, now? You can't say she's not a good worker."

"I neither think it nor say it. I only question the likelihood of her remaining here."

"Why, she blooms here! She wouldn't leave us!"

"Unless she were obliged to."

A paper snapped. Freeman's voice dropped so low Alice had to move dangerously low on the stairs to hear him. "There's more in this paper than news of trade."

Silence, except for the crackling of the paper.

After a time the widow said, "It says 'light hair and blue eyes.' This can't be our Alice. Her hair is far too rich a shade for 'light'; her eyes most clearly hazel."

"You must agree the rest matches."

"It says 'aged fifteen years.'"

"You might recall I remarked the first day I saw her she couldn't be a day over sixteen."

"And 'five feet in height'?"

"You can't say she's greatly over it. Come now, you must consider the chances of two such creatures, two such Alices—"

"All right, then, suppose I consider it. Suppose this is our Alice. What then?"

"According to law—"

"The law! Again the law! And after that fine speech you made to Nate about a higher one!"

"Widow Berry, calm yourself. I'm not about to fetch the constable. I confess I've come to your way of thinking about the girl. In truth, she's won me utterly."

The widow's voice softened. "And don't think I haven't noticed the effort you make with her."

"She has a fine mind, which someone else must have noticed before me. She reads and speaks well beyond what I might expect from someone in her situation."

"And she's been taught to work. And she looks to please. That in itself—"

"You needn't add to her charms on my account. But we must take into consideration those who aren't so charmed, and would see this advertisement and make something of it."

"Who in this village—"

"Anyone in dire need of the five pounds reward he offers."

They fell silent.

At length the widow said, "But indeed, sir, it doesn't sound just like. Blue eyes! Light hair!"

"Well, no, not just like."

ALICE WAITED THE next morning until Freeman had gone into the village and the widow out to the barn to apply a balm to the cow's udder. She picked up Freeman's *Gazette* and made her slow way through the advertisements: *For Sale—two Negro men and Negro woman and child . . . Run away from his master William Brown . . . To Hire— Woman in her thirties capable of all House Hold Business Town or Country . . .* On the third page, Alice found it:

> Run away on the 3rd inst. from Emery Verley of Medfield, a servant girl, indented by the name of Alice Cole, aged fifteen years, five feet in height, light complexioned with light hair and blue eyes, comely features. Whoever secures this servant in any gaol in this or the neighboring governments shall have five pounds reward and reasonable charges paid by E. Verley of Medfield. N.B. All masters of vessels are forbid to carry her off, and any others to harbour her at their peril.

Alice stared at the box, exactly centered in the middle of the newspaper page. The words *five pounds* seemed to leap out of all the other words on the page. Surely, surely, such an advertisement would attract the attention of every reader. It occurred to Alice to wonder how long the advertisement had been out there, and she returned to the front page of the paper to find the date. When she saw that it had been published on June the twenty-fifth she received her second great shock: it didn't seem possible that so much time could have passed since she'd left the Verleys. She closed the paper and raced to the cupboard shelf where the widow kept her almanac. June had indeed run down. July was well along. And so came her third shock: the courses that should have given Alice their usual trouble a fortnight past had never appeared to trouble her at all.

FOURTEEN

At first it seemed some trick of time only; she hadn't been gone as long as she thought and she only needed to recount the days to ease her mind. Alice counted and recounted but she couldn't make any better sum of it: Nabby Morton had married Emery Verley near the end of April; Verley had lain atop her from the end of April until she'd run off in early June; her June courses had never come. Such was the truth of it.

Next Alice decided it was nothing but an ordinary quirk in a usually most reliable schedule. She watched between her legs for the first week, then another; she imagined the griping in her womb that always signaled the dark blood and imagined the streaks on her bedsheet and shift; in the dead of night she felt sure she could feel the stickiness with her fingers. But every morning it was the same: the snowy linen, the dry skin, the still womb.

Oddly, the rest of life continued the same, with the single exception that Freeman commissioned the widow to make him a jacket of the crimson broadcloth, and out of the sum he paid the widow the widow paid Alice a shilling, making careful note in a ledger that showed the hours spent at spinning the yarn for the length of cloth, as well as the subtraction for her keep.

Alice added the shilling to the other coins she'd received for this and that small task from Freeman. She continued to listen at her wheel, and at the stairs, but since Freeman's return he'd made no further mention of either sending her back to Boston or finding her work in the village. In fact, the nighttime chats seemed to have diminished; working a loom was heavy work, and Freeman seemed to have come back from Barnstable in greater fatigue than he'd left for it; most nights the household retired to their beds in unison. Every morning Alice checked her sheets and shift, but she did so as if she were in a dream, as if she couldn't believe the sight of nothing could be made into something to fear.

With Freeman's return came the boy Nate, or that was to say, with his return the boy Nate actually came inside, exchanging the Locke for another book and asking Freeman his questions. Freeman had a way of answering a question with a question so that the boy was forced to talk more than seemed to suit his natural inclination, for if Freeman left the room to fetch a book or paper the boy at once fell into silence, as if he were a bird whose cage had just been darkened. He looked at Alice from time to time, his face such a glowing rose if she caught him out that she found herself taking looks at him when his attention was engaged with Freeman. For a time she thought her oldest brother might have grown to look like him, for another time she thought the younger; in the end she decided no; the boy Nate was too finely made, too fair-haired, too *pink* to have ever been her brother.

The next week a shift occurred in Alice's workday that temporarily distracted her from her womb: the widow took her off the wheel to process the flax. First the full-grown plants were pulled up by their roots, then the seeds shaken off for the next year's sowing. Next the stalks were bundled for soaking in the pond to rot away the leaves and soften the tough bark. There came the work for the men. The widow bartered three cheeses and a hen for a pair of strong boys from the village to haul the flax to and from the pond and then brake and swingle the stalks; the sound of the heavy brake bats pounding away the outer husks continued for days, right up to the edges of dark. Once the braking and swingling were done the widow and Alice set to with the hetchels, combing out the fibers into fine, long strands; Alice and the widow ended many days coated in the fine dust and dirt of the flax work.

When Alice returned to the wheel it wasn't to the great walking wheel she'd used for the wool but to the smaller foot wheel, which allowed for sitting, a thing Alice might have appreciated at another time, but now it only increased the restlessness of her spirit. She pumped the foot wheel in a quick, frantic rhythm and fidgeted the flax through her fingers onto the bobbin; as she worked she tried to distract herself by keeping a kind of chant running through her head—a half skein, one handkerchief, five skeins, one shirt—for Freeman had placed another order with the widow for two shirts and twelve handkerchiefs.

Perhaps it was the fact that Freeman must have known every piece of cloth he bought meant that many more days Alice might work for the widow; perhaps it was the other thing distracting her mind; perhaps it was the talk she'd heard on the stairs about having won him utterly; whatever the reason, Alice found herself worrying less and less about Freeman. She found herself even performing small chores for him unasked. She cleaned his boots, reamed out his pipe, trimmed his quill, and learned to know his smile as she did so, but the most gratitude came down on her when she restitched the loose binding in the book by Montesquieu that he read from often in the evenings.

But mostly, Alice spun. As she spun the widow bleached the thread, running it through many cycles of soaking and wringing in hot water and ash before laying it out over the grass to whiten in the sun, and from the finished thread the widow wove a fine dimity, which she bleached again. Alice took a fair degree of satisfaction in the sight of yard upon yard of snowy cloth, but the whiteness that filled her days only showed up how black her dreams had become.

At night Verley chased her into dark, pulsing caves; he bound her in long ropes, and when he pulled them off, her clothes came too, revealing burned skin like the widow's; he forced bread into her mouth, suffocating her until she swallowed, making her belly expand and expand until a putrid black thing burst up from her belly and into her mouth, suffocating her again.

AUGUST CAME; THE non-importation date came; the widow's house filled with men again. The voices around the table sounded less spirited to Alice, as if the thing they had agreed upon two months past had changed into something else, now that it had turned real; if a man did speak, his voice rang thinly while the others stared at him as if he spoke in a foreign tongue. After a time Freeman took over the floor, urging them all to faith and steadfastness, reminding them what they worked toward; he spoke of his dream of a village full of homespun-clad wives and daughters. He pointed to Alice, to Alice's wheel, to the neatly folded length of dimity "fresh off the widow's loom." He raised his mug to the widow and Alice, to the other men's wives and daughters, to the king, and for each toast the table followed him. When the men spilled out into the night they seemed livelier, and Alice didn't put it all to the cider.

The big excitement for the women, however, was Sears. He paused at the door, pointed to the length of cloth, and said, "Are you selling?"

"Indeed," the widow answered.

Sears turned to Freeman. "Test the waters."

"Yes, yes," Freeman said. "Fine thinking."

The widow said, "Three pounds ten."

THE WIDOW GAVE Alice two and six out of Sears's money; three days after the sale she sent her to the store to see if the cloth had sold. As Alice walked by the big house nearest the millpond she saw the girl Jane coming out of the door with a sack in her hand. At the store she found the dimity uncut on Sears's shelf, and Alice had something of a struggle to remember that it had only been three days, that the non-importation agreement wasn't two weeks old.

On her way out of the store she found the boy readying to come in, with the sack she'd last seen in the hands of his sister.

He said, "I come on an errand for my mother. Allspice, three ounces. A pint of salt. Cloves."

Alice said, "Oh."

As he said nothing more, she added, "Good morning," and moved toward home.

The widow took the news of the unsold cloth with a short nod and climbed the stairs to the loom to lay a web for a piece of check. Alice returned to her spinning.

AROUND THE TIME of the unsold cloth Alice's stomach began to grow unsettled, and with the taste of the bile came, at last, the truth of her situation. She was with child, and once the widow discovered it, she would be sent away, no matter whether Freeman ordered more clothes or Sears bought cloth, or the non-importation plan took hold. This was the thing Alice knew as she now knew the widow's loneliness or Freeman's smile; this was a shame no woman would willingly keep under her roof, and Alice feared the discovery of her shame far greater than she feared the horror of bearing a bastard child.

The next week the widow sent Alice back to the store; when she saw the empty shelf where the dimity had been she didn't believe; she walked the whole store round till Sears said to her, "You tell the widow. I'll take more if she has it."

"Would you like a check, sir?"

"A check? Yes, a check too. And the dimity."

When the widow clapped Alice's face between her hands at the news, Alice's excitement was so great she came close to forgetting. Even Freeman beamed at her, but Alice understood the cloth meant more to him than the money the women had earned; it meant the non-importation plan had indeed begun to take hold. He went out and returned with a fine goose; the widow rung its neck, plucked its feathers, spitted it, and returned to her loom.

THE WIDOW'S FLOOR began to collect more litter and the garden more weeds as the women extended their hours at wheel and loom, working as long as the light held. The days had already begun to shorten, and the view outside Alice's window was now deep and thick with the full colors of summer, the air heavy with the scent of honeysuckle, manure, and, always, ocean.

Alice felt always overstuffed; her stomach grew more troublesome; at night she snuck downstairs to steal bread to settle it down. Her dreams remained full of swollen black things that burst out of her from all her openings, sometimes suffocating her, sometimes beating her with pokers, sometimes lying on her like a Verley.

Freeman came and went, and the boy Nate came, each time

exchanging one of Freeman's books for another, books by men named Coke and Bacon and Fortescue, until one day Freeman held before him, instead of a book, a new pamphlet written by James Otis.

Freeman made to hand the pamphlet to Nate but snatched it back and flipped into its pages, his excitement too great to be borne in silence. "You must listen to what he says here, Nate. 'The end of government being the *good* of mankind points out its great duties: it is above all things to provide for the security, the quiet, and happy enjoyment of life, liberty, and property.'" Freeman ruffled more pages. "And here. 'The people certainly never entrusted any Parliamentary body with a power to surrender their liberty in exchange for slavery.'" Another page. "Ah, Alice, hearken as you wear away your fingers; this is for you: 'No British manufactures can be paid for by the colonists. What will follow? One of these two things, both of which it is in the interest of Great Britain to prevent. One, the northern colonists must be content to go naked and turn savages. Or two, become manufacturers of linen and woolen cloth themselves, which will be very destructive to the interests of Great Britain.'"

Freeman crossed to the wheel and leaned over Alice, holding the page in front of her face. "Do you see this, Alice? According to Otis's calculation, if the colonies were forced to manufacture one suit of clothes per person per year, the cost to Great Britain and Ireland would be two million pounds per annum. *Two million pounds.* By God, I must read this to the widow."

Freeman bounded up the stairs, leaving the boy to stand alone with Alice, his eyes fixed on his shoes. After a time he said, "He makes a fine argument."

Alice was so surprised to hear him speak that she assumed Freeman had just returned. She looked up and saw the boy's eyes fixed on her for a moment only before they flew up to the ceiling, but from that position he managed to repeat, "Do you not think he makes a fine argument?"

"Do you speak of Mr. Otis or Mr. Freeman?"

"Mr. Otis. Although where one differs from the other I'm sure I can't say."

"Mr. Freeman does seem to hold a great love for Mr. Otis's words."

"But what if his words are wrong? I mean to say—" The boy stopped there, but it had been such a fine lot of words for the boy, that Alice tried to think of something to say in the way of encouragement. Knowing herself unequal to the subject of politics, she tried another.

"When do you begin at Harvard College?"

"Michaelmas."

"Why, not two months, then."

The boy seemed to have no further words on the subject, and so Alice decided to leave him be, but after a time he surprised her again by asking, "Where do you come from?"

Alice repeated the lie she'd told Freeman. "Boston."

"I've lived the whole of my life in this village."

"But you go away to college now. At Cambridge, is it?"

"Yes, at Cambridge."

The idea of Cambridge seemed to cast him into a gloomy silence. At that moment Freeman returned, which was lucky, because the boy had now dispensed with both Otis and their geographies, and Alice didn't think he had it in him to take up a third subject.

FIFTEEN

T he pattern of Alice's life grew fixed; the homespun cloth continued to sell at Sears's store, and the widow treated Alice as if she were become a permanent fixture at her wheel, but Alice felt only perched there like a migrating goose, watching, listening, waiting to be sent on her way with the next change in the weather.

Freeman had been in place at the widow's for a solid spell, and the evening chatter had increased again; Alice listened each night on the stairs, expecting to hear some suspicion of her condition, but she heard nothing relating to herself at all. They talked of non-importation, and Otis, and this ship in and this one out, and the rising price of everything, until one night Freeman announced that the Verley advertisement had disappeared from the paper.

"So he found his Alice," the widow said, "and ours is safe, then."

The word *safe* floated up the stairs like a cruel joke. What could be safe for Alice now? Verley would ruin her life just the same whether she was returned to him or she wasn't. The thought enraged her. Sparked her. Shook her out of a monthlong dullness. She hadn't risked so much, traveled so far, just to crumble into ruin because of a thing not her making. Verley might yet hold the right to her labor, but he held no right to her womb, nor did his foul seed. She could, she would, do something, and she knew what to do.

Alice hadn't spent all her fifteen years of life in ignorance. She'd heard talk, she'd seen advertisements in the papers, she knew there were ways to free herself of the thing festering in her belly; she knew about the medicines that could bring on a woman's courses. And not only did she know of such medicines, she also knew where to get them in Satucket village. Alice had heard talk of a midwife named Granny Hall who lived along the south-side road in a cottage climbed all over with honeysuckle; with such direction, Alice believed she could find her. She must find her. She would do.

ALICE WAITED THREE more days until the widow sent her to the smith with a broken ladle in need of repair. The day was as the days were in August, the sun hot, the road dry, the air wet, and a fine layer of dust had coated Alice's moist skin by the time she reached the meetinghouse. The road Alice looked for stretched south from the meetinghouse, but the smith lay just beyond; Alice forced herself to push past the turn she wanted in favor of the task with which she'd been entrusted.

Alice had been to the smith before and disliked the place, not just for all the noise and soot but also for the look the smith gave her, and she disliked it more now, the pulsing fires and hot metal pushing the trapped August air to scorching. She further disliked the look of the black metal hanging everywhere: hooks, spades, hoes. Pokers. The smith was working the bellows chain as she walked in, and the roused flames lit his face as if he held the fire inside him. He looked at Alice and she thought she saw something new in the look, as if he might have guessed her condition; she left off the ladle and hurried as fast as the heat would let her back to the south-side road.

Alice hadn't traveled the road before, and she took her time along it, pausing at every honeysuckle vine, straining her eyes for the midwife's house as she'd heard it described. She'd walked a long way and determined she must have missed it, was already struggling to tamp the panic down, when she rounded a turn and got blinded by the gleam of sunlight off a large pond. She looked away from the glare, and there it sat across the road, a pretty little half-house nearly buried in the delicate, thickly sweet blooms. She allowed herself no pause but went straight to the door and knocked.

Everything about the woman who answered spoke of advanced age: the yellowed hair, the clawed hands, the clouded eyes. Part of Alice wanted to run away as she might run from a death ghost; part of her saw in the old woman her own life. She made her request as she had practiced. Pennyroyal. For worm. The woman too looked at her as if she knew her condition, but she turned away, retreated to a small pantry, and came back with a small cloth pouch.

She said, "Sixpence."

Alice picked out three of the coins Freeman had given her and dropped them into the waiting hand, which closed around the money like one of the vines outside the door.

"The whole of it in the one teapot, steeped a quarter hour, no more. A cup three times a day for a week, hot or cold, and you'll expel what ails you in a fortnight. Take it any longer than a week and you'll start bleeding from every opening, blow up like an udder, and go comatose. Do you hear me, girl?"

Alice nodded.

The woman turned away, leaving Alice to step outside and shut the door on herself, as if she were the ghost. A sign? Alice didn't care. She held her first hope in many months in her hand.

ALICE BREWED UP her tea the first chance she found herself alone at the fire and drank one cup down in long, hot gulps; the rest she poured into a borrowed jug and took it cold and slimy where she could in the privacy of her room. She dosed herself just as instructed, three times a day every day for the week, and then she waited. Over the next several weeks she experienced a few days of sharp cramps, but there appeared no sign on her sheets or shift.

OFTEN WHEN ALICE woke, before her condition left its own sleep state, before her stomach had begun to unsettle, she forgot the thing that grew in her. She smelled the rough salt air and heard the chuckling water and the old joy filled her; then her bile rose, and as she remembered, her spirits fell like an overtipped scale. The breakfast bread eased her; dinner unsettled her again; by supper she felt near to fine and might think the pennyroyal had at last set to work in her. She would go to bed and press and pound on her belly in hope of dislodging what grew there; in the morning she went out to the necessary house and jumped violently up and down. Nothing happened. To Alice's amazement, life went on around her as before. Or almost as before.

One day the boy came to return the Otis pamphlet and surprised Alice by opening it up and reading back a passage to Freeman.

"Otis says here, sir, 'Let Parliament lay what burdens they please on us, it is our duty to submit and patiently bear them, till they will be pleased to relieve us.'"

"Well, now, yes, they may make such *laws* as they please, but they may not tax us without our being represented in that body. Nor can Parliament alter a law of God, or one of human conscience, or logic."

The logic of this escaped Alice, as she believed it escaped the boy; his eyes lifted and met hers in matching puzzlement, although he nodded at Freeman in agreement and accepted another book in exchange for the pamphlet: *The History of the Pleas of the Crown* by Matthew Hale.

Some time after the boy had left with his book Alice went outside to bring in a piece of shirting that had been bleaching in the sun and was startled when the boy stepped silently out of the woodlot like one of the foxes that lived there. He came up and helped her collect the cloth but said nothing, as usual.

"Do you make out all these books Mr. Freeman gives you?" Alice asked by way of easing him, and was startled a second time by his laugh: deep, like a man's; boisterous, like a boy's.

"Not by half," he said. "Do you think I might take it as flattery that he thinks I should?"

"Oh, yes, indeed."

He grinned, still holding his end of cloth. After a time he said, "Do you like living with my grandmother?"

"Yes, I do."

"I liked it when I lived with her."

Alice looked anew at the boy. Was it possible that here lay the answers to the questions Alice hadn't dared to ask the widow? She said, "You lived with your grandmother?"

The boy began to talk, slowly at first, picking his way, growing more sure-footed as he went, the tale a patchy thing one person told another when he thought the biggest puzzle pieces were already laid down. A time or two Alice asked a question, but she didn't risk too many; the boy seemed to think her in a certain degree of confidence, which she didn't like to disprove. Out of the jumble Alice learned that the widow's husband had drowned trying to drive a pod of whales onto the shore in a storm, that the widow had lived with the boy's father and stepmother, the widow's daughter, until a disagreement drove the widow to claim her dower right and return to her husband's home, where she now lived. While making candles one day her dress had caught fire, and she would have died, the boy said, if there had been no one at hand to beat out the flaming cloth and carry her to safety. There he stopped, as if contemplating the way life turned, or didn't turn.

"My father doesn't allow any of us to visit here," the boy said after a time, his face coloring in what Alice took to be half-embarrassment at the behavior of his relations, and half-pride at his own courage in defying them, but it also seemed to remind him of a limit beyond which he dared not travel. He stepped in to push his end of the cloth into Alice's arms, stepped back. "I must go."

Alice was so intent on folding up the cloth, so sure the boy had made the turn for home, that when he changed direction and lurched at her, reached for her, she cried out in alarm.

The boy stopped as he was, eyes wide.

The door to the house opened; Freeman stepped out into the yard. "Here, now, what goes on there?"

Alice turned and dashed past him into the house, all of her—knees, stomach, heart, hands—trembling.

THAT NIGHT ALICE lay awake in a new kind of turmoil. She couldn't close her eyes without seeing the boy's hands reaching for her, couldn't see the hands without seeing Verley, smiling behind them. But the boy hadn't been smiling, and he had looked so shocked at her outcry. But what did it matter how he'd looked? It would be with him as it was with Verley; he would look at her as he pleased, and he would have done with her as he pleased if Freeman hadn't come out and disrupted them.

Freeman.

How quickly, now, he had gone from supposed enemy to proven savior! In truth, how unfair she had been to think he ever meant any harm to her. Hadn't he come to her aid at Boston? Hadn't he admitted he no longer wished to send her to the constable? She must add to his credit too the story the boy had told her. Alice imagined the widow in flames and crying out as Alice had cried out; she imagined Freeman leaping up from his chair and beating out the flames with a blanket or bed rug or perhaps even his own jacket. Yes, it would be his own jacket, Alice decided. He would beat out the flames and wrap the widow gently in a clean, white sheet, as clean and white as the handkerchief he'd handed Alice at Boston, and gently, gently, carry her to safety.

SIXTEEN

A lice spun, and snuck pieces of bread to calm her stomach, and spun, until the garden came into its fullest season. Alice helped the widow pick the fruits and vegetables, but their textile manufacture could ill spare her for the rest; she returned to the wheel and left the widow to the preserving. The widow continued to weave in the early morning to get the most of the east light, but after putting up and serving dinner she stayed confined to the kitchen duties.

When the widow finished off nine yards of check, she sent Alice to Sears's store while she drew in the web for the dimity. All the long walk to the store Alice looked out for the boy Nate; just as she passed his house by the mill she heard the clap of a door and whirled around, but it was his stepmother, the widow's daughter, who stepped through it. She caught up to Alice just outside of the store and fingered Alice's cloth.

"You made this?"

"The Widow Berry wove it, madam."

"She can manage a loom?"

"Very well, madam."

Alice stepped ahead of the woman into the store and carried her cloth to the counter.

Sears said, "How much?"

Alice answered as the widow had instructed: "Four pounds six shillings."

Sears counted out the money and handed it to her.

Alice had a few things to purchase for the widow—a pint of salt, some shoe bindings, an ounce of indigo—when she approached the counter she saw the widow's daughter with the length of check in her arms and heard her ask Sears to put it on her husband's account, but to please mark it as a West India calico.

By the time Alice finished her own purchasing and left the store, Mehitable Clarke had disappeared; the boy was nowhere. Alice had gone three-quarters of the route home when she felt it like the edges of a storm; she turned to see him jogging down the road toward her. She clutched her purchases and ran.

WHEN ALICE TIPPED the money into the widow's hand it brought something to life in the woman's face that Alice had missed before, something that to Alice's mind made her all the more handsome. The widow went to the book, made a mark in it, and said, "I believe we might start you on a wage, now." They agreed that after Alice's keep and care were subtracted she was to be paid sixpence a day; the widow handed her the coins and made a note in the ledger.

Alice carried the coins up the stairs and added them to the others that lay in the bottom of the cloth pouch that had once held the pennyroyal; she bounced the pouch in her hand, taking the weight of it, wondering if the feel of the money had changed her look, too, as it had the widow's. She went back down by the front stairs and through the hall to check her face in the small mirror that hung there.

If the money had changed Alice, it hadn't changed her for the better: her eyes had grown hollow and dark, her cheeks pale and damp, her lips red and swollen. Besides the changes in her face her breasts swelled out the top of her bodice, her arms had plumped, her waist had straightened. It seemed to her that her condition must be plain to all, but as she listened to the widow and Freeman that night from her spot on the stairs she heard no mention of herself anywhere. Tax, trade, Otis, took up all.

THE BOY CAME the next day. While he stood in supposed attention on Freeman he dashed his eyes at Alice so often he appeared to have a tic; when Freeman left the room to get a pamphlet or book or whatever it was he wished to feed the boy next the boy stepped closer to Alice and dropped his voice low. "Why do you run from me?"

"I don't want you near me."

"Why not? What have I done?"

"I don't want you touching me."

The boy blinked once, twice, three times. He said, "Very well, then I won't." He held up his hands for Alice to see, jammed them into his pockets, and said, "Now will you talk to me?"

Freeman returned; he studied the pair standing by the wheel; he would know there was something wrong with it; he beckoned the boy away from her corner.

ALICE NEXT SAW Nate Clarke at meeting, coming out of his family's pew, looking up and spying Alice in the women's gallery. He made a great display of hiding his hands in his pockets, lifting his eyebrows, and wagging his elbows at her; there was something so comical in the pantomime, like an angry chicken flapping around in the yard, that the corners of Alice's mouth lifted, even as her face heated. Nate grinned back, a looser, freer thing than she'd yet seen in him, but he didn't remove his hands from his pockets.

THAT NIGHT THE talk Alice overheard from her spot on the stairs seemed stuck again on politics—Freeman's Otis-says-this, Otis-says-that, the widow's how-this, why-that—and Alice came near to dozing until she realized that somehow the talk had turned to frolics. The Cobbs planned a watermeloning party at the midweek and had asked Freeman to pass an invitation to the widow; the widow had declined it. The discussion grew sharp.

"You might find yourself entertained."

"I might find myself avoided like a pest house."

"By some, perhaps—"

"By any who think like my son or think like the reverend. Too many for my liking."

"You might turn them."

"Into what, hypocrites? I don't care to go, Mr. Freeman. You might take the girl, though. She looks dispirited, and I can't make out the cause."

"I can make it out well enough. Nate's been bothering her. I told him to leave her be."

"Did you, now! You can't think he'd harm her."

Silence. "As to this frolick—"

"I'm quite done with this frolick. Take Alice and your own advice: leave me be."

• • •

FREEMAN AND ALICE left the house together and walked along the landing road toward the water until it swung parallel to the shore along the path that Alice and Freeman took to meeting. They fell in behind several Myricks and a Howe making their way in the same direction; they turned in at the Cobb farm, where nearly a dozen young people milled around a pair of carts at the edge of the watermelon field. Along the far side of the field sat a long board set on stumps and covered with a cloth, the cloth covered with baskets like the one the widow had sent with Alice that held a full-to-brimming pie dish; at the farthest end sat a huge cask, around which a group of men had already congregated. Alice took her basket to one end of the table while Freeman veered toward the other; Alice placed her basket and looked around. She spied a handful of mulatto servants among the women setting up food, and a knot of young people her age around the carts; to which group did she belong? Freeman came up behind and pointed her toward the carts. He said, "The old folk may shirk; you, my dear, must work for your supper."

Alice moved nearer the young group, but not into it. She recognized Nate's sisters, Jane and Bethiah, but didn't see Nate. She knew most of the rest of the group from seeing them around the village, but she felt no ease at the thought of joining them. She stood back and watched as two boys took up the cart handles and the group moved off down the rows, soon pairing up, or so it seemed, into boy-girl, boy-girl. The straight-backed Jane stood beside a young man; Joseph? James? Like her brother, she seemed to have little to say to him.

The melons were tweaked from their vines and hefted into the cart with much jostling and shouting and giggling all around. Alice felt suddenly old. She turned to go, and there was Nate. He said, "Will you partner with me if I promise to keep a melon between?"

Alice flushed. Nate grinned. It was the second time she'd seen such an easy display in him, and both times it had occurred in answer to her own discomposure. Did he only grow free as she shrank tighter? Was this the Verley in him? Or did he only wish to jolly her into a state of greater ease? But why should he want her easy with him? Or need she ask that question? But Nate had already stepped off toward the field, as if unconcerned whether she followed him or she didn't. And after all, what harm could he do with all these people around them, with Freeman yet in hailing distance?

Alice trailed after Nate. He turned to make sure she came, and then set off down one of the emptier rows, finding his way to a plump melon, twisting it free, handing it to her to settle in the cart. They continued. After a time a strip of sweat appeared down the middle of Nate's shirt, and his hair damped around the edges; he had the hard work of stooping and lifting. They finished the row and began another. More than once someone cast a curious eye at them; here and there a boy or girl would call out to Nate and he would answer back; but after a time even that died down, leaving Alice and Nate a quiet core at the center of the noise all around.

The day seemed timed almost to the last melon—the carts returned from the rows just as the sky had begun to shut down. The pickers rolled up to the tables with the carts, the first melons were split open, the bonfire was lit; wedges of cold meat pie, chunks of dripping pink fruit, and mugs of beer or cider were handed around. The pickers dropped into the grass around the fire, not too close to the heat, or the light—most of the pairings of earlier in the day had held.

Nate found Alice a spot on a nearby log, just outside the inner circle of young people. They ate in silence for a time; when Nate got up to refresh his cider mug Alice looked around. As soon as the small children had finished their food they'd leaped up and begun a kind of race around the fire; already couples here and there had snuck off into the darker reaches, some girls being dragged laughing, some doing the dragging, but all looking happy enough to go along. Alice saw

Jane Clarke's young man, but she didn't see Jane, either within the circle or without; had she gone home? Or had she gone off into the dark with the other one? Alice felt oddly curious to know whether that straight spine had bent itself into the grass or no. She looked for Nate and saw that his younger sister had cut him off on his way back, hanging on his elbow again, trying to pull him into the race; she pestered until he tickled her off. Behind him, his cask-shaped father watched him all the way back to the log.

As Nate settled himself beside her Alice said, "Your father doesn't like where you sit."

"He doesn't like many things," Nate said. "But he likes not liking things. Were I to sit somewhere else it would make a dull evening for him."

Alice turned from watching the father to watching the son. "What did your father and grandmother disagree about?"

"As my grandfather's nearest male heir my father inherited title to the house my grandmother lives in. My grandmother held dower right to a third of the house as long as she remained widowed. My father wanted to sell the house, but she wouldn't give up her third."

"Couldn't the law resolve it?"

"It resolved it. Mr. Freeman resolved it. She received life use of the house entire in exchange for releasing my father from the additional charge of her keep and care."

"And yet they remain strange?"

"We were allowed to visit at first, until . . . until some other troubles came along."

"Your stepmother, the widow's daughter, even she doesn't visit now."

"She obeys my father's law. She doesn't ask herself why he makes it and by what right."

Maybe not, thought Alice, but she purchased the widow's cloth.

They fell silent, amplifying the growing noise around: the women picking up the empty plates and calling to their younger children, the men lifting their voices in reverse proportion to the lowering of the cider in the cask, the oldest Myrick boy spitting watermelon seeds at the youngest Winslow girl, the Winslow girl running, and then not running, the boy picking her up and whirling, stumbling—by accident or design—to the ground.

Alice got to her feet.

"Where are you going?"

"Home." She set off in the direction of the road. Nate fell in step beside her, hands in pockets, but she didn't know whether that was by accident or design either.

She said, "You'd best stay with your friends."

"They're naught but a bunch of children. They don't have any idea. Not a single idea. I don't care a thing about them. If I stayed I'd talk to Mr. Freeman."

"You admire him so greatly, then?"

"I admire him above all." Nate looked down at Alice. "But I wouldn't talk to him if you stayed. If you stayed I'd talk to you."

"And what if I'd leaped up to play with the children, as you call them?"

"You wouldn't. I saw how you watched them. I see how you watch Mr. Freeman when he talks of politics. You have a seriousness in you that matches mine. That's why I like you, Alice."

The silence fell down, thick with Nate's words, thick with the thoughts it stirred in Alice. He liked her. Or he liked the girl he thought she was. When he found out about the bastard she carried it would be the end of any liking; he wouldn't wish to be seen within ten miles of her. But what did Alice care? What could this boy mean to the life that lay ahead of her?

For one dream minute Alice thought of another kind of life, of herself as a girl like the ones at the frolick, who might creep out into the dark with such a boy as this and welcome his touch on her. But then what? Oh, she knew well enough! No matter his cute panto-mimes of chickens, once she let him near there would be no hands in pockets unless they were her pockets; he would touch what he wished to touch, put himself where he wished to put himself, and put her in even greater trouble. There Alice paused to correct herself; she could lie down in the road with the boy this minute and he couldn't put her in any greater trouble than she already was; she couldn't be twice got with child. Of course she might put him in trouble if his father chose to walk home by the same route and caught them thrashing in the dust, but how great a trouble would that be compared to hers? Unless she tried to put her unborn child to him . . .

Alice paused in her thinking again, a queer, cold thrill shooting through her. What if she did lie with this boy this minute? What if she did put her unborn child to him? The cold in her began to heat, her face to burn. Oh, so shameful a thing! But what if . . . what if!

The heat subsided. What if? Nothing. Nate was only fifteen, bound for long years at Harvard College. He couldn't keep her or her bastard.

Alice's feet had begun following the road home as her mind had followed another one, and now she saw with surprise that she had tra-versed almost the whole short distance to the widow's, in the dark, far outside Freeman's range, with Nate by her side. She dared a look side-ways and found him with eyes fixed on his own footsteps, hands still secured in his pockets, but still she felt the rush of panic. She looked ahead and saw the widow's house not three rods away, the keeping room windows yellowed with the light of her candle, and she calmed some. She said, "I'm here, now. You may go back to your frolick," and ran up onto the widow's stoop. She took the latch securely in hand and turned, but Nate seemed to have vanished. When he spoke his voice came out of the dark like the invisible call of a wolf or an owl, except for the work of the cider in it. "Don't you like me, Alice?"

The solitary plea drifted across the air, bringing with it a kind of power Alice had never before experienced. If she said yes, she might draw him to her as she might draw a strand of thread from the bobbin; if she said no, he would spin off into the night. It was Alice's choice. She put them both before her, the "I like you" and the "I do not," and could see no great advantage to herself in either.

She called, "Go back to your frolick!"

THE WIDOW DROPPED her knitting pins in her lap as Alice entered. "Why, Alice! 'Tis barely dark! And what have you done with Mr. Freeman?"

"I came away ahead. He talks yet."

"No doubt." The widow peered at her. "And did you enjoy yourself?"

"Yes, madam. I'll soak the beans now."

"'Tis done."

"I've the cheeses to turn."

"The cheese is turned. I hope you didn't come away from your fun thinking me too feeble to turn a few cheeses."

"No, madam. I was only tired. I'll go to bed, then."

Alice climbed the stairs but had only got as far as sitting on the bed and dropping her shoes when the outer door opened and she heard Freeman exclaim, "Is she here? Is the girl here?"

"Yes, yes, gone to bed. Whatever—"

"I look, I turn, I look again, she's gone. With Nate. The pair together. Ben Howe said they walked off toward the road."

"What did you think, they'd run off, then?"

"I thought . . . well, good God! As soon as I heard, I set out after; this was no longer than a quarter hour since—"

"Hardly time to pick a stone out of a shoe, let along tumble around behind a stone wall, if that's what worries you."

"You don't know fifteen-year-old boys, then. Without a word she walks off. Without a look!"

"She grew tired. You were engaged in talk. She came home. Nate walked her. Calm yourself, sir."

A chair scraped. A pair of heels thudded heavily against the floor.

The widow said, "What news of our neighbors?" and so the talk turned, too low for Alice to hear from her bed. She thought to return to the stairs, but she was tired. Beyond tired. She lay down on her bed and thought of how once again her protection had lain in Freeman. If Nate had indeed removed his hands from his pockets and tumbled her down behind a wall, Freeman would have come along in a very few minutes. She thought again of the tale she'd heard from Nate: she pictured Freeman's strong but gentle hands wrapping the widow's burned flesh in a sheet and carrying her to safety. After a time Alice realized that she had changed the tale, and that Freeman carried her and not the widow; the wake-dream lulled her into sleep, and she didn't wake till dawn; if she dreamed a sleep-dream she didn't remember it.

SEVENTEEN

After Alice had collected three more payments from Sears and watched them go into the widow's money jar, after she'd felt the growing weight of her own little money pouch, she began to eat like she used to do. Or more than she used to do. Her waistband grew tighter, her face rounder; she checked herself in the hall mirror more and more now, but as no one commented on her changed shape she began to think she might keep her secret forever. She expected herself to be delivered of her bastard by early March; she made the calculation and then pushed it away as she might push away a turned piece of meat—far enough away from her and it wouldn't smell. Or at least so it worked in daylight. At night she woke with pounding heart and sweating skin and wondered what was to become of her.

It seemed the greatest irony that as her internal situation became daily more alarming, the household around her seemed to settle into a greater state of ease; even Freeman seemed used to her presence now. The point was proved one night after Alice had gone up the stairs and she heard Freeman's voice below, in that softer, looser tone he some-times fell into after an extra mug of cider.

"I declare that girl draws half the light when she leaves the room."

"Does she, now."

"I said *half* the light, Widow Berry."

"But which half sends the spark?"

"I say nothing of any sparks, I say only—"

"'Tis the old, dry wood goes first to flame."

"I only mean to say that I think she's a fine girl, and I'm glad you took her in."

"So I see."

"You might stop your nonsense and admit you're glad as well."

"Glad of what? That I took the girl in, or that you've succumbed at last to her charms? Or is it one and the same?"

Freeman's chair scraped. "The amusement you seem to find in this particular line of conversation escapes me. I believe I shall say good night."

"Good night to you, sir. Enjoy your dreams."

To which Freeman made no answer that Alice could hear.

AT FIRST ALICE took the conversation as nothing more than the widow's teasing, and yet it kept her awake, running over and over through her head, not just the words but the various tones in which they'd been spoken. After a time Alice thought she began to see the problem: Freeman wouldn't admit the widow's jest about the spark, and this had provoked the widow into more jesting, which further provoked Freeman into . . . what? More praise of Alice.

Alice thought on this some more and began to think on some other things: Freeman's statement earlier that she'd won him "utterly," his new ease around her, how he'd warned Nate to leave her be, how upset he'd become when she'd walked off at the frolick. At first the new thoughts caused her flesh to prickle with sweat, but then they took another turn, and a new conversation began to take place inside Alice's head, in another pair of voices, both Alice's. They batted a single thought back and forth, unable to agree between the two selves whether to keep it or let it go.

When Alice woke the next morning it was as if the last night's conversation with herself had continued in her sleep until one voice had won out, so that what had seemed an argument last night was now no argument at all, was, in fact, no choice at all.

The boy Nate couldn't help her. The man Freeman could. It was that simple.

That awful.

BUT COULD SHE do it? Alice would have been a fine fool indeed not to know the kind of thoughts she sparked in a certain kind of man, but what she didn't know, even after all this time, was whether Freeman was that kind of man. It was true he didn't ogle her as did the other men in the village; it was true he was never anything but kind and courteous; it was true he didn't seem to consider himself in any way entitled to her services; but as Alice watched and listened over the next few days she concluded that although he was more careful at it than most, Freeman didn't necessarily live on any higher plane than the other men in the village.

First came a bit of gossip at Sears's store about the death of a mulatto whore who had been "kept at the tavern by Eben Freeman." Alice lingered behind the shelves, selecting pins for the widow and discovered that the word *kept* got taken looser or tighter, depending on who did the talking. It seemed generally acknowledged that at one time Freeman had favored the whore, and she'd favored him; it seemed also acknowledged that she'd been better fed and clothed than most in her situation. There opinion turned left and right. The youngest Myrick sister insisted that the whore had died near Yarmouth's Indian Town in a cabin that Freeman had built for her and where he continued to visit; the youngest Winslow girl countering that the Yarmouth whore was another one entirely and naught to do with Freeman; Mrs. Cobb declared that the tavern whore had gone off for a time with some money everyone suspected came from Freeman, but that she'd come back to work at the tavern and died in the same bed she'd been born in, being no better than her mother had been. There Mr. Sears spoke up to say that he'd not heard such a lot of nonsense since the business about the witch baby; Mrs. Sears then spoke into the new silence to say that if widowers like Freeman insisted on keeping themselves single so long they might expect their reputation to suffer; the older Myrick sister then supposed that one dead whore wasn't likely to harm Freeman's reputation any more than it had been harmed by "that other one." Alice fussed over the pins a time longer, but there the talk cut off, as if all throats had been severed.

Next came Freeman himself. She now knew that he was a man long widowed and that he was a man yet desirous of a woman's company, but because he'd passed that age where he might hope to acquire a woman by virtue of a natural attraction, he'd been forced to go out and buy one. Alice would have thought there might be a number of older widows ready to take him for his money alone, but as none had done it thus far it seemed clear enough to Alice that Freeman wasn't going to settle for any of the toothless old vultures who circled the village.

And, his whore was now dead.

With all that in Alice's mind, along with what she'd heard out of Freeman's own mouth, she decided to attempt it.

. . .

THE DIFFICULTY WAS in finding her chance. She thought she'd found it one day in late August when the temperature dropped down with September-like chill, prompting the widow to head into the yard to pull goose down for the winter mattresses. Pulling down was long, hard work, requiring the catching and securing of the goose under one arm while fixing an old stocking over its head with the other, then fighting against beating wings and pummeling beak to pluck free the soft undercoat of feathers. The widow would have been engaged with the noisy geese more than long enough for Alice to do what was needed; the trouble arose when Freeman decided to take that exact morning to ride to Eastham to visit an ailing uncle.

Alice's next opportunity came when the widow set out for the shore to collect sand for the floors, but Freeman had come upon something in his newspaper that stiffened his neck and cobbled his brow as well as his jawline; Alice didn't feel it just the moment to test the strength of her power to draw him.

Alice waited, and soon enough another chance came: the widow upstairs at the loom laying a web that should busy her for hours and Freeman off to the barn to check on a recent lameness in his horse. Alice didn't like the idea of the barn, as it held a bad association for her, but it had one certain advantage: the widow wasn't in it. True, the sash in Alice's end of the attics remained raised, because she liked to smell and hear all she could of Satucket, but Alice didn't think Freeman the kind of man to make enough noise to reach the widow's end of the attics. Besides, Alice's pregnancy was advancing, and if she waited much longer she would be too far gone to fool a man of Freeman's wit into believing he'd spawned what she carried.

Alice found Freeman in his shirtsleeves, just leaving his horse's stall. "Why, Alice," he said, and smiled. Alice thought herself well acquainted with that smile by now, but in that minute she saw she had long missed one thing in it, something she could only call a well-worn sadness. For a second she thought with shame of what she was about to do, of how it would shame *him*. Alice wasn't so great a fool as to think that someone like Freeman would marry her just to give his supposed bastard his name, but surely he would feel as honor-bound as he would be law-bound to keep such a child fed and safe and warm. To keep Alice fed and safe and warm. And after all, if he'd managed to keep a whore at the tavern without losing the respect of all the village, how greatly could a single dalliance with Alice shame him? And a single dalliance was all she needed of him. As Alice stood under Freeman's smile she felt her edges soften, felt necessity joined with inclination. She began to form a not unpleasant idea that if she stepped closer he might of his own will put his arms around her, hold her. What he might do next she didn't count as pleasant at all, but as it was her only hope she must allow it. The question was, how to begin it? She'd never needed to start Verley in her direction.

Freeman had pulled an old sack off a peg and begun to wipe his hands; Alice watched his long fingers work the cloth around and knew she needed to get them to leave the cloth and light on her, but how? She said, "Do you find your horse fit, sir?"

"Sound as ever."

There Alice stopped, her best effort exhausted.

After a time Freeman said, "Have you come for me, Alice, or has the widow sent you out here on your own chore?"

And there it lay. The thing she needed to start him toward her as plain as the word of God, or if not the word of God, a sign, then. She said, "I come for you, sir." She took another step forward, stretched up tall, and put her arms around his neck, hoping to press her mouth to his lips, but Verley had never troubled to put his lips on Alice, and she wasn't at all sure how to fix them. She paused, and Freeman had just that second's hesitation in which to pull back. He caught her hands from behind his neck and drew them down. "Here, now, what's this?"

"'Tis all right, sir. You want me, you may have me. Right here. This minute." She raised her arms toward his neck again, but halfway there she saw the look on him and thought perhaps he didn't care to trouble with lips, either. She pulled open her bodice strings, caught up Freeman's hands, and fixed them on her breasts—Verley had liked to squeeze her breasts near to rupture—and dropped her hands to his breeches buttons, working the first button through before Freeman came to life again.

"Whoa, now, Alice!" He lifted his hands off her swollen bosom, but there they stuttered in the air, as if he couldn't decide where else to put them. He attempted to back up, but he only had a few inches to go before he came against the stall, and he struck it hard with his bootheel. It startled the horse, causing it to strike the wall a return blow that rattled the stall door, and Freeman looked behind him in alarm; it gave Alice time to work the second button through, and she felt his part stiffen under the cloth; one moment more, she thought, and all will be finished. She lifted her skirt, but there Freeman seemed to have decided what to do with his hands; he clamped them around her arms like a pair of shackles, picked her off her feet, and swung her around against the wall, startling the horse a second time. It thrashed so hard Alice thought it might bring the barn down over them, but she needed so little time now. She grabbed Freeman's bobbing part; Freeman said, "Alice, now! Alice, now! Alice, now!" and another voice said "What on earth is the—" and stopped there.

The widow stood in the barn door, peering at them through the dimness. Freeman spun around, fixing his breeches as he went, attempting to adjust the awkward twist in them.

The widow said, "I do not . . . I *do not*—" and stopped a second time.

Freeman pushed past her into the dooryard. The widow followed him.

Alice leaned against the wall where Freeman had left her, knees puddling, heart thundering, as breathless as if Freeman had tried to strangle her. Tears massed thick and hot behind her eyes, but she wouldn't let them loose. She wouldn't. After a time she calmed enough to hear the raised voices from the yard. She edged nearer to the barn door to listen.

"And so you have nothing else to say on what's just happened here."

"What the devil do you think's happened here?"

"Judging by what was before my eyes, any number of things."

"And judging by what you know of a man who's lived under your roof for the past two years?"

"I know better than to put any of us on any pedestal, Mr. Freeman. I should like to think, however, that you wouldn't further abuse a young girl already—"

"A young girl already in possession of a trick or two!"

"You would blame her for what I saw, then?"

A pause, in which Alice imagined Freeman would very much like to blame her, but he said, "I blame no one but myself, for the sin of slow-wittedness in extricating myself from an entirely unwarranted and unsolicited situation. Now if you will excuse me."

"So you would run off now."

"I *walk* to the water in the hope that it will cool my temper, and if you're wise you'll leave me to it."

Silence.

Alice peered out. Freeman was disappearing around the side of the house, the widow in the direction of the chickens. Alice crept out of the barn, crossed the yard, and climbed the stairs to her room. Her room, but for how many more minutes? The widow had seen her, and she'd heard Freeman; she would send Alice away now, instead of later.

After a time Alice heard the sound of footsteps on the stairs. She sat down on the bed, her hands under her to stop their trembling. The widow came into the room. She didn't look at Alice but went to the chest where Alice kept her loose belongings, and began to fuss with them as Alice used to do, as if a whirling mind could be stilled by busy fingers. The widow picked up Alice's hair comb and put it down, wound and unwound a hair ribbon, thumbed a book by Swift that Freeman had pushed on Alice, and last, she picked up the pouch that had once held the pennyroyal and now held the coins Alice had earned from the widow and Freeman. The widow hefted the pouch as Alice had done so often, as if weighing it. Regretting it. She tipped the pouch upside down and the coins fell out onto the chest, along with a few dregs of pennyroyal. The widow stared absently at the mess for a time, and then as absently wet her finger and picked up a scrap of leaf; she smelled it, set it on her tongue, and slowly, slowly, as if in a kind of trance, her head came up; she turned; she stared at Alice. She might as well have held a mirror before Alice, so clearly did Alice see her own puffy face, her swollen breasts, her tightening belly reflected across the widow's features.

The widow set the pouch down. She said, "You're with child."

Alice said nothing.

"How far gone are you?"

Alice stayed silent.

"Speak up, girl! Who's got this child on you?"

It began in enough anger, but halfway through something went wrong with it; it didn't hold its fury all the way through the second sentence. Alice lifted her eyes to the widow and saw her do a thing Alice had never seen her do before; she glanced away from Alice. As if *she* were ashamed. As if *she* were somehow to blame. Alice didn't understand it, and then she did. Why, the widow had even said it! *I should like to think that you wouldn't further abuse a young girl . . .* She wasn't ashamed over Alice, she was ashamed over Freeman, the man she had taken under her roof and so allowed to abuse Alice.

Alice imagined a faint breeze of hope entering through that tiniest of cracks. Perhaps it didn't matter what had actually happened in the barn, perhaps it only mattered what the widow chose to believe had happened. She had appeared in the door just as Freeman had swung Alice against the wall; for all she could know it was Freeman who had undone her bodice and his breeches. Alice tried to concentrate, to think through the rest of it. If the widow were of a mind to blame Freeman, would she consider Alice as now in even greater need of her protection? Was it possible she would leap to Alice's defense as she'd done on the deck of the ship? Was it possible she might choose to keep Alice under her roof and throw Freeman out the door? After all, how much did she need his money now that the cloth was selling at Sears's store?

The widow cut through Alice's swirling thoughts. "Speak up!" she snapped. "I asked you who's put you in this way?"

Through the open window Alice could hear the sounds of a horse's hoofs scuffling in the dirt. Apparently the walk to the water hadn't cooled him, and Freeman had decided to ride off somewhere. Alice let her eyes float toward the window, and it was enough. The widow came at the bed, grabbed Alice's wrist, and pulled her to her feet.

"Understand me, Alice. You'll answer me in God's own truth, right now, this minute, or you'll go out of this house this minute. You put this child on Mr. Freeman?"

Alice nodded.

"And how long . . . Well, I might figure how long."

The widow dropped Alice's wrist, walked with purpose to the stairs, and down.

Alice hurried to the window. Freeman was still in the yard, tightening the girth on his saddle, when the widow appeared. He didn't straighten.

"So you have no further words for me on this matter?" the widow said.

"Judging by the words that have flown thus far, I'd say fewer were required, not more."

"Even on the subject of the child Alice credits you?"

Freeman laughed.

Alice heard the laugh, returned to the bed, and lay down on it. She needed nothing more to know the sound of a plot failed. No man could laugh so in anything but the purest innocence, and as Alice knew it, so the widow must know it. All was ended there.

Yet the conversation continued below. Alice leaped up and returned to the window. Freeman had at last straightened to his full height, and stood staring at the widow. "My God, you mean this!"

"As I've just been told it, yes, yes, I do."

"Well, if that's what she's told you, she needs a lesson in the animal sciences." Freeman turned back to the horse, and then pivoted again. "Good God, was that the little wretch's scheme? To tempt me into rashness and lay some ill-gotten child at my door?"

Alice returned to the bed, rolled on her side, and hugged the bolster to her. Foolish, foolish girl! To have tried such a thing on such a man! And worse, oh, so greatly worse, to have confessed her condition to the widow! If she'd but kept to her deception she'd have stayed safe there for many months more. Now she would either be sent away as sinner or, if she admitted to Verley's abuse of her, carted away to face Verley in a courtroom somewhere. If Alice knew one thing about herself it was that she couldn't physically enter any room that held Verley in it. So, she would be sent away. She had admitted to the child, and there was no turning back from it now.

A pair of boots crossed the floor below and hit the stairs, not lightly. Alice leaped up as Freeman swung himself around the stair rail into the room, with the widow behind; he stopped short a good distance from Alice. She saw his face and realized she had never until that moment seen anything like anger in it.

"What in all the—" He stopped. His chest and shoulders rose once, and fell. He began over, in another kind of tone, but still not his. "The widow informs me you're in the way to having a child. She informs me further—" He stopped again, and Alice understood his difficulty. He couldn't believe, he wouldn't believe, that such trust as he'd come to put in her could have been repaid with such treachery. Alice made herself look at him, made herself take his anger as her punishment, and was amazed to see that his disbelief in what she'd done lingered yet. Oh, how hard he would try to believe her something other than the thing she was! How hard he would try to turn back, as Alice would turn back, to before her claim against him! But if Alice had her choice she would turn back further yet, to before her claim of a child at all. Oh, if only she could go back there!

If only she could go back there. Alice looked again at Freeman, at the widow. Why, what if she could go back there? Wasn't there a chance of it, right here? Freeman wished so much not to believe. He could be persuaded, Alice was sure he could be persuaded. But could the widow be persuaded to go along? And what if she didn't? What risk did Alice take that could be any greater than the risk she faced now? If she left things as they lay she was already gone from the widow's home. Why not try to go back?

Alice's heart began to pulse until her flesh grew damp. She wiped her lip, her forehead. She said, "Child, sir?"

"Child, child," the widow interrupted. "The one you claim Mr. Freeman's got on you."

"I've got no child in me, sir. Madam."

Freeman whipped around to face the widow. "Did you not just accuse me——?"

"I accuse! 'Twas she accused. What game is this you're playing, girl?"

"I made no such claim against Mr. Freeman, madam. Mr. Freeman may have had certain wishes——"

"The devil I did! I go to the barn to see to my horse as any man might expect to do in peace——"

"Did I not ask you," the widow cut in again, "in the clearest possible terms, if you were with child? And did you not answer me——"

"I didn't answer you, madam. I couldn't understand how you could ask such a question, and so I made no answer."

The widow stared at her. "Perhaps you didn't answer my question, but neither did you deny. And at a moment further on, when I said to you, 'Do you put this child to Mr. Freeman,' you said——"

"I said nothing, madam. I didn't understand your first question, nor your second, except as you might think, after seeing him a short time before——"

"You nodded your assent! As clearly as you shake your head now! What's the matter with you, girl, do you think me a fool?"

"Here, now." Freeman took a step forward, positioning himself more evenly between them. "Let's collect ourselves. Let's attempt to proceed in a rational manner. What matters now isn't what was purported or believed purported at some point heretofore, what matters now is the state of affairs at present. Answer me, Alice, with the fear of God's wrath in your heart, are you or are you not with child?"

With the fear of God's wrath. And what was God's wrath? A vague, unknown, distant thing, no matter how desperately described by the reverend, as compared to the other choices laid before her. "I am not, sir."

The three of them stood in silence for the space of time it took Freeman to expel a breath, the widow to take one in, and Alice to hold one.

"All right, then," Freeman said. "As we have no child, we can therefore have no false accusation. We can have nothing, in fact, but some false assumptions. And let me say to you right now, Alice, whatever you might have fancied as my intention toward your person, that too was falsely assumed. Now I suggest we put this behind us and return to whatever business we'd been engaged in before this unpleasantness began."

He strode to the stairs. The widow peered a second longer at Alice before following him down. Alice sat down hard on the bed, as suddenly weak as if someone had punctured her lungs, but she hadn't sat for a five count before she realized she couldn't afford such luxury. She must know what they said of her yet. She pulled herself up and went to her spot on the stairs.

The widow had wasted no time in laying out her case again.

"I said to her flat out, 'You put this child on Mr. Freeman?' and she gave me a clear nod. Further again, when I entered her chamber I found a pouch that had at one time held pennyroyal—pennyroyal, which you well know will destroy a conception. And look how she's filled out—"

"Widow Berry, you lay too much on a nod. She admitted to a state of confusion over your question; she might have been nodding at anything under the sun in response to it. As to the pennyroyal, it has its other uses, has it not? As to her filling out, no doubt she eats better here than she has in her entire lifetime. Besides, what might she gain by denying a condition, which if true, will certainly show itself down the road?"

Time, Alice answered him silently. She gained time. And she counted as gain every hour she remained safe in the widow's home. Besides, who knew what might happen down Freeman's road?

EIGHTEEN

As hard as Freeman tried to turn them back to the time before the "unpleasantness," it couldn't be done; he lasted only the remainder of that day and night and left the next morning for Barnstable. Alice waited in dread for the widow to confront her about the child, but she did not; after two days Alice began to hope that Freeman had indeed convinced her she'd mistaken Alice entirely. There remained the scene in the barn, but of that too the widow said nothing. In fact, she said little at all. She spoke when she had to in thin, taut sentences, and except for the hum of the wheel and the thump of the loom the house fell into silence, the walls shrinking in around them like a chestnut burr around a pair of blighted seeds.

So they went on, Alice spinning, the widow weaving, Alice making trips to Sears's store with their cloth and listening to the talk of politics that filled the air, even from the women now. They tossed about the men's words as well as the men ever had—non-importation, tyranny, taxes. Alice even overheard Mrs. Cobb quoting the widow's own words, adding in her own embellishment: they might pickle her and ship her to the West Indian Islands in a herring barrel before she'd pay a king's ransom for a bit of cambric.

The widow and Alice took the necessary time away from their textile work to pick and preserve watermelons, cherries, and currants. Nate came often to inquire if Freeman had returned, or so he said; sometimes he waited in the yard or near it to see if Alice would come out on some kind of errand. Alice knew this because she could look out the window and see him lurking. Sometimes, when Alice didn't appear, he would make a slow stroll in the direction of the landing and come back again; if someone passed him in view of the widow's house he waylaid him with conversation, darting his eye at the house as he talked. Most of the men thus accosted seemed willing enough to talk to the boy; once he stopped an Indian girl, and she seemed willing enough too, until the Indian Sam Cowett came out and beckoned to her to get along.

Alice watched Nate and wondered things, the old things, but some new things too. Strange things. What if she went out just now to collect a tow sack from the barn? What would Nate do? Would he follow her into the barn? Would he try to touch her? If he didn't try to touch her would they stay in the barn and talk of Freeman, or Otis, or the widow, or Nate's father, as they'd done before? Or would he ask about Alice's life now? If he did, what would she say?

As it happened one day she did step outside to pick a handful of parsley for a sauce just as Nate came walking back up the landing road, and he saw her and walked slowly over the grass, as if afraid she'd duck back inside if he came too fast at her, as if she were a deer. But as she watched him come into the dooryard she thought he was like a deer too, slender but sure-footed, graceful, strong. He came up to her and reached out a hand, not to touch her but to take the parsley, to hold the parsley. He grinned.

Alice said, "What amuses you so?"

"I'm not amused, I'm glad."

"What are you glad of?"

"Of everything. Of parsley." He lifted it to his nose, sniffed it, bit off a stem.

Alice reached out. "Give it to me. I must go in."

He handed her the greens without argument. He said, "Am I still not to touch you?"

"You're never to touch me." She turned away and moved toward the house.

He said, "Alice!" so violently from behind her that she started.

She said, "What? What is it?"

"Nothing. I just want you to know that you may touch me whenever you like."

Alice ducked inside, her face in flame.

That night she lay awake thinking of Nate, how young and silly he was with all his talk of gladness and parsley and touching him. But after a time of lying awake Alice began to think something else about Nate. She had told him she did not want him to touch her and he hadn't. Alice began to think too that she didn't know a great deal about this subject of touching. She had Verley, who had touched her when she hadn't wanted it, and she had Freeman, whom she had touched when he hadn't wanted it, neither example giving her the least idea how the thing might work when the parties were together on the subject. Nate had said she might touch him, which took care of his part of it, but what of Alice? Why should she want to lay a hand on him? She knew well enough what would happen the minute she tried it. His hands on her. Not like a Verley, perhaps, at least not to start, but it would be just the same at the end, or close enough to it. She might wonder what that soft, pink cheek would feel like against her palm, and whether it had come into its whiskers yet; she might wonder whether a hand slipped under his shirt would discover a smooth, slender back, as it looked, or a collection of lean muscles and sinews, of the kind required to send wood chips flying wildly. She might wonder, yes, but wondering did not cause pain. Wondering did not cause bastards.

When Alice slept, which wasn't until she'd kicked the sheet loose of the bed tick, she dreamed of Nate, and Freeman, and Verley, all mixed in together, and of herself, running away from them down a long, narrow, stinking street that she didn't recognize in the dream, but on waking she knew it to be her old street in London. As the street came out of the grayness so did the little house, and her mother and father lying on their bed in the corner of the kitchen, their limbs all tangled up in each other, her father's hand gripping her mother's buttock as he slept, her mother's hand curled around her father's cheek. The buttock would have been smooth, the cheek rough as bark, until her father got up and scraped at it with the razor. Alice remembered this too: her mother touching her father's cheek in the morning after he'd worked it over and saying, "Better."

FREEMAN STAYED AWAY until September, when his uncle died, as they said, from drinking cold water, and he was forced to return to see his affairs to a close. His arrival brought the men to the widow's house as usual, where a few hasty condolences were voiced over the uncle, but soon enough they returned to battering away at the same old subjects. Trade. Taxes. Non-importation. From the discussion Alice learned that Boston held strong on the agreement, with Rhode Island, New York, and Pennsylvania following behind. At the end of the meeting they again toasted their king, but it seemed to Alice that Freeman did so with something akin to hurt feelings.

In the few moments Alice had spent in Freeman's company since his return he had barely spoken to her or looked at her, and if he said more than two words to the widow, Alice didn't hear them. Alice imagined that although Freeman's singular laugh had cleared him of the charge of actually penetrating Alice's flesh, an acceptable accounting of the events in the barn must still be wanting. Freeman stayed only the single night and rode off again, this time to Boston.

THE VILLAGE NOW smelled of an odd mix of fresh-cut hay and fetid oil as the whalers returned from the north with their holds full of blubber and began to boil it down. Neither the sickly sweet smell of the hay or the cloying smell of the oil disturbed Alice's stomach, and again she hoped it meant that the pennyroyal had belatedly taken hold, but even as she hoped, she knew it to be less hope, more dream. Yet the face in the mirror regained its color; with the cooler weather Alice was able to add a light shawl to her dress to conceal her fullness; the deception held.

The cloth went faster off Sears's shelves, and on Alice's trips to and fro she noticed the talk among the women turned to what each had done to support the non-importation plan. To save the sheep for wool, they wouldn't eat lamb; they used beet sugar or honey or maple syrup to sweeten their bread or pudding; they traded recipes for tea made from goldenrod and blackberry leaves or made a kind of coffee out of rye and chestnuts.

Alice saw Nate now and then, sometimes at a distance as he attacked his father's hay with a scythe, sometimes near to, if he happened to come along as she was leaving the store or stepping out into her dooryard. He kept his hands to himself, but at the same time he seemed to grow easier in her presence, as if assuming that Alice liked him near. Alice couldn't think what she might have said to cause the change in him; she continued to act toward him as she always had; if she dreamed confusing dreams of him he couldn't have known.

At the end of the month Nate came to say good-bye as he prepared to leave for Harvard College; the news saddened his grandmother and surprised Alice—she'd lost count of the days. He began by reporting to them that the Sugar Act had taken effect, displaying the same hurt surprise over this news that Alice had seen not long ago in Freeman. The widow received the news in solemn silence, but as Nate made to leave the widow said, "'Tis a time that needs men well versed in the law. Attend to your work and make me proud of you," a little speech that surprised Alice, as from the widow's previous talk she'd not understood her to have any great love for lawyers. Nate left but not without making a great show of rolling his eyes from Alice to the door; he would have her go out after him.

Alice didn't want to go anywhere after Nate. She didn't trust the new ease in him. She stayed at her wheel until it became time to collect the cow from the meadow, well ahead of sundown, it was true, but only because the wolves had made such noise of late. She stepped into the dooryard, and there was Nate, coming out of the wood much as he'd done the day he'd helped her pick up the cloth. He fell in alongside her as she walked but said nothing, more like the old days of the hot face and stopped tongue.

After a time Alice said, "Your father will be angered that you've kept away so long."

Nate shrugged. "'Tisn't so long. 'Tisn't so long as I'll be gone from here."

"You're unhappy to be going to the college?"

"I'm unhappy about a number of things. I wished to see Mr. Freeman before I left. I wished to go to another frolick with you. I wished—" He broke off.

They walked onto the meadow, the sun just low enough to blind them; Alice couldn't at first spot the cow and thought it must have chewed its tether and wandered off.

"There," said Nate, pointing at the scrub along the edge of the meadow, and Alice set off after it, slowly at first, but liking the swish of the grass against her skirt, liking the path of the sun on the grass, liking the crisp breeze that peaked the waves in the distance, she started to run. She heard Nate behind her, beside her; she put on a burst and pulled ahead; he caught her up and pulled ahead, then ran backward until he tripped and went down, spread-eagled in the grass. He leaped up and began to hop around, clutching his ankle; Alice came up in all concern, but once she got close she saw he was clowning, wagging his elbows like a chicken again, just as he'd done at meeting. Alice began to laugh. Such a silly thing, to run like children, to hop around like a chicken! Nate saw the success of his clowning and joined in with the laughing, making Alice laugh the more, until she hiccupped, until the tears ran. She bent low to untether the cow, hiding her face; she set off the other way across the meadow, the tears on their own plan now. Nate pulled up alongside, peered at her, and stayed silent.

At the barn he pulled open the door for her, bent down, and peered at her again. He said, "Why do you cry, Alice?"

Alice didn't know. She didn't in the least know.

Nate said, "I should like to think it's because I'm to leave soon and you won't see me for ages and ages, but I think it more like a bee sting, or some dirt in your eye. Or perhaps you wish to kiss me good-bye but don't quite know how to enter upon the subject."

Alice couldn't help it. She started to laugh again. Oh, he was so silly! So young! She said, "'Tis nothing but my eyes mistaking happy tears for real ones. Thank you for finding the cow. Good-bye. May you do well at the college." She tugged at the cow, but Nate held on to the tether.

"Will you miss me, Alice?"

Yes, she thought, surprised; yes, she would miss him, but she said nothing.

He said, "I shall miss you too, Alice."

They stood with the cow between. What *would* it be like to touch him? What harm, now that he was going off? She leaned over and laid her palm against his cheek; she felt the remnants of morning whiskers, but soft ones. Nate put his hand over hers and slid her fingers onto his lips. How soft his mouth was! She pulled her hand away. "Good-bye," she said. "Good-bye and good luck to you."

She yanked the cow into the barn and pulled the door closed.

NINETEEN

I n October, while out in the orchard helping the widow pick apples, Alice felt the first quickening in her womb, and the shock of it dropped her onto her knee. The widow rushed over to her.

"Alice! What's the matter?"

Alice struggled to right herself and collect the scattered apples, already nesting half-hidden in the grass. She pointed to a vague spot on the ground and said, "Skunk hole"; of all the lies she'd told the widow that seemed the most awful because of how easily it fell off her tongue. She moved away from the widow to the next wind-stunted tree in the row, but she had some trouble settling again to her task. With that first kick of life everything Alice had been attempting to push away to some distant point in her future came plummeting down into the present. The seed Verley had planted in her was no longer mere seed but life, a life that would grow and grow until it got born and ruined her own.

THAT NIGHT THE widow stayed even quieter than usual throughout their supper. After Alice had been in bed some time, sorting through all the old daydreams in search of sleep and not finding it in any of them, she saw the quivering light of a candle working its way up the stairs. The widow rose up out of the dark stairwell, her loose-bound hair a mix of night-gray and candle-gold. She crossed the floor to Alice's bed and held the candle over her as Verley had done so often; either that or the fear of what the widow had come to say set Alice trembling.

The widow said, "I've come to ask you this again, Alice, while Mr. Freeman is absent, in case his presence hindered you from answering as forthrightly as you might have when we last talked of it. Before you answer know this: you needn't fear telling me the truth. Never the truth. Are you with child, Alice?"

Oh, to tell the truth! To remember how large a heart stood before her, and how it might, oh, surely it might, take pity on her again, as it had done before on the deck of the *Betsey*. But the voice that spoke to Alice now wasn't the voice that had spoken to Alice on the *Betsey*. It had lost some of that heart. Alice understood that she had cut away at that heart herself, that the hollowness she heard now was the off-spring of her attack on Freeman and the lies she'd told after it. She understood too that to tell the widow a new truth now was to con-firm the old lie; what more certain way to provoke the widow's rage at her? She didn't know what else could happen along the road that might save her, but she knew it wasn't this, now.

"I am not," she answered.

THROUGHOUT OCTOBER THE days stayed unseasonably warm, but the nights grew chilled; the widow and Alice turned away from flax and went back to wool; as the yards of worsted and broadcloth and shirting reeled off the loom, Alice carted them to the fulling mill and then to Sears's store. Foreign cloth still appeared on Sears's shelves, but it seemed to Alice that it sat there longer than it used to do, and so it also seemed that homespun gowns had begun to blossom through-out the village, whether made from the widow's cloth or no. Once Alice saw Mrs. Cobb stop and speak to a young woman in silk, flap-ping her own homespun skirt in the air like a flag until the young woman's face reddened. A week later Alice saw the young woman at the store purchasing the widow's homespun.

FREEMAN CAME. HE was all bright, crackling cheer, and the widow was in return; Alice couldn't bear to be near them. After clearing away the supper she went upstairs, not interested in listening from her near-worn-out stair tread, for what could they say that Alice didn't already know? Even if Alice managed to conceal her condition through winter under layers of thick clothing, by March there would come a thing impossible to conceal, and Alice and her bastard would be sent away together. So why did Alice's feet drag along the stairs? Why did she sink down and cant her ear to catch each stilted, stumbling phrase from below?

"How do your textiles sell?" Freeman began.

"They sell faster. Alice moves slower."

"I saw a fair display of homespun as I rode through town. More so here than at Barnstable."

"You might have noticed both Alice and I have made new gowns, although Alice covers hers with both shawl and apron at all times now."

"We should send you to Barnstable. How their silk parade must burn Otis's eyes whenever he comes home!"

"'Tis mild weather yet for a constant shawl."

"Yes, it has stayed mild."

"Mr. Freeman, you don't hear me."

"I hear you, Widow Berry. I merely struggle to determine if your words are informative or accusatory."

"Informative or accusatory! Can you not tell a cry for help when you hear it? I'm beside myself, Mr. Freeman, as to what's to be done with the girl! You saw the truth the minute you walked in, I saw it take you. Have you nothing to offer in this dilemma?"

"What the devil would you have me offer?"

"I don't know. Indeed I don't. If she won't admit to the thing—"

Silence. After a time Freeman said, "I have my own dilemma, not entirely unrelated. Nate has written her a letter. I confess to a struggle as to whether or not to give it to her."

BUT THE NEXT day Freeman did, indeed, hand her the letter.

Dear Alice,

I took up my pen with the idea of writing to my father and in thinking of the great divide between what I wished to say and what I would be compelled to say I set my pen back; in no long time the idea came to me that the two might better meet if I addressed my letter to you. Perhaps you are now thinking that you have come up a poor second, but as you hold the only letter I shall find time to write this entire week you must conclude that you have triumphed over all.

I see your soft, solemn eyes as you read this, and although I don't dare imagine any great joy lighting them, I hope I may feel convinced of some curiosity to read on, as I have long detected a share of that commodity in you that equals mine. The question now before me is what shall I tell you that might satisfy it? Perhaps as you have inquired of me about the College from time to time I'd best begin there.

On my arrival here I expected to find myself surrounded by souls most kindred to my own, eager to begin their instruction not only in the way of advancing themselves on a profession, but in the way of educating themselves on the many other subjects that would better qualify them for learned discussion. I have found instead a silly gaggle of boys more determined over a bottle of rum and a game of cards, not at all deterred by the fines for this behavior, which of course are paid by their parents and so don't disturb their gaming at all. You wouldn't wish to converse with one of these lads more than two minutes altogether, I assure you.

As to the place itself, it is more farm than town and overrun with livestock most of the time. The marketplace is busy enough, but with few stores. They have given me a room in the new dormitory, Hollis Hall, which should please me well enough if it weren't for the closeness, the smokiness of the air here. I know how you must feel for me, trapped in such a place while you bathe in the sweet breezes of Satucket!

My main study this term is in English and Greek literature as well as oratory in Greek, Latin, and English; I have a fine tutor in mathematics and natural philosophy, a Professor Winthrop, and get on with him well, but I miss my talks with Mr. Freeman. He has sent me a fine letter, even enclosing a word of advice from Mr. Otis, that "a lawyer ought never to be without a volume of natural or public law, or moral philosophy, on his table, or in his pocket," which I beg you to tell him I now follow. Please also give Mr. Freeman my warm regards, and my duty to my grandmother. How I miss my happy, happy visits to her home! How much I wish I could feel your hand against my cheek again! I must stop my wishing there or ruin all.

I am,

Yours Most Respectfully,
Nathan Clarke, Jr.

Alice was greatly surprised to get such a letter. She read it and wondered at it, and read it again and wondered again. She didn't know her eyes to be soft or solemn. She didn't think herself greatly curious. She didn't remember inquiring about Harvard College beyond asking when he was to go there. Nor did she feel at ease passing on his regards to Freeman or his duty to the widow; she didn't feel it her place to be the keeper of his regards, nor did she think Freeman or the widow would feel it her place.

Alice read the letter once more and began to think that she and Nate must have talked a good deal more than she remembered.

TWENTY

T he days darkened, and Alice saw the threat of winter all through the village. Wagons full of hay rumbled to and fro, hog and cattle carcasses hung bled and skinned from barn rafters, woodpiles grew, extra layers of clothing were pulled on in the chill morning and discarded at midday only to be reclaimed again by late afternoon. Along with the smells of hay and warm blood and fresh-splintered wood the air lay thick with the sweet scent off the apple presses and the tallow vats heating up to dip the winter's supply of candles. Within doors at the widow's, pumpkins and squash were sliced and dried or stored whole in the cellar; a meaty, thick mince stewed at all times over the fire, and the loom was now continually warped with the coarser yarns for cloaks and blankets.

Alice also saw winter in the faces around the village: a new alertness appeared, a new wariness, a certain testiness, all drawn that much tighter by the politics, which lay like a smoldering ash over all. Alice heard it at Sears's store, where she seldom walked into silence now, someone either arguing with Sears over something missing from the shelves, or, more often, something still appearing on them, and she heard it at home, where the men still came to discuss it with Freeman. Alice had heard it so many times now it had come to sound to her like the weaving of a check, the warp and weft of each side laying down their own bright color, the places where they crossed forming a third, muddier version of the other two shades.

The Crown's threads were two: they wished to be paid for the great expense of defending the American colonies in the late wars against the French and Spanish, and they wished the American colonies to trade only with Great Britain, so as to more easily market their own goods. Looking to one measure to serve both, the Crown had put down a new tax on any imported French and Spanish goods and stepped up its search and seizure of smuggled items.

The American colonies, in their turn, laid out their own pair of threads, but whereas the Crown laid fresh ones, the colonies preferred to keep to the old favorites: they wanted to keep their French molasses and Spanish wine without the costly duties, and they wanted their own legislatures to lay down their own taxes, as they'd previously been allowed. Looking to make their point they determined not to buy any goods made in England, which meant they had to provide the goods themselves or smuggle them in from the West Indies, despite the British men-of-war lurking off the coast. The names of French and Spanish ports rolled off the men's tongues as familiarly as the names of their children: Madeira, Azores, Canaries, Guadeloupe, Martinique, Santo Domingo, places, it seemed, where the shipmasters had all been many times, places where they still went, and perhaps this new danger also helped to drop that dark, wintry edge down over all. Or perhaps it was the fact that the non-importation plan seemed to be taking hold.

Myrick raised the specter first. "I tell you what troubles my mind. What if the agreement holds, but nothing changes? What if Parliament just orders their merchants and manufacturers and tradesmen to tighten their belts and goes on taxing us as it pleases? What then?"

The men all looked to Freeman.

"Then we tighten our belts, gentlemen. Don't forget, they need us more than we need them. They'll not hold against a strong non-importation agreement. They can't hold."

The men quieted, but when Freeman raised his mug in his traditional toast to the king, the echoes rang thinly.

And the edge within the widow's home lived and breathed yet. Despite Freeman's long absence the "unpleasantness" hadn't been forgotten. He walked around the keeping room like a stiff, wood-carved doll, giving Alice wide buffers of space, addressing her with brittle courtesy if at all, and in the lack of the old attentions Alice saw what she had forfeited. Between the widow and Freeman things hadn't come right, either; it was as if a husk had grown up around each that neither would strip off.

And then, as if overnight, without any cause that Alice could discover, the mood in the house lifted. One night Freeman beckoned Alice to the fire to show her a sketch in a book of a fine castle in Austria, the next the widow admired a pair of worsted stockings Alice had knitted in only two evenings. The widow and Freeman no longer sat up talking at night as they used to do, but they developed a strange habit of finding humor in each other's conversation where Alice could see none. Freeman might prod the fire and the widow would say, "Watch the sparks," at which Freeman would smile. Freeman might ask whether the night's rain was sufficient to settle the dust, and the widow would smile. They together seemed to think an ad in the newspaper offering a new kind of horse liniment the most amusing of all.

Although Alice didn't understand it, she greeted the improved air in the house as she'd greeted her first breath of Satucket air after two days in the sail locker. She stayed up late mending or knitting with the widow; she cleaned Freeman's boots each night and she brushed his coat each morning. The widow thanked her for her late hours by chiding her and attempting to send her to bed, while Freeman gave her an extra coin, or a new hair ribbon, or a packet of raisins. Alice could feel her face begin to relax into its old answering smile, and she noticed that once it did, Freeman's began to answer her as it used to do. One morning he thanked her by patting her hair, perhaps without thinking, and something live began to grow again from the bare ground of Alice's heart. She lay in her bed at night and thought out all the things that fed it: he had said she'd won him utterly; he had said she drew half the light from the room; he had warned Nate away; he had stiffened under her hand; perhaps above all he appeared to have forgiven her a most vile transgression. Who could do that without the underpinning of a great deal of affection? Perhaps he was no Verley who would have her simply because he could, but perhaps he would have her because he cared. Perhaps he missed his old dead whore. Perhaps a sad, crag-faced, aging man now realized he might better keep a young girl such as Alice instead of an old whore, even if she came with another man's bastard.

Alice's new hope lived only until the hunter's moon. She'd always slept fitfully during a full moon, and the October one troubled her more than ever, riling up the thing in her womb until it jerked her around in her sheets. The moon had dropped low enough to fill the room with a cold white light when she finally yanked away her coverings and went downstairs, thinking if she ate something it would calm the tumult in her.

The moonlight had done its work below as well and drawn a clear path on the keeping room floor; Alice walked across it without faltering to the pantry. She unwrapped the remains of the day's loaf, broke off a piece, and dipped it in the beer barrel. She stood in the darkness to eat it, and almost at once the thing inside her quieted. She stepped out of the pantry into the light path again, but as she did so she heard the latch to the widow's bedroom door lifting. Alice ducked back into the pantry, not wishing to be caught thieving, but then considered that the widow might be on her way to the pantry herself, and it would look worse to be caught lurking. She stepped forward again and froze there. It wasn't the widow backing out of the room but Freeman, his shirt hanging loose to his thighs, his breeches unbuckled at the knees, his feet and legs bare, carrying his shoes and stockings. He set the latch down with care, laying his fingers against the widow's door in a silent, unseen good night, and Alice had never felt a blinder, deafer, dumber fool in all her life.

ALICE LAY IN her bed shivering, not troubling to close her eyes, tracking the moon shadows on the rafters. She would understand what she had seen. At first it appeared a simple enough case of another Verley, but after a time Alice found something troubling in that version: she couldn't make the widow another Alice. If there was one thing certain in life it was that the widow held no fear of Freeman; Alice had witnessed the widow's lack of fear the first minute of their acquaintance as she'd followed the couple through the streets at Boston. *I'm glad to see you noticed something.* No, the widow was not an Alice. Freeman wasn't the widow's master; he didn't own her; she didn't even have to keep him under her roof now the cloth sold; why should she give way to him in such manner? But as Alice thought a little longer she reconsidered. Perhaps, in a way, Freeman did own the widow. Perhaps she did have to keep him under her roof. Surely she couldn't have survived before the textile manufacture without the money he paid her for his room and board; what would happen to her if the non-importation agreement ended? She must, indeed, depend yet on what he did for her.

What he did for her. Why, of course! The man had saved her from a fire; no wonder she'd think she owed him her person! Yes, Alice thought, she could cut open the widow's head and find an Alice inside it, just as she could cut open Freeman's chest and find a Verley there. He may not have held the widow by the throat, but he had shamed her. Boarder and landlady they might well have been at one time, but somewhere in the two years Freeman had claimed to live under her roof he had left his room for hers, and all the town knew it. Why, of course all the town knew it! Clearly, clearly, the widow was the Myrick sisters' "other one" that Freeman's reputation had managed to survive, the "other troubles" Nate had mentioned that now estranged her from her son-in-law. And of course although Freeman's reputation might have survived the widow, no such courtesy would be offered the widow. The men of the village might come to visit Freeman, but no one came to visit the widow except one grandson, and he did that against his father's orders, no doubt because his father well knew what went on within the household. Freeman could enter the meetinghouse with head held high, secure in having been forgiven both the widow and the whore; the widow would never, ever, be forgiven Freeman. The widow might be past bearing Freeman's bastard, but she wasn't past shame or ruin, and this Freeman had put on her as callously as Verley had put his seed in Alice.

Once Alice understood she understood all, including all that had followed her attack on Freeman. The widow had been sorely angered, yes, but more at Freeman than at Alice, at his supposed unfaithfulness to her. In his turn Freeman's greatest rage had come not over the trap Alice had set for him but over the widow's mistrust of him. So it was that they could fight and make their peace, finding in their peace their old charity toward Alice. But could such a charity extend to March and the arrival of her bastard? Alice doubted it. It was true that the widow could no longer stand in all innocence and point the finger at Alice, but neither could she afford to house the evidence of the very kind of behavior she worked so hard to conceal.

Only after Alice had worn down her brain with such thinking could she sleep, but it wasn't the old sleep, with Verley chasing through it. She dreamed again of the hot flames, the cool sheet, the strong arms carrying a bundle of burned flesh, but this time he carried them toward the flames, not away from them, and the face swathed in the sheet was sometimes the widow's, sometimes Alice's.

TWENTY-ONE

Alice watched with new eyes, listened with new ears, and saw and heard things she supposed she might have seen and heard anytime since her arrival at Satucket village. The free way of talking, like no boarder and landlady would talk. The way they might say "Widow Berry," or "Mr. Freeman," with the air of a line learned. The way they looked at each other, now that Alice knew to watch for it, as if they knew everything about the other, as if they were entitled to know everything, as if they couldn't wait for Alice to climb the stairs and leave them to each other. Alice couldn't bear to be around them. She begged a sore finger that prevented her from feeding the yarn evenly onto the bobbin so she could escape to the loom in the attics, but soon enough she couldn't bear that, either, and returned to the wheel to watch and listen.

One night Alice heard a carelessly shut door and crept down the stairs to put her ear to it; at first she heard nothing but soft, strange murmurs, but after a time it turned to the familiar gusts and groans that set her trembling.

Alice took to going to bed soon after supper, leaving the widow to work her needle alone. In the morning she stepped over Freeman's chalky boots without touching them.

A STRETCH OF fine, dry, gold November days set down, and then another stretch of heavy frost. The view outside Alice's window lost its shape and color, turning to flat, gray lines of trees and ground and water. Alice took some of her pay in cloth to make herself a stiff, loose-waisted apron with gaping pockets, a heavy shawl with long ends to trail down in front, and a thick cloak, which she wore whenever she went into the village. The wind outside began to compete with the noise of the wheel inside; the stockings the women knitted were all of thickest worsted; the men who came to visit Freeman brought in the smell of salt spray and other evidence of the wind's work: reddened cheeks, watering eyes, disrupted queues.

Nate came back. The widow started up out of her chair at the sight of him, and Freeman cried, "Here, now, Nate! What's brought you away from Cambridge?"

"Some business for my father."

Alice studied him. He looked heavier. More solemn. He came to talk to Freeman of the state of things in town, or so he said, but he seemed to lose the thread of Freeman's talk again and again, looking often at Alice's corner. At first Alice looked away, but after a time, as she saw Freeman's eye come after them, she lifted her chin and gazed back at Nate as she pleased. Who was this man to direct them?

That night Alice woke to a sound like the washing of waves against her window, and she looked out to find Nate standing in the dooryard under the light of a gibbous moon, throwing handfuls of sand against the glass. He motioned to Alice, to draw her down. Alice put on her shoes and cloak, wrapping herself well, and went as silently as she could down the stairs and out into the darkness.

Nate had moved into the moon shadow of the barn, and Alice crossed the yard to meet him. "What do you do coming here now?"

"I wished to talk to you. Alone."

"You'd best go home."

"I'd best do as I like, which is to stand here. And you'd best do as you like. If you wish to go inside, then go."

He's changed, Alice thought; the new solidness outside had gone clean through. No silliness in him now. It should have frightened her, but somehow it didn't. How odd, she thought, that she could stand alone in the dark with him and fear nothing. Why was it? Because he would have her do as she wished. He would have her go in if she wished. He wouldn't hold her there.

She said, "What did you want to talk of?" Her eyes had begun to adjust to the dark, and she could see him better now, the shape of him, the white of his smile at her question. He stepped closer.

He said, "Well, for one thing, I wondered how you'd got on with the kissing question."

So he was silly yet. Alice felt a ridiculous surge of gladness. She felt glad of his silliness, and yet she also felt glad that he had grown more solid, but how close that solidness had come to her now! Or had she moved? She could reach out and touch him if she wished; she could, if she wished, kiss him. She peered through the dark and thought of how soft his mouth had felt against her fingers.

He said, "Alice," and she put up her hands to stop him as she'd done before, but he was so close to her already. Why, she could feel the heat of him! One step, one step only would bring him into her, but he wouldn't take it. If any step was to be taken it was to be Alice's. But of course she wouldn't take such a step. And yet there he was, closer, yet! No step was needed at all! She could reach out and touch her fingers to his coat sleeve. . . .

Alice reached out. Touched. The cloth felt like skin, as if she'd gone straight through and rested her palm against his muscles and sinews; she felt sure, very sure, that if she kept her hand there it would burn straight through to the bone. She picked her hand up and laid it against his cheek as she'd done before, let her thumb slide down to his mouth and run over it. His cheek so cool, his mouth so warm. And soft. So soft!

Alice lifted up onto her toes and put her mouth against Nate's mouth, holding on to his coat sleeves to keep her balance; it felt odd, different than she'd imagined, but she didn't mislike it, didn't mislike it at all. Nate brought his hands to either side of her face to keep her there while he took his mouth away to look at her; he put his mouth back, still holding her. But Alice didn't want to be held there. She pulled back; Nate let go. He stood still. Alice stood still.

After a time Nate said, "If you'd like to try that again I shouldn't run off," and Alice laughed. How odd that felt too! But then she was afraid, although she couldn't have said it was of Nate, exactly. She stepped back. "Truly, you'd best go." A gentle enough phrase, but Nate responded by a shout that sent her back another step.

"Oh, blast this going! Blast college! Blast my father! Blast it all!"

"Shush!" Alice said, but too late.

The door opened. A voice carried across the dark. "Who's out there?" Freeman stepped into the moonlit yard, breeches pulled up under a loose shirt, stockingless feet shoved into his shoes. Alice thought to shrink back into the shadows, but Nate stepped out into the clear. Alice followed.

"Nate," Freeman said. "And Alice. Well, now."

"I mean Alice no harm, sir. I only wished—"

"Whatever you wished, lad, this meeting in the dead of night makes it highly suspect. Get on home."

"Please, sir—"

"Mr. Freeman knows what he speaks of on meetings in the dead of night," Alice said. "Best do as he tells you."

A chill silence closed on Alice from both sides, squeezing her between.

Freeman broke it first. "You might think you've naught to lose and perhaps a deal to gain by this behavior, Alice, but Nate, I should think you'd know your situation is something different. Think what you do, lad. Think what you do."

He returned to the house and closed the door.

Alice stared after him. She felt unsteady, as if the ground had canted sideways and was about to tumble her into the road. How many times a fool could one girl be in her lifetime? *Think what you do.* So Freeman had said, but to Nate, not Alice. Freeman wouldn't save Alice from Nate, he would save Nate from Alice, as he had no doubt meant to do all along.

FREEMAN DIDN'T MENTION the night visit to Alice again. There was no need. He rode into the village the next morning and didn't come back till suppertime; over his toasted cheese and cider he mentioned that the two Nathan Clarkes had set out by chaise for Cambridge that noontime.

Alice returned to her work and put Nate out of her mind, or attempted to do so. During the daylight she did better at this than at the nighttime; during the daylight she could say to herself that she had kissed a boy and it was no strange thing for a girl her age to do. At night she could think only how different she felt now that she had touched her lips to another's, how nothing on her was left virgin now, but how different it felt when a thing was given of her own free will.

As the nights added up, one atop the other, Alice also wondered why Nate didn't send another letter.

IT CAME, FINALLY, just after Christmas, carried by Freeman's hand, however willing or not willing, and bearing a date three weeks old, which was in itself no odd thing, and yet Alice wondered. She took it and a candle upstairs to read.

Dear Alice,

I attempt to read my Virgil and find it little use to turn the page, as each one seems to hold naught but the image of you. Should I write these words? My father would say no, just as he has said no to my returning to Satucket and managing his tannery. I think of some of the other places I might go and the work I might do, and I think of you with me. What right have I to say such things to you? None. Every. There are such things as natural rights that outweigh those imposed by either parent or society or the content of a man's pocket.

This is a sad place to be just now. Parliament has crippled the province with its trade laws, and many merchants have entered into bankruptcies. More than one son has been removed from this college for lack of funds to go forth, and I only wish I might count myself among them. I see the lawyer's life as nothing near so noble as I once did. Besides, what sense in studying the law in this colony if a Parliament in England may countermand it as it wishes? I therefore see no sense remaining in this cold and barren place at all. All hope for happiness lies there at Satucket. I think of the night we were last together and that alone is all my solace.

You don't write to me. I don't expect you to write to me. I
don't expect a thing on this earth but what I make for myself
and so I tell my father when he tries to hold his pocketbook
over me.

If you would but write to me.

> I am Always,
> Most Respectfully Yours,
> N.C., Jr.

Alice sat considering the letter a long time. She wondered what
had turned Nate from his chosen profession so abruptly. She wondered at his dreaming of going away and taking her with him. She
wondered what he would dream if she told him what she carried. She
wondered about writing him, about what she might say and might
not say, but in the morning Freeman left early for Boston, without
inquiring after a return letter from her, as was the usual custom.

FREEMAN WAS NOT gone long, returning soon after the turn of the
year, accompanied by every man who'd spied his passage through the
village, and he trailed with him a black rumor: not only had Parliament refused to read all petitions sent by the Massachusetts colony,
but they had also ignored the warning of the non-importation agreement and were considering a new tax requiring stamps on newspa-
pers, licenses, deeds, shipping papers, and all other legal documents.

Alice helped the widow wait on the jammed table but could take
little interest in the men's railing, although she noted that this time
Freeman brought no quotes or pamphlets from Otis, and Cobb mut-
tered blackly about Otis voting twice with the governor. Her ear
turned again when they talked of the same string of bankruptcies
Nate had mentioned in his letter, and Freeman reported that a man

he described as the "treasurer and banker of all the colony, or indeed the continent" had stopped all payments, equating the effect to an earthquake.

Alice never did know what Freeman might have said or not said to the widow about her night meeting with Nate, but she could detect in the widow none of the new stiffness that had become so plain in Freeman.

A week later he left again for Boston.

TWENTY-TWO

The cold struck at Candlemas and didn't lift. Through the month of February snowstorm followed snowstorm, the sun melting just enough to form an icy crust on top before the next batch fell, so that walking became a series of awkward reaches and drops, the crust holding for one held breath before giving way and trapping the boot underneath. Because the going was so poor, the widow rarely sent Alice to the village, and it seemed to Alice that her fingers now spun not a fine wool yarn but the sticky fibers of her own cocoon.

The snow crust had compacted into something like blue glass, and Alice had just made an exhausting trip to the barn, bucking the wind all the way, when she felt the first dull, griping pain in her womb. She ignored it and worked her way back to the house, where she resumed her spinning, her step hitching only slightly with each weak pain. After several hours she felt the urgent need of her night jar, but halfway up the stairs the pressure released, and a warm wet flow coated the insides of her legs. She removed her petticoat and wiped the stairs; she worked her way up to her room to change and then returned to help the widow with the dye tub, taking care to keep any sign of internal disturbance from the surface.

The two women sat to dinner alone as usual, and if the widow noticed that Alice ate little she made no remark. After the meal Alice returned to the wheel, but the dull repetitiveness of the work only turned her thoughts to the occasional turmoil in her belly. At supper she again ate little but drank long from the beer pitcher, and although the widow watched her closely, she said nothing.

Alice passed a long night, falling into a shivering sleep for a few minutes and then waking with her belly griping hard, her skin painted with sweat. Sometime before dawn the pains began to come so hard and fast there was no hope for further sleep. As soon as first light brushed the window Alice got up, made up her bed, and tried to put on her clothes, but almost at once she was driven back to the bed with a racking that left her trembling. She rose again, dressed herself, and had reached the top of the stairs when the storm assailed her again. She returned to her bed and stayed there.

More light.

Steps on the stairs.

The widow's hand on her belly.

"Alice, tell me now. How long have you been in travail?"

Alice closed her eyes.

"Alice, answer me. How long have you been in this way?"

"I woke with a stomach gripe. If I might rest—"

The widow picked her up by the shoulders and shook her. "Hear me, Alice. I'll not play at this game another minute. Answer me. How long since you began?"

Alice tried to think of what to say, how to get the widow to go away so she could deal with her trouble in secret. She said, "At first light."

"How often do the pains come?"

"Not often."

"How severe?"

"Like a common gripe."

"If you can call it so you've not come on strong. Stay as you are. I'm off for the midwife."

The next wave took Alice as the widow clattered down the stairs, and she set her teeth against it. She heard the clunk and hiss of fresh wood on the fire, the clang of a kettle, the scuffle of boots being dragged on, the door latch snapping up and down.

Alice lay with her knees tucked tight through the next pain and the next, the goal in her head to fight it back, to keep it in. For some minutes she was able to believe that the pains had indeed softened and lessened; the next minute they forced her to roll on her side and vomit on the floor. She sweated and shivered at once; she pushed away the blanket and pulled it over and tossed it back again; the next pain came like a hammer and an ax together, and there Alice's goal changed; to get it out, not keep it in. She pushed, and the pain was so great she thought she would die inside it; as the room blurred she thought she had indeed died, except that she couldn't believe the dead felt such pain. She pushed again and felt such bursting relief she thought that too might be death, but a lump lay between her legs, and as she reached down to get it away from her she found she was still bound to it by a slippery, pulsing cord.

Alice fell back and lay there under a woozy cloud, unsure if she were alive or dead. After a time she felt the urge to push again, and a pulpy, bloody mass joined the other bloody thing where it lay between her legs. She pulled the blanket over the mess to cover it up and pushed it aside. She couldn't stop her shaking. She rolled away from the sodden blanket, drew the bed rug over her, and closed her eyes.

ALICE WOKE TO a strange voice. "I see no mark on it. But covered as it was—"

"She mustn't wake to such a sight," the widow whispered. "Take it below-stairs."

The bed heaved slightly. Footsteps faded off across the room, and Alice drifted away. When she opened her eyes again the widow's face hung over her, sagging, as if freshly aged. She raised Alice's head and held a cup to her lips. Balm. Sage. Rum. Alice sipped and lay back. The widow began to wash her face with a cloth, warm and wet and smelling of mint; a shadowy memory of a similar comfort so old it couldn't form either a face or a circumstance flooded over her. The widow raised her again and eased off her soiled clothes; she washed her arms and hands, between her legs, down her legs, rolled her over and washed her back. She raised her again and pulled a clean shift over her head, worked it down around her legs, and covered her with fresh blankets. When she was finished she sat back and looked at Alice in silence, let Alice look at her in silence. She said, "Alice, the babe is dead."

After a time she said, "Alice? Do you understand me?"

Alice nodded.

"'Tis downstairs. Granny Hall will bring it to you when you wish it."

Alice shook her head violently. She didn't want to see it. She closed her eyes.

Someone said, "Alice Baker."

Alice didn't recognize the voice or the name. She kept her eyes closed.

The widow said, "Alice."

Alice opened her eyes. The midwife stood over her, but she carried no shrouded babe in her arms. She looked taller than Alice remembered. Older. Darker.

"Alice Baker, you must answer this question I put to you in the full fear of God's retribution if you give false answer. When this babe was born, did it have life in it?"

Alice looked to the widow. The widow picked up her hand and held it. "Alice, you needn't—"

"Hush, widow, and let her answer. Was there life in your babe as you bore it?"

"I don't know."

"Did it cry?"

"I don't know."

"Did it breathe?"

"I don't know. I didn't touch it."

"You wrapped it in the blanket."

"I didn't touch it."

"You wrapped it in a blanket and pushed it on its face and suffocated it."

"Here, now!" the widow cried.

Granny Hall turned to her. "Say what you wish, but I know my duty. A bastard child, born alone, suffocated—"

"You know nothing of what you're saying."

"I know what I see."

The two women jabbed back and forth, making Alice's head ache. She closed her eyes.

ALICE SLEPT, AND woke, and the midwife was gone. The widow gave her more rum and a strong soup; she helped her to the night jar on still trembling legs; Alice slept again, or perhaps she'd been asleep all along and had dreamed the soup, but she dreamed it again and again. She roused to the sound of voices shouting below-stairs, some she knew and some she didn't. Heavy-booted heels addressed the stairs along with a softer tread, and a strongly built man with a face as close to blank as Alice had ever seen stood next to the bed. The widow came up beside him, her face lumpy with anger.

"This is Sheriff Stone," she said, her words bitten and brittle. She turned on the sheriff. "You might look at the girl, sir, and think better of what you would say to her. She's not been out of this bed since the birth."

The sheriff cut across. "Alice Baker, you are hereby placed under arrest on the complaint of the coroner of this county for being accessory to the death of a bastard male child born of your body on the twenty-seventh day of February in this the year of our Lord his Majesty King George III seventeen hundred and sixty-five. You will remain in the custody of this authority until it is judged you are fit to travel, at which time you will be confined in the gaol at Barnstable to await your trial."

TWENTY-THREE

Alice marked time by the increase in her strength, the decrease in pain in her breasts and loins. The widow remained in a constant state of great excitement, her voice rising from below at frequent intervals. At first Alice thought she argued with Freeman, but after a time she came to understand that Freeman wasn't there, and that the widow argued with the guard they had assigned to Alice until she could travel to the gaol. Alice's strength had returned enough so that she might have rekindled her old habit of creeping to the stairs at any time to listen to the on-again-off-again struggles below, but she could think of no reason to take the trouble.

The widow too seemed to wish to keep her where she was. She fed her, washed her, and helped her to the night jar as she was able but asked her nothing, and Alice made no offer. The hours and days since the first pain had struck seemed to weave together and fall apart, reconnecting themselves in no kind of pattern. She recalled great pain, and one moment of such bliss she wished she might have died at that minute to keep hold of it as it was, but the next thing she recalled with any great certainty was the sheriff. She drifted in and out of sleep, ate, sat up, and walked the length of the room as the widow directed, but sleep was the thing she craved, although it was never peaceful.

She dreamed of the babe, a great bloody babe, lifting bloody hands to strangle her; she dreamed of the widow raising scarred hands to strangle her; she dreamed of Verley come after her, and Freeman accosting him, not to rescue Alice but to demand his five pounds reward for her capture. She dreamed of her mother, finned and swimming across the floor toward her, tears puddling around her, and her father, kicking the trunk, which had a dead, bloody babe inside it. If she dreamed of Nate she didn't remember it.

She woke to more shouting below: men, at least two, neither voice recognizable, and a woman she thought a stranger also until she realized it was the widow, in as hot a fury as Alice had ever heard her. At length the widow appeared with a bowl and a plate, her face raw red, her jaw a ridge of locked, jumping muscles. She sat down on the bed and fed Alice a salty broth along with some soft, sweet bread; it tasted very fine, and Alice felt very warm under her coverlet; it occurred to her that if she could have erased the commotion around her she would have said that her life had come around to a good spot. She was out of pain, she had been shed of the babe, she had kept her bed at the widow's.

The widow put the dishes on the floor and went to the pegs to collect Alice's quilted petticoat and wool flannel gown. She set them on the bed. She said, "I've held them off as long as possible. They say you must come down now, or they'll come up and get you."

Alice didn't move. The widow fetched a thick pair of worsted stockings from the chest, then another. She returned to the bed, and as Alice still hadn't moved, drew down the covers and began to push on her stockings.

"All right, now, Alice, you must get up."

But Alice couldn't move. It was as if her legs understood that if she once gave up her bed under the widow's eaves she would never return to it. The widow said, "Do you want them to carry you out like a trussed hog, Alice?"

Alice didn't. She jerked her legs to the side of the bed and stepped into the skirt as the widow held it, but it had been made loose for an expanded girth, and the widow had to cross the tapes to fasten it. She held out Alice's boots, and Alice pushed her feet into them. She stood up, the widow helping her. She walked to the stairs and worked her way down, holding on to the rope rail.

The two men waiting for her in the keeping room were built in similar blocky shapes like a pair of matched oxen. They stared and shuffled back and forth, looking at each other in between, until one of them stepped forward and captured Alice's elbow. The widow came up and brushed him aside to fix Alice's cloak around her, tie on a muffler, hand her a pair of mittens. The men, both of them together this time, stepped in and took hold of Alice's arms. They led her outside to a heavy wooden cart filled with straw and lifted her in. One of the men—Alice made no effort to distinguish them—reached into the wagon, grabbed Alice's ankle, and clamped it in an iron band fixed by a chain to a heavy metal ring in the wagon floor.

The widow reappeared with a bundle, which she thrust into Alice's arms; she tossed two bed rugs over her. One of the men climbed up onto the seat and the other mounted an already saddled horse that had been tied to the wagon; they each clicked to their beasts, and the cart wheeled off into the road. The widow called something after her, but Alice couldn't make it out against the wind off the water.

The wind followed the cart, and Alice pulled up the hood of her cloak; after a time she lay down in the straw and pulled the bed rugs closer. The wagon jolted over the ice-crusted road; the light turned from dull gray to bright gray to dull purple. The wagon took a sharp turn up a hill and wobbled to a stop. The driver jumped down, the rider jumped down, and they came at Alice, urging her to do this or that or say this or that, or perhaps that was later. She remembered being taken into a room that had a fire and being allowed to stand close to it but not long enough to warm her through; she remembered a third man speaking to her and perhaps she spoke to him; she had some trouble remembering anything but the cold, and the heat, and the cold again when they took her to the gaol.

A WOOD BOX, a tiny, barred window, a pallet to sleep on, a bucket. Alice dropped onto the pallet and pulled her rugs over her; she slept, but the bad dreams still found her, the old dream, of Verley coming at her, Verley reaching for her throat. She clawed at his hands, but he caught hers up and said, "Whoa, Alice! Whoa, Alice! Whoa!" But the voice wasn't as Verley's was at all. It began to say things like, "Look at me, Alice, settle now, Alice, look at me. Look at me."

Alice wrenched her eyes open and saw it was Freeman who had hold of her. She lay back, panting.

"I've frightened you, Alice, and I'm most sorry for it. I shouldn't have waked you if we had more time, but we've none of it; I only just received the widow's letter. Are you well? Dear God, look at you. Tell me you're well."

"I'm well."

"Very good. Very good. Now, then, you must collect yourself and talk to me. First, do you understand the charge against you? That you murdered your infant?"

"I do not understand. I did nothing to it."

The lines that divided Freeman's forehead softened. He got up off his knees and walked the box in the tight square allowed him, once around, twice, three times. He stopped.

"All right, Alice. The thing now is for you to tell me everything as it happened. Everything, do you understand? We've no time for you to blush or demur or speak in roundabout terms. Can you do that, Alice?"

Alice nodded.

"Very good. Very good, Alice. Now let us begin with your entering your travail. Were you alone?"

Alice nodded again. "Until the widow came."

"Had you delivered of your child when she came?"

"No. She went for the midwife."

"She left you alone?"

"She thought I'd some time remaining. I made her think it."

"Why? Why would you make her think that?"

"I didn't want her to know of the babe."

Freeman closed his eyes. "Alice. Child. Surely . . . all right, now. You entered your travail. The widow found you. She set off for the midwife, thinking she had time to fetch her. Now, then. What happened next?"

" 'Twas great pain. A very great pain. I wanted it gone."

"You wanted what gone?"

"I wanted the pain gone."

"Very good. You wanted the pain gone. And what of the babe?"

"I wanted it out of me so it would stop hurting. I tried to push it out of me. I pushed it out of me."

"Very good. You pushed it out. And then what did you do?"

"I don't know."

"Think, Alice. The babe is out. What did you do with the babe?"

"I don't know. They took it downstairs. The widow wanted me to have it back and I didn't want it."

"You didn't want the babe?"

"It was nothing of mine."

"What do you mean, it was nothing of yours?"

Alice made no answer.

Freeman studied her. "All right, Alice, perhaps now is the time for us to go backward. Perhaps now is the time for you to tell me how you came into this circumstance."

Alice turned her face away.

"Alice, understand me. I wish this information only so that I may help you. You do believe I wish to help you?"

She didn't. She couldn't. Why should he wish to help her, after she had caused him such great trouble? Why not see her hanged, and then he and the widow could keep in one bed all the night long?

He said, "Alice, I would ask you to look at me and tell me if you see anything in my face that might cause you to think I mean you harm."

Alice looked at him and couldn't say she saw any such thing. And yet she couldn't give him Verley's name. She couldn't risk going back there.

"All right, then," Freeman said. "Tell me this. The midwife Granny Hall thought the child had been brought near to term. Do you think this true or false?"

Alice thought. "What was the date it came?"

"The twenty-seventh of last month. The twenty-seventh of February."

"It was near to term."

"All right. Now tell me again what you did with the babe. After you pushed it out, what did you do with it?"

"Nothing."

"Did you pick it up?"

"No."

"Did you touch it in any way?"

"No."

"The widow in her letter says they found it wrapped in a blanket. Did you wrap it in a blanket, Alice?"

"No."

"It was found wrapped in a blanket. Who might have done that if not you?"

Alice remembered the bloody lump between her legs; she remembered the pulpy thing that came after it. She said, "I didn't want to see it. I covered it in the blanket."

"It was cold in the room?"

She remembered shaking, shaking so hard she thought the bed tick might slide off its frame. She nodded.

"So you covered the babe to keep it warm. And then what?"

"I don't know."

"Did it cry?"

"I don't know."

"Did it breathe?"

"I don't know! I don't know! I didn't look at it! It was naught to do with me; I had naught to do with it!"

"Alice. Please." Freeman took a step toward the pallet; Alice crabbed backward. Freeman stepped back, folded his arms, and peered down at his boots for some time. At length he said, "I wonder if you understand how a lawyer works in a court of law, Alice. As defendant you are not allowed to testify in your own defense, so your lawyer must do it for you. Your lawyer must tell your story. The king's attorney will speak too, and he will tell his own story. The one this king's attorney will tell is of a wanton young girl with no moral fiber who got herself into some trouble and wished to rid herself of the evidence with the murder of her bastard. I don't believe this is the true story, but I need another to tell them. Can't you help me with that story, Alice?"

Alice couldn't. She couldn't.

After a time Freeman said, "Perhaps you could tell me something of your young life, your parents."

Her parents! What could her parents have to do with it? Alice looked for the trick but could find none. So she told him of the ship, and her mother and brothers, and of Mr. Morton taking her away in his carriage, but she didn't tell him Mr. Morton's name, or where he took her, or anything of the Verleys. Freeman then launched a long series of odd questions, such as did she ever have any younger brothers and sisters, and did her first master have any more children after she came to live with him, and had she ever stood watch at a woman's travail. He asked her many more, and came near to the place where she didn't wish him to be, but he didn't push into it.

After a long time he ran out of questions. He said, "All right, Alice, do you have any questions for me?" And she asked him what date it was, and he said it was the sixth of April.

April.

The word sounded new and strange, because for so long Alice hadn't allowed of its existence. If she had she might have imagined it anything other than what it was, and yet here it was, perhaps not as bad as it might have been, for here was the gaoler come for Freeman, and here was Freeman paying him for her food and asking her if she needed more of it, asking if she needed more clothes or blankets, when she might have been out in the cold with a newborn babe in her arms, looking for a night's shelter.

But April also meant that somewhere in the confusion of days at the widow's the twenty-first of March had swum by and Alice was sixteen now. Which made Alice think of a second question. "How long will they keep me here?"

"They'll keep you here until your trial. A capital crime allows for no bail. The circuit returns to Barnstable in July."

And so the line Alice couldn't think beyond moved from March to July.

TWENTY-FOUR

Alice came to know her box well. A man named W. Bartlet had carved his name in a beam, with "13d October 1698 and 27d he went out." Another man, or perhaps the same man, had whittled a ship into one of the thick oak planks, another had carved out a huge, thrashing whale, yet another had covered both sides of the doorjamb with diagonal lines, possibly to pass the time, or possibly to mark his days in gaol. Alice thought what she might do if she'd had a knife: carve her name, perhaps, but which name? Her dates? She didn't know them. Her life story? If she began at the floor and climbed the wall how far up would it take her? It seemed to Alice that a great many things had happened to her in fifteen years . . . no, sixteen now. She was only grateful that she'd passed her birthday in the widow's attics and not in Barnstable gaol.

In the end, Alice marked the days, not with any knife mark but with Freeman's visits. He came bearing gifts, but not the same kinds of gifts he'd brought her in her past life. He brought a foot warmer, a woolen cap, a thick blanket, a meat pie made by his

Barnstable housekeeper. But Alice also noted the increasing tightness of Freeman's mouth and jaw as he greeted her, and she knew well enough what that meant. Alice didn't wish to be hanged; she wanted to help Freeman help her; but she couldn't give him Verley's name or any more of her circumstance; she couldn't give away any clue that might take her back to Medfield. She thought many times what might happen if she told Freeman what he wished to know, and when she wasn't lying awake thinking it, she dreamed it. In her dream she stood before a row of justices, with Verley towering beside her within an arm's length, his height and breadth nearly filling all the space around them, his hands pulsing to get at her. Alice never came as far as the actual judgment in her dream; the nearness of Verley was all the nightmare she needed to cause her to wake sweating.

Alice had other visitors besides Freeman. The gaoler, a reedy man with a pinched face, came to let Freeman in and out of her box, to bring her the food that Freeman bought her, to take away her full chamber bucket and return it emptied. He made an early point of telling her he had ten children of his own and didn't take well to people who murdered their infants. The sheriff came, seemingly just to stare at her through the tiny square of bars in the door, and the king's attorney came, a man not as tall as Freeman but half again as wide, who seemed to think if he stood in the box long enough and let Alice drink him in she would let loose a different story than the one she'd already told him. When the king's attorney came, Freeman came with him, and when the king's attorney asked the name of the babe's father, Freeman cut him off with, "That's not the issue before this court, sir," after which the king's attorney gave Freeman the kind of look that suggested he'd learned what he'd come for.

One day of visits stood out among the others. It began with the widow. She brought things Freeman couldn't have thought of: beeswax for her chapped skin, clean linen for when her courses returned, cornstarch to clean her hair. She said, "You look like death," and sat down and combed the starch through Alice's hair herself, brushed her cheeks and lips with the balm, and tied a new woolen shawl around her shoulders. She didn't talk of Alice's troubles but talked of affairs in the village, and the half-wit she'd hired to take Alice's place at the wheel, "whose mouth works faster than her fingers." Before she left she said, "Do as Mr. Freeman tells you. I need you home," and Alice would have given much to have been able to speak at that moment, but she knew of no words that would say all she owed.

And Nate came. It so happened that Freeman was in the box when the gaoler unlocked the door and ushered the boy in. "Nate!" Freeman exclaimed. "How now? Why aren't you at the college?"

"I came away."

"Do you know the fine for that?"

"Two and six. Another one and three per day for tarrying." He looked at Alice and back at Freeman and said nothing more.

Freeman said, "What news have you from town? What's said of the stamp tax? We hear rumor of its passing."

"'Tis passed. To take effect the first of November. A ream of bail bonds goes from fifteen pounds to a hundred."

"The devil! And what does Otis say? Has he waked from this odd sleep of his?"

Nate drew a pamphlet from his coat pocket. "He's just come out with this. He says in it that Parliament has the 'just, clear equitable and lawful authority' to impose taxes on the colonies. He says that the colonists are 'virtually, constitutionally, in law and equity to be considered as represented in the honourable House of Commons.' He does add that an American member in the house would be a 'reasonable indulgence.'"

Freeman snatched the pamphlet and began to read.

"They say in the street that Otis has made a deal to keep quiet on the stamps in exchange for his father's appointment as probate judge and chief justice of the Court of Common Pleas here at Barnstable."

Freeman lifted his eyes from the pamphlet. "No. No. This no rational man can believe who knows him. Or his father. Or the relation between them."

"As I hear the people talk, your Mr. Otis won't get reelected to the legislature. They call him reprobate, apostate, traitor. I hear it on every corner."

Alice looked at Nate, puzzled. Was it a note of glee she heard in him? Did he wish to torment Freeman? He hadn't yet looked at Alice, but this Alice could understand better; she was no longer the girl he'd thought her.

But the news of Otis's doubtful future in the legislature appeared to perk Freeman to a degree. "That itself disproves any theory of deals made with his enemies," he said. "Why boost a father's paltry career compared to his own stellar one? 'Tis madness to consider it."

"All I can say for certain is that Otis had best do something to earn back the people's trust in him, and he'd best do it in a hurry."

Freeman didn't answer, his gaze again directed at the pamphlet.

Nate said, "I must go," and there he looked at Alice for the first time. She would have given much for another kind of look, one with something of his old silliness in it, but even as she completed her thought he had already turned away, banged on the door for the gaoler, and disappeared through it.

After Nate had gone, Freeman stood as he was some time, gazing at the pamphlet he held, so that Alice assumed it was Otis that occupied his mind, and was greatly surprised when he lifted his eyes and said, "I wonder what I must do to earn your trust in *me*, Alice."

It had been a wearing day. That was all Alice could think to account for it. The widow's visit had swelled her bruised heart near to cracking; Nate's visit had cut her; it had also reminded her that she had taken Freeman away from events of more import than her own poor life, and that if Freeman saved her life she would owe him a debt she could never possibly repay. There Alice thought of the widow and how the widow owed Freeman her life as well; she thought of how the widow was repaying him. She thought of the noise she'd heard through the door of the widow's room. This was the best Alice could explain it: the day, the debt, the memory of the widow and Freeman together. She burst out, "You might leave the widow be!"

Alice supposed that if she'd drawn a knife and sunk it in Freeman's back unaware she couldn't have more greatly surprised him. He stared at her long until his features sank into a depth of sadness Alice had never seen in him, but that sadness only spurred Alice the more. "Don't you see how you shame her? She's been cast from the church! She can't go about the village! You save her life and then you take away her life as pay for it! Why didn't you leave her to burn, then?"

Freeman's face turned from sadness to puzzlement. "Save her life? Take her . . . *burn?* Let her *burn?* Upon my word, I haven't the least . . . Oh, good Lord. The fire. You've heard somewhere about the fire, and you assume it was I . . . It wasn't I. I wasn't living there. But what in the name of—"

He broke off. A flush overtook his face and neck, deeper and darker than anything Nate Clarke had yet managed. "You think the widow gives as pay . . . you think I *take* as pay—" He turned around and banged on the door for the gaoler. He swung back at Alice. "I won't debase either the widow or myself by giving answer to that allegation. As to my shaming her, I assure you, my suffering on that account is by far the greater."

"Then why don't you marry her?"

The gaoler's key scraped in the lock, the door swung open, Freeman stepped into the frame, turned back to her. "I would marry her today, or tomorrow, or yesterday, for that matter. She will not consent, for the dower rights her husband left her to her home would be canceled on her remarriage. You see by this how much shame troubles her."

ALICE LAY AWAKE that night as usual and yet not as usual, for instead of herself and her troubles filling her thoughts, they were filled with the widow and Freeman. Or she supposed she would have to say they were full of Freeman; Alice felt she understood the widow no more nor less than she had ever understood her. To trade a house for a husband who had another fine house in Barnstable, seemed no bad bargain, but Alice had long accepted that the widow's actions would run contrary to Alice's expectations. Freeman, though. She must rethink Freeman entirely. If he wasn't the thing she had first thought him, he wasn't the second thing she'd thought him either; she supposed—oh, she more than supposed—she might have concluded this before now without the words of explanation just offered her. She might have looked only as far as the image of a man's hand touching a woman's door in a gesture that could speak of nothing but the greatest tenderness to come to a proper understanding of Freeman's nature.

But in truth should Alice have needed even that? Shouldn't she have taken his true measure in his treatment of her? If he were a man who would take what he could, why had he not taken Alice, if not before she'd made him the offer of it, as a Verley would, then afterward, when few would have blamed him for it?

Thinking thus, understanding thus, Alice could only lie on her pallet in misery at the thought of the harsh words she'd dare to throw at him. How easily now she could see the widow as he painted her, a woman without shame! How easily she could see the truth of Freeman's statement that he was the greater sufferer! But if he suffered so, why did he continue so with the widow? Alice supposed she could see why. She had put the case before, but in another consideration entirely. An aging man alone and lonely, a man of little physical attraction, a man with little but his money to recommend him, where else would he find his comfort?

But there too, as Alice considered the old description she'd assigned to Freeman, she began to see how poorly it fit him, how shallow had been her assessment of him. He wasn't a young man, it was true, but neither was he past his physicality, as she'd discovered with her own fingers. He wasn't a handsome man, it was true, but he possessed the kind of face that, although slow to give up its secrets, once opened, warmed him into something as good as handsome. And little but money to recommend him? No, Alice had been another kind of fool to think so. She thought of what she'd said to Freeman and flushed hot. She'd greatly wronged him, twice now. He'd forgiven her the first, but what man would forgive the second thing too? No doubt she'd seen him for the last time; no doubt he would leave her case to another now.

FREEMAN STAYED AWAY the next morning, just as Alice had feared, but the widow came in his place. Alice couldn't look at her.

The widow said, "Mr. Freeman asked me to come to see you before I leave for Satucket with Mr. Cobb. I've neither the time nor the patience to go 'round and 'round with you as he's done. He says he's attempted unsuccessfully to discover how you came by this child, but as you wouldn't tell him you might feel more comfortable telling me. He said also that if you didn't tell me you were lost. Understand that by the word 'lost' he means you will hang."

"He . . . he spoke to you of what we talked of?"

"He said nothing but what I've told you. He was quite distressed. I dislike seeing Mr. Freeman distressed, and when I see him so, I like to do what I can to remedy it. I should think you might too." She waited, but not long. A scarred hand snaked out and captured Alice's chin, bringing her eyes level with the widow's. "I shall make but one last attempt to make Mr. Freeman's position clear to you. He must know all your story, Alice, not just such parts as you wish to tell. It makes no difference what that story is; he must know it in order to know how to build his case. *He must know it,* Alice. If you lay with the reverend's son, he must know it. If you lay with the *reverend*, he must know it. If you lay with a sailor, or two sailors, or three sailors—"

"My master lay with me against my will. He got the child on me."

The widow dropped her hand. She said, "This would be Verley? Of Medfield?"

The name out of the widow's mouth stopped Alice. How could the widow know it? How?

The widow said, "Don't look so stricken, Alice. I'm not out to claim the five pounds he offers."

So there it was. Straight out of her dream. Straight out of the newspaper. Of course the widow and Freeman would have remembered the newspaper. Of course they had never truly believed in that other Alice run off from her master. They could have sent her back to face Verley at any time they chose. Alice began to tremble, or did she only feel that she trembled? If she did shake, the widow took no notice; she picked up Alice's hand and turned it over to expose the three ridged lines across her palm. "And how came you by this? Verley also?"

Alice nodded.

"And the marks on your neck when you first came to Satucket? And the cut cheek, the injured arm? Verley as well?"

"And Mrs. Verley."

The widow blinked. She said, "You must tell me the whole of it, Alice."

Alice told her. When she finished, the widow fixed her eyes on the floor and didn't lift them until Alice said, "Madam?"

The widow looked up. "I've long ago stopped blaming or thanking God for the workings of a man's heart. I'll not squander the remainder of my time in further pondering the workings of this one. The woman's, I'm ashamed to say, I understand well enough. Right now I've but one question for you, Alice. Why on earth could you not tell me this before, if not when first you came, then later, when you'd come to know me something better?"

"I was afraid you'd send me away."

"For a sin not your own?"

"I'd heard it put the other way, madam."

The widow peered at her. Alice knew the widow's quiet rage by now and watched it as it grew, but just as she'd learned to grasp the difference between similar words as a child, she now grasped that she was not the object of this anger. The widow said, "How differently disguised our courage comes. Yours has my admiration. Now I must speak with Mr. Freeman," and she banged for the gaoler.

FREEMAN CAME. ALICE had been so afraid of how he might look at her, and indeed, his face appeared less open than it had before, but he spoke gently. "I must hear it for myself, Alice."

So she told him. He didn't interrupt her, despite her many stops and starts, but when she was finished he bade her tell it again, and that time he interrupted often. When Alice had finished with that telling, he picked up her hand and said, "Hard as it may be for you to believe, Alice, this Verley is the saving of you."

Yes, it was hard for Alice to believe, for without Verley there would have been no dead babe and no charge of murdering a bastard in the first place, but she looked at Freeman's face, opened to her once again, and decided that perhaps she could trust him after all.

TWENTY-FIVE

May came, and along with it a splash of pink on the single branch Alice could observe through her small barred window. She might have described a greater light and fresher air in the box as well, but she had some trouble deciding if the improvement in the light and air were real or imagined, as Freeman's mood had lifted so markedly she suspected that alone accounted for the difference. He came in smiling and left smiling; he brought frivolous gifts like a doll on a string that danced when you pulled it, and candied plums, and a new hair ribbon. Indeed, he seemed to have forgiven Alice every transgression against him. He didn't come every day, but he came often enough that Alice doubted he'd taken time of late to travel to Satucket, and she wondered if her saying the word *shame* out loud had made him think another thing about his relation with the widow.

During each of Freeman's visits he talked to Alice of her upcoming trial. He spoke, always, with a soaring confidence in its outcome, but Alice believed she could recognize the places that troubled him, and one in particular. He asked her if there was anyone in Satucket besides the widow that might speak to her character, and at first Alice said no. Freeman expressed no dismay at her answer, but she saw that it troubled him; she gave it greater thought, and the next time he came she said, "I wonder if Shipmaster Hopkins might speak well of me, sir. He came to the widow's more than most, and he never made such remarks as the others."

Freeman's face brightened so markedly that Alice tried to think some more. "And perhaps someone at the frolick."

"No."

"They might say they saw me do my share of work, that I didn't run about wild like—"

"No, Alice. Not the frolick."

Alice couldn't think why not, and then of course she remembered. They might also say they'd seen her walk off into the dark with a boy.

No, not the frolick.

IN THE MIDDLE of May a Spanish pirate captured off a ship wrecked on Truro's outer bars was pushed into the cell in manacles. Freeman arrived soon after to find him leaning over Alice and jabbering at her in a foreign tongue; Freeman roared as Alice had never heard him roar, not at the Spaniard but at the gaoler, and not long afterward the same two men who had fetched Alice from Satucket came and carted the Spaniard off. To anyone else the Spaniard might have seemed of little significance, but to Alice it meant all. Freeman might have wished to save Nate from Alice, but so too did he wish to save Alice from the Spaniard.

Five days after the Spaniard's short stay Alice fell ill. She got the first idea of it when the cold and damp stopped troubling her; the fever was well in command by the time she understood that a sickness had fallen on her. Next came a flaming throat that thickened her speech, and there Freeman sent for the doctor. Alice was still sensible when the doctor arrived and heard him label her affliction the putrid malignant sore throat, adding that it had killed many children in the village. He seemed quite sure she would die of it too, and the gaoler seemed so satisfied with the idea that Alice determined not to. She gargled with the cold water root tincture the doctor had left for her, applied the onion poultice Freeman's housekeeper sent, and lulled herself into healing sleep with an old song about a bird on a cradle that she remembered from nowhere.

Somewhere in the height of her fever the sheriff returned and read her a passage from a paper that seemed to do nothing but restate the old charge, until Freeman explained to her that she was now charged as Alice Cole, not Alice Baker. After the reading of the charge the sheriff and Freeman stood in the box and had some words back and forth about another case to be judged at another county court; their long, measured words lulled Alice to sleep even better than the old song had.

The widow came again, this time bringing honey cake, brandy, and a flannel soaked in hyssop tea to wrap her neck in. The widow stayed at Barnstable some days; Alice wondered if she stayed at Freeman's house, and if she did, in which chamber she slept, and what Freeman's housekeeper thought of the arrangement. The widow busied herself at her visits by repacking the onion poultice on Alice's feet or rewrapping her neck in the flannel, and while the widow visited, Freeman stayed away, which caused Alice to wonder if she'd been correct in supposing a change in their relation.

The widow returned to Satucket. Alice began to feel better. As her health improved, Freeman secured permission for a daily walk in the yard, and he took her walking himself, clamping her hand tight in the crook of his arm. On these walks Alice saw the things she'd seen on her first days in Satucket: the plum blossoms, the pinking oaks, the pine pollen that had scraped so at her eyes and throat. She'd come full circle through an entire year, but the idea of the circle made her uneasy, like a bad sign. Like a rope.

Alice began to dream of circles, being trapped inside a circle of towering, angry, strange men; she dreamed of being strangled by ropes instead of hands. She woke almost every night sweating and trembling, in misery because of her fear, in misery because she feared, but in the very depths of it, at the absolute bottom of it, she sometimes came to a place of peace. If they hanged her, she would be rid of it all: the dreams, the sweats, the shakes. The fear.

As Freeman walked with her he began to fill the conversational space with talk of politics, much the way he'd filled his talk with the widow, and Alice thrilled at this change in their relation. He told her of Otis's reelection after his enemies published a lampoon of him in the *Gazette*, which proved to the townspeople he'd not been bought by them after all. Freeman also told her of the Virginia colony passing their own resolves denying the authority of Parliament to tax the colonies, a thing Alice imagined would have pleased Freeman, but he took on a look and tone she could only call something akin to jealousy. Virginia forged ahead while Massachusetts sat silent! While Otis stayed silent! Worse than silent! Otis had been overheard on the street calling the Virginia resolves an act of treason!

ALICE GREW STRONGER. She counted the days in the yellowing, and, finally, the greening of the tree branch outside her window, wondering what the view from her window at Satucket would look like now, and then stopped counting the days altogether, knowing too well where they ended.

One day Freeman came in the highest of spirits and didn't wait till they'd left on their walk to tell her what had caused it: Otis was back. He'd presented a resolution to the House of Representatives to form a committee of correspondence with the other provinces, to assemble representatives of each colony at a special congress to consult together over the late acts of Parliament. The committee had in fact been formed; Otis had been named to it, he was further named as representative to the new congress. Freeman then led Alice out into the day and told her how fine she looked and how strong she grew and how she needn't worry about what lay ahead. They walked long and far, Freeman securing her hand to his elbow with his own palm, and Alice couldn't think of a time when she'd felt happier. But that night the dreams were the worst they'd been, with nothing at the bottom of the fear but a new fear. What if she never saw such a day again?

Sometime after the tree branch had buried itself in solid green Freeman announced three days remaining to the trial; over the next days he came to Alice's cell and talked to her of anything he could find to talk of besides the trial. He told her of his housekeeper's distress over a hole he'd burned in his breeches, of a sloop aground in the harbor, of a fuss in town over who owned a tree that had dropped a branch through the meetinghouse window.

The day of the trial the widow appeared with clean clothes and a bucket of fresh water; she set to work scrubbing Alice down. Once Alice was washed to the widow's satisfaction she pulled a simple gown of sky blue linen over Alice's head, combed out her hair, tied it in a clean white ribbon, stood away from her, and said, "You look as you should, child. You look your own lovely self. Now I have no advice for you; you'll have got all you need of that from Mr. Freeman. You must take from me nothing but my honest belief that you're none of the things they'll call you in that courtroom; you must wear your innocence around you as you wear this fine cloth, as if it were your suit of armor," and she brushed her fingers over the new gown made of thread Alice had spun herself that past summer.

The widow left. Freeman came. He picked up Alice's trembling hand and said, "All will be well, Alice. Do you know why? Because we meet fabrication with fact. With truth. With truth we will win. And after we win, the widow and I will take you home."

The gaoler opened the door. Alice stood up and smoothed her skirt over her knees. *Armor*, the widow might call it, but it couldn't disguise the pudding that lurked beneath it in the place of knees. Freeman went out first; the gaoler gripped Alice's elbow and led her after. She walked out of the stinking box into the soft, sweet air, Freeman's last words ringing in her head above any others. *The widow and I will take you home.*

TWENTY-SIX

T he minute Alice entered the courtroom she felt the weight of it: the long tables, the solid boxes, the heavy rail that divided the principals from the crowd jamming the room from wall to door in anticipation of some fine entertainment. Freeman pointed and whispered in low tones so Alice might know who was who—the five justices seated behind the longest table in front of the fireplace, the twelve members of the jury in their boxes ranged at either side, the clerk at his table, the lawyers at theirs, the witness box, the prisoner's box.

Alice's box.

The first row of seats behind the rail contained the witnesses, ready and waiting to be called before the bar; among them Alice spied the widow, the midwife Hall, Mrs. Sears, Mrs. Winslow, and Shipmaster Hopkins. Alice might have guessed what some would say of her, but not all.

The sheriff led Alice to her box and shut her inside. She watched Freeman walk to his table and settle himself; the space between them seemed as long as the Boston road. It might have been the heavy tread of the king's attorney as he entered, or it might have been the pounding of Alice's heart that so rattled the floorboards, for he stared hard at Alice, twisting something of disgust into his mouth as he walked by. How could a stranger wish so desperately to see her hang?

Alice removed her eye from the king's attorney and looked at the men on the jury, determined not to be fooled by their surfaces. She hoped she had learned at least that one lesson by now: to look through the skin for a sense of the core, taking eyes and mouth as the doors that would let out the inner warmth or chill. Some of the men were young, some old, some fine, some ugly, some richly clothed, some roughly so, but they all sat grim-faced, either staring at Alice fixedly or casting their eyes up and down, up and down; she understood they looked at her in just the way she looked at them, trying to take her measure, but beyond that she saw the king's attorney twelve times over. Oh, that twelve strangers could look at her so!

The sheriff's *oyez* brought silence, his *hear ye* the attention of all as the charge was read aloud: that on the twenty-seventh day of February in the fifth year of His Majesty King George III's reign seventeen hundred and sixty-five the spinster Alice Cole of Satucket in the county of Barnstable brought forth of her body a living male child, which child being a bastard, the said Alice Cole, not having God before her eyes, did on the twenty-seventh day of February aforesaid at Satucket with force and arms feloniously and willfully and of her malice aforethought assault the said living male child in the presence of God with both her hands, wrapping said living child in a blanket and laying said living child down upon its face, and the said Alice Cole feloniously and willfully with malice aforethought neglecting to relieve or sustain said living child, said child there and then died.

The courtroom hummed as if full of a swarm of bees, and then fell silent. Alice sat in the stillness that followed and wondered how in all the world she had somehow become the "spinster of Satucket." After a time the fantastical in the situation began to die down in her, and Alice considered each thing as it had been charged, keeping the faces of the jury before her. Had she had God before her eyes? Had she done something with both her hands that morning that could be called willful or malicious? Had it been done with forethought? And was it not a child of her body, that thing that had lain on the blanket between her legs, that intruder on her life? Its coming had been nothing of her doing, but what of its going?

The chief justice spoke. "How does the prisoner plead?"

As Alice debated it within herself Freeman's voice rang out, "The prisoner pleads not guilty, Your Honors."

The chief justice motioned to the king's attorney, who rose from his table, stepped into the small space beside, and looked around him at the justices, the jury, Alice. His voice rang out louder than Freeman's. A sign?

"May it please Your Honors, and you, the gentlemen of the jury, the charge before the court, to which the defendant Alice Cole has pleaded not guilty, is a charge of willfully and with malice aforethought causing the death of an infant. Her infant. A child born of her own body. There can be no doubt that you, the gentlemen of the jury, must sit in the same horror in which I stand before you at the thought of so selfish, so ungodly, so monstrous an act. Now I understand that you may look at this pretty young woman in the prime of her life, cloaked as she is in the raiment of innocence, and disbelieve that she could commit such a crime, but before this trial is over you will have another opinion of Alice Cole, for we shall have proved beyond all doubt that Alice Cole is not innocent, gentlemen of the jury; she is not innocent of the sin of fornication, which needs no further proof, nor is she innocent of the sin of concealing her fornication, for which the evidence will be shown to be most bountiful; nor is she innocent of the sin of causing the death of her own infant, the guilt of which the king's witnesses, as well as the defendant's own shame, demonstrated by her efforts at concealment and denial, will prove beyond all question. In short, gentlemen, what you may now perceive to be a young and innocent girl will prove to be a deceitful, devious, morally devoid young woman who has put herself before her child, who has put herself before her God, who has put herself before her king, and has willfully and in full understanding, that understanding proven time and again by her attempts at denial and concealment, committed the most abominable of all crimes against a child of her own body."

At first as Alice listened she wondered who the king's attorney spoke of, because it certainly wasn't Alice, but then she saw the men of the jury take the king's attorney's words from his mouth and carry them back to her face. She saw the Alice Cole the king's attorney proclaimed her to be mirrored in their faces. So, no doubt, would she see that same Alice Cole mirrored by every person in the courtroom, if she dared to look. She braced herself to search out Freeman's face, or as much of it as she could see in the one side so exposed; he sat as still as a log on a forest floor, looking hard at the king's attorney without a single glance at Alice, as if he couldn't bring his gaze to rest there. Alice thought again of how little reason she had given that man to wish her well, thought again of all the kindnesses he had showered on her during her period of imprisonment. Perhaps Freeman never truly believed he would win her case; perhaps his kindness was only an attempt to march her to her death in happy ignorance. But how much greater the shocked misery when that ignorance got knocked to the floor! And how fast a fragile, newborn trust could die with it!

TWENTY-SEVEN

T he king's attorney first brought the midwife Granny Hall to the bar, her age alone enough to cause the room to settle into grave silence. She lifted her chin in all confidence as the king's attorney addressed her.

"You know the defendant, Alice Cole?"

"I know the face. When I first met her she was called by the name of Alice Baker."

"And when did you first meet her?"

"When she came to me for pennyroyal."

The bees hummed again.

"And when did she come to you for pennyroyal?"

"In August of last year."

"And why did she say she wanted pennyroyal?"

"She said she wanted it for worm."

"Pennyroyal expels worm?"

"It does."

"And what else might pennyroyal do?"

"It brings on a woman's courses."

"It brings on a woman's courses. Do you mean to say, that if a woman had begun a conception, a dose of pennyroyal would remove it?"

"It could. I'd have to say this time it didn't."

Laughter.

"And you say Alice Cole came to you in August?"

"Yes. August."

"And when did you next see Alice Cole?"

"She was still Alice Baker, or so the widow told me."

"This widow would be——?"

Granny Hall pointed. "The Widow Berry. She came to me on the twenty-seventh of February to ask me to attend the girl's childbed."

"And you went with her?"

"I went with her. Through deep snow. Ice. Hard walking. By the time we got there it was over."

"Tell us, please, what you found once you got there."

"I found that girl, whoever she is, lying on her side in the bed, and a dead babe lying at the foot of the bed on its face, wrapped up in a blanket."

"Did you examine the infant?"

"I did."

"And what did you find when you examined it?"

"Nothing, 'cept its being dead."

More laughter.

"And what did you consider the likeliest cause of the infant's demise?"

"I considered that the girl smothered it."

"Smothered it!"

"Well, seeing I knew the girl to be unmarried, and seeing the widow told me on the way over how she'd tried to conceal her condition, and seeing how she'd come to me for the pennyroyal, and seeing how the blanket covered its face and its face had been pushed down into the bed tick, I considered that the girl smothered it."

"Very well. And what did you do then?"

"I cleaned the babe and wrapped it and left, and on the way home I stopped and told the constable, and once the road cleared the constable sent for the sheriff."

"Thank you, Widow Hall."

The king's attorney returned to his table, and Freeman rose.

"When you examined the infant, Widow Hall, did you think it to term?"

"I did."

"So that when you saw Alice in August, when she came to you for the treatment for worm, she would have moved into her pregnancy only two months or so?"

"Thereabouts."

"Are you familiar with the laws of our colony regarding the removal of a conception, Widow Hall?"

"I am."

"And you understand that it is not a crime before quickening?"

"I do."

"And when does that first sign of life usually appear?"

"The fourth month would be the earliest."

"So that if Alice Cole had come to you for pennyroyal to remove a two-month conception, you would have violated no law in selling her the medicament, nor would Alice Cole have violated any law in seeking it?"

"Nobody said she broke any law."

"I beg your pardon, Widow Hall, but certainly this is why we're here today—because *you* said that Alice Cole violated the law. Not that day, but on a later day, in February, when she lay alone and afraid in the midst of a difficult travail. Which next leads me to ask you,

Widow Hall—you say you examined the dead infant on February the twenty-seventh and found 'nothing, 'cept its being dead.' No mark on it?"

"No marks, no."

"For example, no bruises around its neck, or bleeding from its nose or mouth, anything at all to indicate some violence done to it?"

"Like that, no."

"Like what, then, Widow Hall?"

"Like I said before. Like it was suffocated in a blanket."

"Suffocated? And what mark on its body proved to you it had suffocated?"

"No mark on its body. 'Twas all wrapped inside a blanket and pushed facedown on the tick. Suffocated."

"*Pushed?* You saw the babe's face being *pushed* into the bed tick?"

"Put, then. The face put right down into the tick and smothered all over in a blanket."

"Was it cold in the room, Widow Hall?"

"Cold?"

"Cold. This is February. The room in question had no fire. Could it have been cold enough that a newborn babe fresh ripped from its mother would need to be covered in a blanket?"

"Well, covered, but not its face covered. Not its face pushed down into a bed tick. *Put* down in the bed tick."

"Have you attended many births, Widow Hall?"

"I've attended near two thousand, sir."

"Any of them young girls of Alice Cole's age?"

"A fair number. I don't know it exact."

"And would you say this birth was a difficult one, from what you saw of it?"

"No, I wouldn't. She did it all without aid and in no great time."

"She did it all without aid. A young girl, fifteen years old. And you say it was done with no great difficulty. I presume, then, that when you came upon this young girl after this trouble-free birth she was sitting up in all her strength and able to talk to you with sensibility?"

"She wasn't sitting up, no, but she answered my questions as I put them to her."

"Tell me about some of these other young girls whose birthings you assisted, Widow Hall. Were any of these girls awkward in their first ministrations or did they all take up their babes with the ease of long practice?"

"If they had apt instruction—"

"Apt instruction! But you say that you and the Widow Berry arrived at Alice Cole's travail after it was all over and the babe was already dead. Who then might have instructed her?"

"Not then, perhaps, but at some time before—"

"By whom, Widow Hall? The girl denied the pregnancy, even to the woman closest to her. Why, then, might anyone attempt to instruct her?"

The Widow Hall fell silent.

"Thank you, Widow Hall," Freeman said.

The king's attorney next called Mrs. Sears to come forth and asked, "Do you know the defendant, Alice Cole?"

"I knew her as Alice Baker, yes."

"And when did you see her last?"

"At my husband's store, in February."

"And what thought you of her appearance?"

"I thought her to be with child, and well advanced in it."

"And did you speak of this to anyone?"

"I spoke of it to the Widow Berry."

"And why to her?"

"Well, she kept the girl in her home."

"And what did the widow tell you?"

"That the girl had been eating way too much for her size ever since she'd arrived in Satucket."

"And you took this statement to mean—?"

"I took it to mean it was either the story the girl chose to tell the widow or the one the widow chose to tell me."

"And why do you think either the girl or the widow would tell such a story?"

"To conceal the girl's condition."

"And why might they wish to conceal the girl's condition?"

"So no one would know her sin."

"Thank you, Mrs. Sears."

Freeman asked Mrs. Sears no questions.

The king's attorney next called Mrs. Winslow forward, who told a similar story. She had last seen Alice Baker, or Cole as she now was, in February, walking to the fulling mill. The wind had pushed her cloak back and pressed her skirt against her belly and she'd looked well gone with child.

Freeman had no questions for Mrs. Winslow, either.

The king's attorney next called the Widow Berry. She rose and walked up to the bar with a lively step, as if eager to say her piece; just before she reached it she turned around and jerked her head in one quick nod at Alice.

"Widow Berry, will you please tell the court the events as you remember them of the morning of February the twenty-seventh."

"I went upstairs to find Alice Cole in what appeared to be travail."

"This was a surprise to you?"

"It wasn't."

"It wasn't! She'd informed you of her condition?"

"She hadn't. But it could easily be observed by anyone living in the household."

"And to some outside it. And yet you took no steps to expose her condition. Why not?"

"'Twasn't my condition to expose."

"Very well, then. You found her in travail. And how advanced was she in it?"

"I falsely determined she'd a time to go yet, so I set out for the midwife."

"And how long did it take you to fetch the Widow Hall?"

"A long time. The roads were in poor condition from the snows."

"And what did you tell the Widow Hall when you reached her?"

"I told her that my servant girl was in travail, that she'd denied her condition to me but now there was no doubt of it, and that she was so small a girl that I feared for her safety."

"And the Widow Hall accompanied you to your home?"

"She did."

"And what did you find on your return there?"

"The girl already delivered and lying in a stupor, with much blood around her, and the babe dead, lying on the bed beside her."

"How was the babe lying?"

"Under a blanket."

"All of it or part of it covered?"

"All of it."

"On its face or on its back?"

"On its face."

"Thank you, Widow Berry."

Freeman leaped up. "Widow Berry. You say you found the babe 'under a blanket.' Do you mean 'wrapped in a blanket'?"

"I do not. 'Twas a loose-thrown cover, as if by a weak hand."

"A weak hand wishing to extinguish the infant's breath?"

"A weak hand wishing to cover it over."

"Was the room cold?"

"Very cold. I'd not had time to properly feed the fire below. I was distressed when I returned to feel the temperature."

"And Alice Cole. Was she covered?"

"She lay half under the bed rug, as if she'd managed to pull it up so far and no farther in her weakness."

"And what did she say to you when you told her that her babe was dead?"

"She said nothing. She was too worn out to speak."

"Have you been party to many such travails, Widow Berry?"

"I've been party to enough. I've seen dead babes come of it, and I've seen dead mothers."

"And what did the evidence before your eyes tell you in this case? Was this a difficult travail? Was this mother in danger?"

"By the blood let and by her weak condition I should say it was difficult indeed, and for such a small girl and the size of the babe I should say she was in every kind of danger."

Freeman said, "Thank you, Widow Berry."

The king's attorney called one last witness, the coroner who had examined the dead infant; he declared that the babe was of full term and had been born alive and had died soon after.

Freeman asked the coroner if there was any evidence whatever of any violence done to the infant, and the coroner answered, "None, sir."

The king's attorney then rose and began his summation reviewing the charge and the evidence at hand in a light most unfavorable to Alice. He concluded by saying, "Does it not seem clear to you, gentlemen of the jury, that in Alice Cole's desperation she saw hope for her future only in the death of her bastard? Does it not seem clear to you that once she saw that hope, she went toward it like a hawk after a field mouse? Does it not seem clear to you that Alice Cole did with her own hands maliciously, willfully, and with malice aforethought smother

her infant in a heavy cloth and press it into the bed tick? I warn you, gentlemen, do not let beauty or youth cloud your eyes; do not forget that a smooth, green husk can conceal a worm-riddled ear of corn. Likewise do not let the syrup of the defendant's attorney stop your ears. Do your duty as men and fathers obedient to the will of God and declare the defendant guilty of this most heinous crime of murdering her newborn child."

TWENTY-EIGHT

They returned Alice to the gaol to eat her dinner, a fine stew thick with salt beef like she'd not seen at her gaoler's hand since she'd been brought there. She pondered the significance of it and could make only one conclusion: someone had taken pity on her. She could think of only one reason to deserve such pity at that point in her trial. She pushed the stew aside.

When they returned to court after the adjournment the air had grown hot and stale; as Alice stepped inside she wished nothing in life but to step backward into the air, but instead of stepping backward she was edged forward. She looked at the men in the jury ahead of her and found only two now looking at her, one a rough-cut young man with a crooked nose and the other an old man who fingered his waistcoat buttons as he stared. What did it mean if ten men could no longer meet her eye? Oh, she knew what it meant! She knew! For a minute Alice didn't believe her legs would carry her to her place; the pudding knees wouldn't stiffen; she wavered, thinking who would collect her if she fell, and thought of Freeman, and her old daydream of being carried to safety. She removed her eyes from the jury and let them float without focus, but as she passed the crowd she thought she saw Nate Clarke, his usually pink cheeks gone pale as his hair.

Freeman stood and began to speak, his wigged head and robed form turning him into someone as much a stranger as the king's attorney and the jurors.

"May it please Your Honors and the gentlemen of the jury, I'm here today to ask you to believe, not what I tell you to believe, but what your own eyes and ears and rational minds will tell you to believe, as you listen to the story of Alice Cole, a young girl just fifteen years of age at that time of her life which is the focus of this trial. But Alice's story begins long before that time of her life; Alice's story begins at the tender age of seven, when her father bound her into indentured servitude off the very deck of the ship that carried her here from London, her mother and brothers freshly dead and buried at sea. I ask you to think of that young girl as you look at this one standing in the prisoner's box, gentlemen, standing today as she once stood on that dock at Boston—alone. I will ask you to remember that aloneness, for it is the key to much of Alice's story. That aloneness allowed her to be preyed upon by an evil man; that aloneness forced her to run away to a strange land full of strangers; that aloneness suffered her to experience a time of panic and fear and confusion without a mother's supporting arm or guiding voice; and that very aloneness was the only thing Alice Cole had beside her during a single moment of pain and swooning, her own untaught, untrained, unskilled hands the only hands to aid her. Perhaps those hands did not lift to tend her babe as they should, but certainly, *certainly*, gentlemen, they did not lift *feloniously*, *willfully*, or with the least degree of *malice aforethought*, toward the only creature on earth that might have put her less alone—her own cherished infant.

Now let us consider how Alice Cole came to be in this position in the first place. You've heard the king's attorney's fabrication; now you may hear the truth of it."

And so Alice's story was told. The 'tween decks of the London ship became a room in hell, Mr. Morton's household became a dark, motherless, loveless place, the Verley home a filthy cage. Freeman described other things Alice had never spoken of at all: the fear, the panic, the pain, and yes, the ignorance. He might have said something of her foolishness as well, but he left that off. Alice heard the audience murmur and gasp as he told of the rapes, the burning, the blow from the poker, but when he asserted her right to leave such a scene of horror, no assenting rumble touched her ear. They would have their servants keep to their laws.

"Gentlemen of the jury," Freeman concluded. "I ask but one more thing of you now: as you listen to the evidence presented to you I ask that you look at the young girl who stands before you and you remember the long, tortuous road that brought her here, a road she did not choose of her own free will, a road that was roughly thrust upon her by the evil deeds of others, and, yes, thrust upon her by her own innocence. And as you listen to this evidence I want you to think of Alice Cole as you would think of your own wives or daughters or sisters, upright, moral women, as Alice Cole is moral. The king's attorney has told you that she is devoid in this particular, but how then, could he next talk of her shame? How might one feel shame if one were devoid of all morals? Isn't Alice's shame the best proof of her morality? Isn't her attempt at concealment of a condition brought on against her will by the evil deeds of others only another proof of her godliness? Look at her, gentlemen of the jury! She sits before you not draped in concealing cloth or false paint to trick you as the king's attorney would have you believe, she sits before you as who she is, a courageous young girl, a faithful and obedient child of God, an innocent, misused victim of a most heinous crime. This is all I ask of you, gentlemen: that you do as English legal tradition requires you to do and allow her her innocence until her trial is completed."

How odd, Alice thought, that she should not know the girl Freeman talked of either.

FREEMAN BEGAN BY calling to the bar a midwife of his own, a Mrs. Crowe from Barnstable, a raw-cheeked, cheerful-looking woman who might have been Granny Hall's daughter. Mrs. Crowe testified to the necessities required of newborn infants, of pinching off and cutting the cord, of clearing the air passage, of chafing it into its first breath, of keeping it warm. She testified to all the mistakes that an untaught young girl giving birth alone might make.

The king's attorney asked Mrs. Crowe how many births she had attended; when she answered "just under one thousand, sir," he looked at the jury to make sure they noted the great difference in the two midwives' numbers, and dismissed her.

Freeman next called the shipmaster Hopkins and began by asking him to describe the condition of Alice Cole when she'd been discovered in his ship's locker. The shipmaster fumbled about with a vague description of dirty clothes and mussed hair; Freeman prompted him about cuts and bruises and he said, "Oh! Yes. She looked to be banged up some."

Freeman moved it along. "You might have charged this girl with stealing passage from you. You might have turned her over to the constable. Why didn't you do this, sir?"

"Well, she was just a girl."

"You weren't concerned that if you let her loose on your village she might cause trouble? Do harm?"

The shipmaster looked at Freeman. "Alice? Harm?"

"I'm speaking of what you thought of the girl at the time."

"Well, at the time, I'd say she was looking for a good supper more than she was looking to do any harm."

"And later, once you got to know something of the girl, once you saw her at work in the widow's home, what was your opinion of her then?"

"Why, I thought she was a fine little thing. Fine."

Freeman waited.

The shipmaster added, "Oh! Yes! She seemed in every way a good sort of girl."

"Thank you," Freeman said in something of a rush, and sat down.

The king's attorney rose. "Mr. Hopkins. You say that Alice Cole looked in need of a good supper. Didn't it occur to you that a penniless, hungry stranger might have wandered about the village, found an open door, and pilfered someone else's supper?"

The shipmaster said, "No."

"It didn't occur to you that an unknown girl from unknown circumstances and of unknown character might, in desperate circumstances, indeed do harm?"

"No."

"And if your ship had a hole in it, would it occur to you to plug it up?"

Freeman shouted, "Object!"

The shipmaster said, "My ship's got no hole, sir!"

The chief justice said, "Sustained."

The king's attorney sat down.

Freeman next called on the Widow Berry, to speak for the defense this time; she looked much the worse for the day's efforts. Freeman began as he'd begun with the shipmaster, asking the widow to describe Alice Cole's condition when she first arrived, and the widow did a better job.

"She could barely walk. Her arm hung limp. She carried a bloody wound on her cheek, and a festering burn on her hand. In addition, she was starved and exhausted."

"Did she tell how she came to this condition?"

"Not at first. At first the subject was far too painful for her; she couldn't speak of it without shaking all over. But later she told me, at great cost to herself, and I might add, at great cost to me when I heard it. This Verley used her against her will in as rough and offensive a manner as a man can. Why, he tortured her. He—"

The king's attorney rose. "I object! This is naught but hearsay!"

The chief justice said, "Sustained."

Freeman said, "You decided to hire Alice Cole to do some spinning for you. What prompted this decision?"

"I could see by the look of her she was an honest girl. And she proved to spin like the wind."

"Were you ever made uneasy in any way about her character?"

"Never. She was a fine, hard worker, faithful in her attendance at meeting, and devoted to her prayers."

Freeman thanked her solemnly a second time, and the king's attorney stood up.

"Did you witness Alice Cole receiving her alleged burns and bruises, Widow Berry?"

"I did not."

"So as far as you know she could have received them in a tavern brawl. Now you said a moment ago that you 'could see by the look of her that she was an honest girl.' What specifically about her looks proclaimed her honesty?"

"She was in no tavern brawl, sir!"

"I ask you to address my question, Widow Berry. What revealed Alice Cole's supposed honesty to you?"

There the widow faltered. She flung an arm wide at Alice. "Well, look at her."

The courtroom looked at Alice. The king's attorney did not. He said, "Of course, when you discovered the girl to have lied to you about her condition you then changed your opinion about her honesty."

"I did not."

"You did not! You did not consider a lie to be dishonest?"

"I considered the cause of the lie. I considered what had been done to her. I considered the courage it took for her to come as far as she'd come and how afraid she must have been. I took the lie as nothing but her belief that not a single soul on all God's earth would wish to help her if her condition were known."

"And so you attempted to help her."

"Yes."

"As you attempt to help her now."

"I *attempt* nothing but telling the truth about the girl."

"Truth or lie being one to you."

Freeman leaped up. "Object! Object! Object!"

The chief justice said, "Sustained."

The king's attorney said, "Very well. I have every confidence that I might leave the question of the girl's honesty to the gentlemen of the jury. Thank you, madam." He sat down.

FREEMAN ROSE TO begin his closing argument. First he reviewed the evidence, marking the glaring lack of it. He further reviewed the charge and then said, "Gentlemen of the jury, if you believe Alice Cole *willfully* and *maliciously* and with *aforethought* caused the death of her infant, than you must find her guilty as charged. If, however, you have any doubt regarding any single one of those three things, if you think it entirely possible that a young, innocent, brutalized girl, alone, uninstructed, and frightened, having survived a most difficult birth, did what she could to protect her infant from the cold, thinking only secondly of attempting to cover herself, and in her innocence and ignorance, not knowing what other things might need to be done to secure her infant's life, if after exhausting her last reserve in the act of protecting her child, she then dropped off into a swoon, not waking until the women arrived to inform her of the most unfortunate death of her child, if you think any of that possible or, indeed, probable, if you are honest, moral, godly men, perhaps fathers or grandfathers of your own young girls, perhaps brothers of the same, you must in all conscience declare Alice Cole innocent of this charge."

Freeman sat down.

The chief justice said, "Gentlemen of the jury, you will need no further instruction, since your good sense and understanding will direct you. Go now and do your duty."

The jury departed. Alice peered at each face as it passed, but she seemed to have lost whatever skill she had gained over the past long year; each face looked as opaque and colorless as a stone wall.

TWENTY-NINE

As hard as she'd studied them, once the jury left the room Alice couldn't remember them as they'd been. Oddly, now, they all seemed to look like Mr. Morton. What might he have thought if he'd been sitting on the jury? Would he have argued in her defense if the others had turned against her, or would he have gone along, thinking to cause himself the least trouble? She tried to remember what she'd thought of Mr. Morton's face when she'd first spied it on the deck of the ship from London, but she saw only its later versions. She gave full credit to its many kind looks along the years, but she couldn't escape his final one. She closed her eyes to block it, as if he actually sat there in the room, and saw a circle. A rope. She opened her eyes and tried to conjure another image out of her old library of comforts: the house in Philadelphia, the high-walled ship, the widow's house; Freeman carrying her from the fire and wrapping her in a white sheet. She trusted Freeman yet. She did. She did. *The widow and I will take you home.* That was what he had said.

So then, she would imagine that.

Alice saw herself at the widow's house, sitting at her wheel, the widow at the fire stirring a sauce, Freeman at the table studying the newspaper. She saw Freeman look up at her and smile with a new affection born out of all those days together at Barnstable; she saw the widow look up and smile. Alice could feel her own smile. And yet something was wrong. Three smiles, and she could not connect them one to the other, all at the same time.

The sheriff announced the jury's return, and the courtroom came awake like the Satucket marsh birds at dawn. Alice studied the jurymen's faces as they entered, but all appeared bent on maintaining the look of a wall; she could make a case for one Morton among them, but for the first time she believed she saw a Verley too.

The chief justice said, "Gentlemen of the jury, are you agreed in your verdict?"

One of the older jurors stood—the one who had played with his waistcoat buttons—not Morton, not Verley. "We are agreed, Your Honor."

"How say you?"

"We find the defendant not guilty."

A great noise went up in the courtroom, a noise Alice didn't know whether to take for good or bad. She looked to Freeman and saw that he stood beaming on her like the sun itself; that he could smile so at her swelled her heart with an exquisite ache, as if it were full of laughing and crying both, as if it were full of all of life. Her life. Oh, how could she ever have thought him unhandsome? How could she have failed to trust him?

The chief justice quieted the court. He said, "The prisoner shall be remanded into custody to await trial at Suffolk County Court on the secondary charge. This court is adjourned."

The crowd rose to its feet in a boisterous, choppy wave and began to spill over itself for the doors. Alice looked about in confusion for

Freeman; he stood bent over the clerk's table signing papers. The clerk spoke to the sheriff; the sheriff and Freeman worked their way to Alice's box, and the sheriff unlocked it. Freeman took her arm, drawing her back with him, away from the mob. Alice stumbled alongside him, as if dazed from a blow. What had the chief justice said? What secondary charge? She tugged at the hand that gripped her elbow. "What did he mean, sir, 'secondary charge'?" Freeman didn't seem to hear her, so she called out again, "What secondary charge, sir!"

Freeman continued to draw her toward the rear door; he continued to smile. He said, "You're exonerated of the murder charge, Alice; there lies the important thing. But you must answer yet to the charge of running away from your master, and this must be done at the Suffolk County Court in Boston, as we discussed in gaol."

Alice pulled free of him, backing away from him. It couldn't be. It couldn't. He couldn't betray her so! She had trusted him, she had told him of Verley, she had told him every terrible private shameful thing, and he had used it only to get her out of one court and into the next. Could he not know, could he not see, that it meant nothing, *nothing*, to walk free of this courtroom if it meant walking into that other? She couldn't do it. She couldn't. She couldn't move one foot closer to that road. She felt herself sinking to the ground; she felt so certain that she'd sunk she couldn't understand how the courtroom walls appeared to be moving past, as if Freeman had her by the arm again, as if, indeed, she walked with him out the courtroom door.

He was speaking yet. "You mustn't let yourself get lost in the one small dark thing while the larger one shines so bright. I've arranged with the court to stand surety on your recognizance; you'll return to Satucket to await a date at Suffolk when the circuit returns there in August; I'll see you there myself, where we'll tell your story to the justices there as we told it here, and with just such result. You need fear nothing, Alice. You may trust me with Suffolk as you trusted me with Barnstable. Now come, we must find the widow."

They made their way outside and toward the street. The widow came up and hugged her violently. Nate was there, staring at her as if he'd never seen her in his life, making no move to ride in on the same wave and offer his own hug, but his hands weren't in his pockets, his elbows didn't wag; it was no joke now. The crowd moved in to gather around Freeman and offer their congratulation; it seemed to Alice the crowd was all that held her upright for her shivering. She felt as cold as she'd felt in that bloody bed in February and would have welcomed a fire despite the July heat, but Freeman looked in no great hurry to be shed of the people around him.

Alice endured what seemed a longer time than the jury had taken to form their verdict before Freeman began to ease them into the road. She looked around for Nate, to see if he followed, but she couldn't find him. They stopped and started and stopped before they burst free of the well-wishers and continued at a decent pace until they reached a plain, solid, two-storied building bearing a small but determined plaque declaring it the office of EBENEZER FREEMAN, ESQUIRE, ATTORNEY-AT-LAW. Alice saw the house and sign and thought that if she'd seen them before she might have understood better what would have happened to her; Freeman wasn't a man to boast of his skills, but he would apply them with a quiet will; he wouldn't veer before the wind; he would do what it took to gain his verdict. He would return her to Suffolk.

Freeman's housekeeper must have been put on alert, for a fine roast turkey awaited them, and in no long time the celebrants had gathered around a deeply weighted table to feast on food and merriment. Freeman and the widow chatted over the various turns in the courtroom for a time, and then the widow addressed her.

"You sit quiet, child. You must be quite wrung out from this."

"Yes, madam."

"Indeed, you must feel it far beyond what I do, and I feel it to my teeth."

"Yes, madam."

"And you, Mr. Freeman," the widow said. "All these months—"

"Yes."

Alice looked up at the brittle sound of the word and found Freeman's eyes fixed on her, not happy. Well, of course. He would expect her to be merry. He would expect her to be grateful. That Alice might expect him to know what his verdict cost her was her poor luck; if he hadn't known it when she told him her story, he wouldn't know it on this earth. But she knew what she owed him. She said, "I wish to say, sir, how grateful I am," but to her own ears it sounded poor stuff to weigh against a life. She tried it over. "I know that in my life I cannot repay my debt to you—"

"You may repay me by looking the least bit glad of that life, Alice."

"Yes, sir." And she tried, indeed, she tried, but it didn't come near, and she knew it. Freeman knew it. He set his tankard on the table with the kind of care that spoke of an internal violence. He said, "I must speak to Davis," pushed back his chair, and went out.

FREEMAN'S HOUSE CONTAINED a finished second story with two comfortable chambers; the housekeeper put Alice and the widow in the east one; the west one no doubt belonged to Freeman. The bed tick that the women shared had been well stuffed, the linen cool and crisp; it was that bed more than any words of Freeman's or the widow's that brought Alice to an understanding of what Freeman had done for her. She might have slept this night on her old, damp pallet in the gaol; she might have wakened to a ride to the gallows, perhaps in the same rough cart with the same rough men who had taken her from Satucket.

The widow seemed in no mood to chat with Alice, which pleased Alice well enough. She pretended to fall quickly asleep and lay still until the widow's breathing had dropped into the slow, shallow rhythm of real sleep, but Alice knew she would be experiencing no such thing for herself. She lay and listened to Freeman's house sounds: the scraping of a shovel against the hearth as the housekeeper banked the fire, the tap of her heels as she retired to her bed, the click of a downstairs bedroom latch, the muffled striking of a clock, the distant noise of the tavern, the occasional pounding of a horse in the road. She couldn't hear the ocean. After a time she heard the outer door open and close, a man's tread on the stair, the west chamber door opening and closing: Freeman, in for the night then. Alice listened some more but heard nothing. She thought back to how she lay and listened to the house on the night of her escape from Verley; she thought, again, of circles. Oh, to be brought back there! She began to tremble. The widow stirred. Alice lay breathless until her trembling subsided, but after a time her limbs began to ache from the effort to keep them still; she slid from the sheets and crept down the stairs into the keeping room.

The banked fire gave off a faint, peachy glow that guided Alice to the candles on the table; she took one up, went to the fire, picked up a coal in the tongs, and blew on it until it fired the wick of her candle. Alice's mental state on entering Freeman's house had been such that she'd noticed little of its furnishings; she lifted the candle now and looked around her. The keeping room was as any keeping room was, full of the ordinary workings of day-to-day life; Freeman hadn't spent his money here to excess, although the candle did pick out a modest gleam of brass and silver among the earthenware and iron; the keeping room told her nothing of the man she hadn't already guessed. She looked at the closed door to a small room next to the pantry, no doubt where the housekeeper slept; she crept past it into the parlor. She stood in the middle of the parlor and turned in a circle, the candle held high, to discover what clues to the man this room held: a pair of smoky portraits of a wigged gentleman and a woman in a lace neckerchief, their eyes the only spots that took up the light of candle; two ladder-back chairs and a card table along the wall; a case of drawers along the other; two stuffed chairs by the fire; a pair of closed cupboards framing it. She crossed the parlor to the front hall, crossed the hall to the door opposite, and stepped through.

Freeman's office. A long desk held two neat squares of piled papers, an inkwell, and three quills; one ladder-back chair sat behind the desk and one in front; a pair of well-worn stuffed chairs had been divorced from each other, one to hug the fire and another the window. But the walls were what took her; except for an additional outer door and the window, they were covered floor to ceiling by bookshelves. The light picked up the gold letters that ran across the worn leather spines packed cover to cover, thick between thin, short between tall. Alice stepped close and let her eye wander at random, picking up names familiar to her from Freeman's discourses with Nate: Locke, Cicero, Plutarch, Homer. She stepped closer and pulled out a thin pamphlet too narrow to carry its title on its spine: *A Lecture on Earthquakes,* and was surprised that she could recognize the name of Nate's Harvard tutor, John Winthrop, as the author. It sat on the shelf flanked by *The Theory and Practice of Brewing* on one side and *The History of the Pleas of the Crown* on the other. Next came Sir Edward Coke's *Reports of Cases* and Sir Francis Bacon's *New Abridgement of Law.* There at the earthquakes, then, sat the line between Freeman's professional life and his personal one, the two halves strangers to each other's contents, perhaps, but their spines touching just the same, the line between them invisible.

Had Freeman read all these books? Alice little doubted it. She drew the candle along the shelves, trying to pick out which spine looked the most worn; she settled on a single, small volume of the *Works of Shakespeare.* She pulled it from the shelf and examined the contents: *Much Ado About Nothing, The Merchant of Venice, Love's Labour's Lost, As You Like It, The Taming of the Shrew.* The book fell open at the middle; a swamp maple leaf had been pressed between the pages of *The Merchant of Venice.* Not Alice's favorite tale, but one did not press leaves between the pages most frequently turned. Yet as she turned the page she noticed faded pen marks against many of the lines: *But love is blind, and lovers cannot see the pretty follies that themselves commit . . . Who chooseth me must give and hazard all he hath . . . in such a night . . . Troilus methinks mounted the Troyan walls, and sigh'd his soul toward the Grecian tents, where Cressid lay that night. . . .* Alice turned from the *Merchant* to *Much Ado* and again found marks: *Is not marriage honorable in a beggar? Is not your lord honourable without marriage? . . . By my troth, my lord, I cannot tell what to think of it but she loves him with an enraged affection. . . .*

Alice closed the book and replaced it where she'd found it. If the marked passages held new clues to Freeman, they weren't the clues that Alice wanted. And besides, how many years ago had he marked them? Since that time he'd used the book to press his leaves in.

Alice looked around the rest of the room; she spied the stuffed chair by the fire and saw that it had kept the imprint of the man; she crossed the room and sat down in it, the arms of the chair enclosing her. She stared, again, at the shelves. The man of law, who had read all these books, who had *bought* all these books, who had freed her from the gallows, surely, surely, such a man could free her from Verley as well. In the courtroom, after the verdict, after the news of the second trial, she had thought of the word *betrayal*, and so she had felt it then, but she wondered if she could use that word now, having seen the man's house, having seen his books. He wasn't a man to bend to trickery. Indeed, as Alice thought, she remembered that during her sickness in the gaol there had been some talk of Suffolk, talk of another case she hadn't dreamed could be her own. If Freeman had indeed explained the risk to her then, if he believed Alice to have understood him then, if Alice had in fact made no objection, how could she accuse Freeman of betraying her now?

But what if Alice *had* objected? What would Freeman have done? The same? Alice couldn't know. She might stare at the man's face until it blurred and she couldn't know.

Alice made her way back to the keeping room, snuffed the candle, returned it to the table, and fumbled her way to the stairs. Freeman's door sat tightly closed. She entered the room opposite and slipped quietly between the sheets; the widow's breathing changed, but she didn't move or speak.

Alice lay quiet, trying to pull up some kind of waking dream, any kind of dream, to lull her into sleep, but the old one of Freeman saving her from the fire wouldn't work with the widow so near. She came closest with the image of the widow's house, but the three smiles that wouldn't meet disrupted her again.

By morning Alice could count for certain only one brief moment of sleep, from the first quail song to the first real fingers of sun, but Verley had managed to camp even there. He and Alice stood at the bar in a courtroom much like the courtroom Alice had just left. Freeman stood between. Verley's hands reached for Alice, as they usually did in her dreams, and Freeman said, "I don't want you to touch her!" But Verley towered over Freeman, his arm span wider than Freeman's; Freeman couldn't stop the hands from coming across.

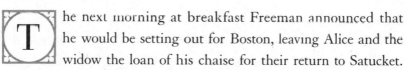

he next morning at breakfast Freeman announced that he would be setting out for Boston, leaving Alice and the widow the loan of his chaise for their return to Satucket. The business of preparation took up half the morning, the good-byes themselves less than a minute. Freeman rode off first, spurring his horse into a lively canter the minute he'd cleared the gate, leaving Alice with a half accusation that she quickly buried. What did it matter that Freeman and the widow together didn't take her home, as he'd promised they would? Home was home.

The widow and Alice climbed into the carriage, the widow to drive with Alice beside. For a time they rode in silence, but at the outskirts of Barnstable the widow's thoughts seemed to move ahead; she began to tell Alice of what awaited them at Satucket—a large order for dimity from Hannah Cobb; a treadle in need of repair; a field of flax overdue for pulling. That subject done, she again fell silent.

Left to her own thoughts, Alice's head filled, of course, with Suffolk, until at the outskirts of Barnstable she happened to glance up and catch the sun on her face. It shone dry and clear out of a bold blue sky with just enough breeze to cut its edge, and Alice thought of all the long days in gaol without the touch of either. Oh, how fine it felt! And oh, how pretty the woods and fields looked, all dressed out in the full flush of summer! This might have been her last day on earth; how foolish she would be to give it over to thoughts of Suffolk! She must put up the old wall, this time around a vague day in August, and again not go beyond, a trick she had by now perfected. At the far side of Yarmouth the widow helped her: she broke out a loaf of chewy brown bread, a wedge of pungent cheese, and a bottle of spicy beer; afterward Alice put her head back and floated into a sleep that required no urging beyond the steady rocking of the carriage.

THE SUN HAD turned from white to gold when Alice opened her eyes and saw that they were approaching the mills at Satucket. She spied Mr. Myrick, his sisters, and Mrs. Thacher in the near distance; their heads turned and followed the chaise as it drew past.

The widow twisted in her seat. "Prepare yourself, Alice," she said. "You're now famous."

WHAT ALICE MIGHT better have prepared herself for was her return to the widow's house. When they turned down the landing road and the squat walls and high-pitched roof came into view it took her like a dose of salts. The tears she had managed to keep from light and air all the long months in gaol now oozed out beneath her clamped eyelids. She'd hoped for this minute, of course; she'd tried to cling to that hope; but it hadn't been a solid thing until now.

Alice must have made a sound that hinted at her struggle, for the widow leaned over and patted her knee. "'Tis a fine sight, is it not?"

Oh, so fine a sight! And so different from the one Alice had left in February! No churning gray sea in the distance but a sun-flecked blanket of indigo, no bare-branched trees but softly fanning sprays of green, no empty square of earth but a thick stand of flax, no barren dooryard beds but neat rows of dark leaves splashed with yellow squash, velvety cucumbers, and pink-and-green-striped rhubarb.

The widow pulled the chaise up outside the barn and climbed down to tend Freeman's horse. Alice went inside at once. There too all had changed since her last look at it, the winter dimness replaced by midsummer light, the usual chill replaced by the heat of a too-long closed-up house. Alice propped open the door and moved around the keeping room, tossing up the windows; as she passed she noticed that the cord on the great wheel had fuzzed with a fine dust. She turned to the fireplace and took up the tinderbox from the cupboard beside it; she set up the kindling and struck the tinder over it, blowing it into a gentle flame, feeding it with more small sticks from the wood box until it took firm hold.

Alice collected the bucket and went outside to the well, taking into her lungs the brew of honeysuckle, pine pitch, salt flats. She drew up the water; in the act of drawing she fell backward through the past year, back to the day she'd first arrived and the widow had sent her to the well. What had she thought on that day of what lay ahead of her? Or had she thought at all? Perhaps she'd just breathed, and looked, and drank, as Alice did now, intent on the minute she lived. But no, Alice remembered it now; she'd stood at the well, crawling with trepidation, not over the unknown events ahead, but over the unknown people with whom she was about to share bread. Well, Alice supposed she knew those people now as well as she ever would; the one she stood unsure of was herself. She peered into the well, waiting for the disturbed surface of the water to settle into a smooth, silver coin. The face it reflected looked shriven and colorless, the eyes too big, the mouth too blurred, but just the same, Alice.

Alive.

Alice picked up her bucket and returned to the house. By the time the widow came in, Alice had the kettle near steaming. She would have given much for an old-fashioned cup of tea, but instead she readied the dried blackberry leaves that filled the widow's tea canister. The widow set out the usual bread and preserve, and Alice fell back again to another image of that first day, a meal nervously begun and more calmly finished by virtue of a stranger making the effort to chatter a young girl into easiness. She could trust such a man. She must trust him.

The widow and Alice took their supper and afterward worked together for an hour or two to right the house, but both were tired, and a pale gray light still clung to the walls when they said their good nights and parted. Alice climbed the stairs, went straight to her bed, and lay down atop the coverlet, testing not the bed itself but the strength of the memories that had been born in it. The bed had cradled her hopes and her despair alone and together; it had cradled her full heart, her sore flesh, her dead infant.

Her dead infant.

All right, then, this was to be the first, the most insistent. She put out her hand and felt the coverlet, pulling the cloth around her, not from any need for warmth, but to feel the weight of it in her hand, to imagine the weight of it thrown over an infant. Had she suffocated it? Alice closed her eyes and was surprised at the clear picture of the babe that came to her now, where it hadn't in the gaol or in the courtroom: head thick with dark hair neither hers nor Verley's, skin as blue-white as milk with the cream skimmed from it. She remembered an open mouth formed by a perfect pair of bow lips, but no sound coming from it, no breath warming her cold fingers. But how odd it was: Alice could now conjure a sound like the keening of a gull at a great distance, the gentlest brush of air on her knuckles, as if they'd been dusted with a feather.

She could feel the weight of the blanket.

Alice got up and went to the far window, the one that looked out across the ocean, seeking comfort in the old view, but instead of looking out she looked down into the landing road. The Indian Sam Cowett had just rounded the turn and stepped into a shadow as long as his own; he came out the other side of it, swinging along the pitted road with the sureness of one who had trod it many times, with the sureness of one who knew where he came from and where he was headed. How did one get such sureness? Alice wondered. She turned around and went to the other window, the one looking over the dooryard, and felt again that odd sense of past into present, a trick kind of certainty that she would look down and see Freeman dismounting from his horse, just come from Barnstable or Boston. She thought of Nate, throwing sand at her window, of looking down and seeing him there in the moonlight. She thought of touching him, kissing him. She thought of what Nate now knew of her, of his silence in the gaol, his silence outside the courtroom.

Alice returned to her bed, undressed, and climbed into it. To be where she was should have been comfort enough to soothe her to sleep, but she found her thoughts pulling away from Satucket to a place she might least expect to find her comfort: the gaol at Barnstable, on one of her walks with Freeman near the end of her illness. They had come upon a muddy patch of ground riddled with potholes, and Freeman had put a hand under her elbow, then slid it down to grip her hand as they came to a particular bad section. When they'd cleared the rough place Alice made some small effort to free herself, but Freeman only tightened his grip. "We're not done yet, Alice," he said. "Look ahead of you."

THIRTY-ONE

The next day Alice understood what the widow had meant when she'd called Alice famous. It had seemed odd when the widow insisted she accompany Alice on her first trip to Sears's store, but when they met up with the Myrick sisters Alice understood something better. The widow shoved Alice ahead toward the store and lingered behind to talk to the sisters; Alice walked as far as the first screen of trees and stopped to listen.

"My goodness, Widow Berry, what an ordeal for you!"

"'Twas Alice's ordeal."

"But your courage, Widow Berry! To have kept her here! And to take her back now, after everything! What she owes you!"

"She's allowed me to make my way; I feel the debt well balanced."

"Well, you may say so . . . Tell me, Widow Berry, when do you expect Mr. Freeman back? You must tell him we stand in awe of such a wondrous achievement."

"I shall tell him."

"And such generosity of spirit! The whole village remarks on it! All the long hours, why I don't think we saw him in the village for the three months altogether." A pause. "I understand the girl's master is being blamed for her condition?"

"As he caused it, yes."

"But one can't blame him for the murder charge. What do you say of it, widow, the murder charge? I must say the evidence did little to change Granny Hall's opinion."

"Then Granny Hall's hearing must be failing. I must get on. Good day."

Alice leaped ahead and gained Sears's store a respectable distance before the widow. Mrs. Sears stood behind the counter, in apparent confusion as to what to say to Alice; when the widow came she greeted her in an unaccustomed wave of spirit. Alice decided to try the previous exercise in reverse; she said to the widow, "Excuse me, I've picked up a stone," and stepped just outside the door to listen. Mrs. Sears at once commiserated with the widow over the problem of engaging honest help. Alice heard no sound from the widow whatever. But as they made their way home Alice found she couldn't in fairness argue with any of the ladies' assessments of her. The murder charge hadn't been proved, but it hadn't been disproved either. And as to honest help, how many times had Alice lied to the widow? Too many to remember.

SHIPMASTER HOPKINS CAME by in the afternoon, and the widow left off pulling the flax to take him inside for a cup of tea. Alice left off pulling flax as well and crept near the window to listen, thinking to discover another perception of events, but it appeared the shipmaster had no perception whatever. He'd not once suspected Alice's condition, but once he'd heard the charge he'd taken it for the fact as it was presented until he'd heard the jury's verdict, and there he'd taken her innocence as fact as well. He said "quite the surprise, quite the surprise" several times, and "Girl's come through all right, has she?" twice over, but in neither case did he wait for the widow to answer.

At the end of their first day back in Satucket, Alice felt she could say in fairness that the widow went to her bed more worn down from it than Alice.

SO THEY WENT on, Alice feeling the widow's fatigue as great as her own as she faced the villagers' talk, as if walking into a constant stiff wind. In the long months in gaol Alice hadn't pictured her return to the widow's home as requiring such stretching and straining; nor had she pictured the growing weight of obligation that caused her footsteps to drag across the room.

Nate didn't come. Alice heard of him only through the shipmaster, who had seen him at the tannery, where his father had put him back to work until he returned to the college in the fall. Nate had spoken rudely to his father, the shipmaster said, and had been soundly cuffed for it; the lad had been rude and sullen ever since to all.

FREEMAN RETURNED AT the first of August, bringing an oppressive damp heat with him and more of the great weight of obligation that already dragged at Alice, but debt aside, Suffolk aside, Alice discovered in herself the same pleasure at the sight of him that she'd experienced in the gaol at Barnstable. He seemed, again, to have forgiven her sins against him, treating her with the same kindness he'd shown her at Barnstable; it appeared to Alice that the smile he turned on the widow held nothing warmer than the one he reserved for her. Alice watched the widow closely for signs of her own pleasure at the sight of him, but if she felt it she kept it well tamped down.

The men of the village appeared more openly glad to see Free-man. They came as before and could barely wait to accost Freeman over the state of affairs at Boston, but they took time to stare at Alice as before. Or not as before. Alice read a new question in their looks now: innocent or guilty? She also saw the question was twofold; they would know if the death of her child had been murder or accident, and they would know if the act that had got the child had indeed been forced on her or engaged in with a free will.

Freeman collected his own share of new attention, Cobb giving him a quiet congratulation on a "fair job at Barnstable, sir," Winslow adding, "Good that's over, then," and Myrick summing up, "Lucky girl to have had *you*, sir," but they wasted little more time on it. All went back to politics, with Freeman reporting Otis's latest contention put about in town, reflecting the Otis of old, that no Englishman could be rightfully taxed without his own consent or the consent of those chosen by himself to represent him. To that the table cheered, and in the few seconds before she remembered Suffolk, Alice might have believed that the older, happier days had come back full circle.

To further prove it, as soon as the men dispersed and Alice and the widow had cleaned away the remains of the meal, Alice returned to her old position on the stairs. The talk began as it usually began, with Freeman reporting on his Boston trip, then moved to the state of affairs in the village, the weather, the crops, then back to Barnstable and some of Freeman's recent pleadings: a case of trespass, a broken covenant, an action for scandalous words, until at length Freeman said, as if it were the subject all along, "How does she fare?"

"Not poorly. Not well. She hears the talk. She worries over Suffolk. Is there a date?"

"The fourteenth of August."

"You continue confident of the outcome?"

"Unless this Verley has some unforeseen trick in mind, I've not the least doubt of it. No man can listen to her story unmoved. You saw them at Barnstable. But I confess to you my puzzlement at how little the outcome at Barnstable seemed to move *her*."

"I believe it takes her more now. It will take her more after Suffolk. You must consider what she's endured. What she yet fears."

"She's a brave child. If you'd but seen her those first days in gaol. And what it cost her to lay out her ordeal to me! I'll never forget how she looked at me as she spoke, her very life in her eyes. . . . I declare, I'd have seen those eyes in my sleep till I died if I'd let them hang her. Hang her! Can you imagine it, hanging such a girl?"

"You've seen it done, sir."

Silence. After a time Freeman said, "I've not told you something I should have told you before. The girl knows what goes between us. She made hint of it some time ago here at Satucket, but as it came to naught I saw no need to trouble you. She accosted me with it flat out at Barnstable."

"Did she!"

"She accused me of shaming you." A pause. "I'm afraid I didn't answer as I should have. It would appear old wounds lie fallow just waiting for the turn of the plow. I as much as admitted the situation by laying the blame on you for not agreeing to make our relation a lawful one."

More silence. Alice counted: one, two, three, four, five, before the widow said, "Perhaps 'tis just as well she knows. Considering."

"Yes. Well."

"After all, she's not likely to run about the village shouting it."

"You believe this village lies in ignorance?"

"They may suspect, but how can they accuse without some proof?"

"And what comprises proof in such situations? A rumor twice-told?"

Another pause. "Perhaps you'd prefer to take your old room at your brother Shubael's."

"This is your best suggestion?"

"You have a better one?"

"Indeed, I believe at one time I did have a better one. But no lawyer enjoys arguing the same point twice, least of all absent new evidence."

Silence again. Alice counted again, to three this time. "Were you to argue so now, it might appear you think of naught but Alice's tongue. Of course, were you not to argue so, it might appear you do so out of another kind of thought entirely."

A chair scraped. "You would have made a fine lawyer, Widow Berry. You box me completely. You leave me nothing to say but good night."

Alice heard no answering good night; she heard nothing but the scrape of another chair and the sound of doors opening and closing. She counted them: one, two.

inally, Nate came. When Freeman asked if he were prepared for his return to school he said, "I've not at all determined on going."

Freeman and the widow exchanged a look but made no remark,
and after a time Nate left, without a look at Alice, or at least not while
Alice dared look at him.

THE PLAN WAS settled between Freeman and Hopkins that the
party would travel to Boston by ship as soon as they could secure a
wind. The widow arranged with the Indian girl to tend the livestock;
Freeman rode about the village, settling his own affairs, collecting the
usual pouch of letters to be delivered to the various relations and com-
mercial connections in Boston. He also gathered the usual commis-
sions for this buckle or that book, but no one would have dared ask
him for a bolt of Irish lace or a barrel of West India molasses.

All the activity distressed Alice, for it meant she could no longer keep the line ahead of her fixed at a vague distance. As the new week broke upon her she found her stomach growing uncertain; she woke each morning with a tightness around the eyes that by nighttime ran from her temples into her neck and down through her shoulders. Her dreams were wild black things, with both the Verleys chasing through them; once in the dream Mr. Morton came and held Alice while Nabby fetched the poker, freshly heated from the fire. He said, "Take care, you don't burn yourself, daughter," whereupon Nabby raised the poker and brought it down on Alice's already scarred hand, somehow managing to turn the star into a moon. A circle.

THE WIDOW ORDERED Alice to sponge and air the same dress she'd worn at Barnstable, thinking it good luck for her. She helped Alice pack her few things into the widow's trunk; together they put up a chicken pie and some cheese and a pan of corn bread, cut and wrapped for the journey. Alice looked at her money pouch; to leave it meant her confident of her return; to take it meant she doubted. Alice emptied the shillings and pence onto her coverlet and counted: nineteen shillings eight pence, one pair of buffed shoes away from a pound. She would leave it.

But the water sat as becalmed as if a large, phantom hand pressed down on it. On the tenth of August Freeman and the widow began to form plans to set out by carriage. On the morning of the eleventh Alice got out of her bed and felt a fine, steady breeze coming through her open window. She dashed for the night jar and puked a vile, yellow acid into it.

Within the hour the shipmaster arrived, their trunks were loaded into his cart, and they were taken to the water; all had been rowed to the ship, and the crew stood ready to make sail when they were hallooed from shore. Alice peered over the rail with the rest of them and saw a pale-haired, slender form in gray breeches and bleached shirt waving a mustard-colored coat over his head. Nate. The longboat was again lowered and rowed to the beach; Nate threw a canvas bag into the boat and leaped after it; he was rowed to the ship and monkeyed himself up the ladder as neatly as any seaman. He'd been sent on business for his father, he said; he had a letter, which he waved at the shipmaster, at Freeman, at his grandmother. He didn't wave the letter at Alice, nor did he speak to her. Alice determined to pay him no attention, which was easy to do, as the ship itself engaged her entirely.

Alice had by now traveled twice by sea, but on neither journey had she been positioned to witness any of the ship's workings in detail. She stood transfixed by the change in the village men she had come to know as one kind of thing and now saw as something other. Idle bodies turned to a synchronized row of straining backs and pumping muscles; the wavering shipmaster turned into a barking mastiff. "Stand by to make sail! Ready on the throat! Ready on the peak! Haul away throat! Haul away peak!" The men rolled back their answering chant: "One, two, heave! One, two, heave!" with the fine rhythm of psalm singers. The mainsail jerked up the mast, whipped against the wind with the crack and rumble of distant thunder, and bellied out against the sky. The shipmaster cried out for headsails. "Trim! Ease away! Make fast!" The boat took on a gentle cant and flew over the rippled sea as smoothly as any osprey or gannet.

There Alice's own mood turned on her; she saw what a fair, fast journey it should be and could take no enjoyment in it. She could only wish a mightier wind that would force them to turn back, or a lesser one that would cause them to slow, anything but this fine, steady breeze that pushed them so effortlessly toward Suffolk.

The shipmaster had packed the hold full with barrels of salt cod, mackerel, flaxseed, corn, and rye. He had likewise packed the deck full with passengers. Besides Freeman, the widow, Nate Clarke, and Alice, he carried two Snows, four Crosbys, one Howe, and one Doane. Alice heard distant talk on deck of where each was going and what they were going for, but she didn't turn her ear to it, afraid of being drawn into a discussion of where she was bound. If the widow or Freeman wished to toss her business back and forth with the others they were free to do so, but if they did so, Alice didn't want to witness it.

They ate their first meal off the gently sloping table below-decks at noon; they ate their second near dusk. Alice took only a small lump of corn bread and a mug of beer at each, but she might have taken an entire pie for the length of time it took her to work it down.

They slept in the bunks in shifts, in their clothes, or rather Alice lay awake in her clothes, listening to the sounds of waves smacking wood, the half-whispered giggles of the two small Crosby boys, the full-throated snore of Mrs. Snow. Only an hour into her shift Alice gave it up and returned to the deck.

A slightly flattened moon had blossomed out of the dark shoreline while Alice had been below, and now it hovered just under the great triangle of stars, marking so bright a path over the water that Alice imagined she could climb atop the rail and step off onto the white road below. As she gazed at the moonlit water she thought of her mother and her brothers; she imagined a pair of wide child's eyes, the teary gleam of a mother's.

A voice said, "Alice."

Alice made a small, startled leap back from the rail, and Nate dropped a hand onto her back to steady her, then plucked it off, as if she'd burned him. He said, "I must talk to you."

Alice said, "You have business for your father in town?"

"I've no such business."

"But your letter—"

"'Tis written by myself to myself. If anyone had asked me to open it and failed to recognize my father's hand I'd have been put back to shore in an instant."

"I don't understand you."

He said, "Alice. I don't know the least thing to say to you. I can't sleep for thinking what happened to you. Good God! You told me not to touch you, and now I know the reason for it! To think on what you suffered! What *I* might have made you suffer!"

Somewhere a hatch thumped. Nate reached for Alice's arm but dropped his hand before it touched her. "Come," he whispered, and backed away from the rail toward the shadow of the after cabin. Alice followed. Nate sat down, leaning against the wall of the cabin, and after a minute Alice slid down near him. It seemed such a strange thing, sitting on the ship's deck in the dark beside Nate, that Alice missed the first words he said to her, but it seemed the second words were the key ones.

"I don't go back to school. I don't go back to Satucket. My father will be enraged to find me gone. I stay with a school friend in town until I find a boat for the eastward."

"The eastward!"

"I go to Pownalborough. 'Tis a fine place; trees one hundred feet high and seven feet thick through the middle. There's work at lumbering there for anyone with two strong arms. I go to live at Pownalborough."

Alice was silent. She hadn't thought of Nate as greatly connected to her life in any way, and yet the thought of him gone away unsettled her. After a time she said, "I've not heard of this Pownalborough."

"'Tis on the Kennebec, in the province of Maine. 'Tis no wilderness, Alice; it has a new courthouse, a fort, two mills—" He broke off. She could see nothing of him but a brown rectangular shape. "I don't like what Mr. Freeman does with you, Alice, marching you to court just because some justice orders him to. I don't like giving this Verley any kind of chance at you. Who knows what trick they'll spring at you? Who knows what will become of you?"

Alice could feel the beginnings of the old, torturing shakes again. Oh, she was so tired of shaking! She'd tried so hard to lay her trust in Freeman, to push August fourteenth away into the distance, and here Nate's words put her right back to the beginning. She leaned forward and hugged herself into a tight bundle to still her flesh, but it did nothing, until after a time she realized it wasn't just her own arms that contained her. Nate had put his arms around her too, caging her against him as gently as if she were a live pigeon. She thought to break away from him but then realized a wonderful thing: her shakes had begun to subside.

Alice stayed still, quiet. Nate stayed so. After a time Alice discovered that she could rest her head along his shoulder, just fitting it between his chin and collarbone, and so they sat, Nate's arms drawing more snuggly around her. A new calm settled into her. It felt like something she'd never known but always wanted; it felt like the thing she'd spent so many fretful nights in hunt for. After a little more time Alice discovered another thing: if she turned her head a quarter turn and tipped her chin to Nate he could move a very little himself and fit his mouth on her mouth. She discovered that she could take her mouth away and he would wait there for her to put it back again; she discovered he could take his mouth away, and if she didn't move, he would put it back again. Soon enough Nate formed his own ideas of where to put things, his hands sliding down her back, over her shoulders, his mouth finding her cheek, eyelid, temple. She remembered touching his cheek and mouth with her fingers and touched them again; in fact, she felt his next words with her fingers.

"Come with me, Alice. Come with me to Pownalborough."

Alice took her weight back from him and sat upright in surprise.

"You must! You must come! You can't count on some lawyer's trick to save you! We would have a fine life, a wonderful life, free of all of them!"

Alice wanted to laugh at how insane the idea was—a runaway sixteen-year-old boy trailing a runaway servant with him to some-place like Pownalborough. They wouldn't be in town a minute before they'd be accosted by the constable. This was Alice's first thought, but soon enough she thought of another: how much more insane was Nate than Alice? How different had her situation been when she'd run off from Verley? Indeed, how mad would it really be to go with him? To escape Suffolk and Verley, to escape all that had happened, to start over, free of all of them.

All of them.

Alice said, "Mr. Freeman's 'tricks' as you call them saved my life."

Nate's hands came up fast, one to grip her shoulder, the other to lay two fingers across her lips. A shape had risen up out of the com-panionway and into the moonlight: the widow, her hair come out of its pins and blowing out behind her like its own kind of sail.

She called, "Alice?"

Nate pressed his fingers harder to her lips, but Alice pushed his hand away and shrugged out of his grip. She stood up as soundlessly as she was able and moved along the rail, into the moonlight, until she came into the widow's line of vision.

"There you are! I'd begun to fear you'd gone over."

"I couldn't sleep."

"You take a bunk when offered at sea. You'll not get another."

"I'm sorry to have worried you. I didn't think you awake."

"I must confess I sleep poorly at sea myself. Though perhaps 'tisn't all the sea in this circumstance."

Alice said nothing.

The widow dropped her hand over Alice's on the rail. "All will be well, Alice."

"But how do you know it?" Alice cried. "You can't, you can't know it!"

"'Tisn't I alone who says it. Mr. Freeman assures me it will be so."

"And how can he know?"

"He knows the law. He knows the human heart. He knows your heart."

No, thought Alice. He couldn't know a thing she didn't know.

THIRTY-THREE

B oston rose up ahead of them with the late-summer sun, striking Alice as a grander thing than it had appeared in her childhood, perhaps because her memories of London had drifted so far and faint behind. But as they wound their way around the islands and up to the great long wharf Alice noted things that had certainly escaped her before, if they'd been there at all: the hulking British man-of-war anchored off the point; the row of warehouses like tall, multiwindowed dovecotes lining the far side of the wharf; the skeleton of a ship in dry-dock, waiting for rigging and sails before it could be set free; and so many carriages, carts, people, noise. *Mackerel! Oysters! Cod! Fresh in this morning!*

The ship itself carried its own noise: the beat of the sailors' shoes across the deck, the rattle of the block, the creak of mast and boom, the snap of stagnant sail being secured. Nate attempted to move close to Alice, but the widow and Freeman were likewise too close for anything like private speech. She read something like panic in his eye until she heard him speak with Freeman over where each planned to stay in town; there Nate winked at Alice. He would know where to find her.

People and barrels began to spill off the ship together, and Alice lost Nate. Freeman had moved ahead to secure a carriage, but before he could do so he was accosted by a tradesman, a man he appeared to know, who spoke to him long and feverishly, his arms waving in a westerly direction. After a time Freeman broke away from the man and hailed his carriage. The trunk was loaded, Alice and the widow were loaded, Freeman climbed in behind and gave his order to the driver: "School Street."

"School Street!" the widow cried.

"I must see Otis."

The carriage reeled into the knots of well-dressed and ill-dressed people, a greater knot of the latter than Alice had remembered from her last brief passage through town: a mix of workingmen and boys, apprentices, what seemed a great lot of sailors. She peered through the crowd for Nate but couldn't see him. The sun being low didn't help her, either blinding her or turning all she looked at into rusty shadows, reminding her of her long-ago struggle to make out her father's shape in the wagon as it drew away. Had it been this very street where she'd last seen him? Had she come again through another circle? Alice looked wildly around her. She saw boarded-up buildings, brand-new street signs on all the corners, new even since her flight the year before; she couldn't recognize her past here.

The carriage whirled down King Street, a wide, inviting avenue crowned in the distance by a stately brick building whose corner facades were decorated with the gold lion and unicorn of the royal crest. Freeman pointed. "The Town House."

The carriage swung past the Town House onto Corn Hill, then onto School Street. It stopped in front of an elegant house that somehow frightened Alice and seemed to give Freeman pause as well; he sat in the carriage and sent the driver up to the door. A Negro servant appeared and disappeared; the door blew back wide, and a great, looming giant of a man leaped down the steps toward the carriage.

A whale, Alice thought, looking at him, a suited and shod whale, but as the man drew closer and she saw his startling eyes she changed her mind. Not whale, but eagle.

"Freeman, by God," the man cried. "I'd have conjured you if I could! And Widow Berry!" He grasped the widow's hand, kissed it, and helped her down onto the cobbles. Freeman and Alice followed.

"I've just landed," Freeman said. "I ran into Edes at the wharf. He tells me there are plans."

"Plans! What good are plans when you put them in the hands of a mob? 'Tis all Sam Adams's doing, you may be sure of it. He's called out McIntosh and his Pope's Day gang. A mess of cudgel boys who wouldn't know a Stamp Act if it bit them. Add to them the bankrupt shipwrights and sailmakers and soap boilers and braziers with naught to do but look for someone to blame—"

"Edes spoke of a peaceable assembly."

"He may speak as he likes. When the pot boils the scum arises." Otis turned to the steps, still talking, eyes dancing wildly, as if struggling to follow his own thoughts. A woman appeared in the open door, as handsome a woman as Alice had yet encountered, but to Freeman's greeting, "Good day to you, Mrs. Otis," she lifted a silky hem and turned back into the darkness in silence.

Otis laughed. "She knows your politics, sir, and dislikes them as much as mine. Take heart that she denies you naught but her company at the tea table; for me, alas, my sacrifice extends to another piece of furniture entirely." He pointed up the stairs and laughed again. As he turned around his eye fell on Alice; fooled by the laugh, she was surprised to meet up with such grimness.

"So this is the girl?" he asked. "This is our famed Alice? I understand all, my friend. All and more. And now you come to town to wait on the court at Suffolk?"

"We do."

Otis came down a step until he stood on the same plane as Alice. "I see a scar on the cheek. How reads the law? 'If any man smite out the eye or tooth of his manservant or maidservant or otherwise maim or much disfigure him, unless it be by mere casualty, he shall let them go free from his service and have such further recompense as the Court shall allow him.' Would we call her 'much disfigured'? Not on any other cheek, perhaps, but on this one. . . . Is there any other marking?"

Freeman pointed to Alice's hand. Otis bent low. "Would you allow me, please, miss?"

Alice held out her hand, and Otis picked it up, as if he were to kiss it as he'd kissed the widow's. His hand felt warm and chill at once, as if heart and nerves had met together in the tips of his fingers. He turned Alice's hand over, flexed her palm as far as he could, extended each thumb and finger, took up the other one. "The scarred hand doesn't extend to quite the degree of the other; could we call it 'maimed'? Indeed, you might make the case. You might indeed make the case. The scars, the reduced efficiency . . . at any rate, 'twould be a thing worth testing."

Otis dropped Alice's hands, snapped upright. "And why do I keep you standing here in the damned street? Come in. Come in. Freeman, we've much to discuss, you and I. I hear talk they would put you up for the legislature. We need you there now, sir, above all others. We must argue reason over riot, a peaceable resistance over a bloodletting; I beg you, my friend, to join us."

He turned from Freeman to the widow. "And you, madam. 'Tis your skillful hands this province needs, not some bloody trampling feet of a Pope's Day gang. Let them keep to November and Guy Fawkes!

Or would they like to raise him from the dead now, and this time help the papists blow up Parliament?" He laughed again. They stepped into the hall, Freeman and Alice following, but as soon as Alice had planted her second foot inside the door an elderly woman in home-spun appeared, separated Alice from the others, and brought her to the kitchen.

The first thing Alice noted was that the political divide in the household stretched into the kitchen as well; the housekeeper sent a servant with a pot of real Bohea tea up the back stairs with the Negro while she carried another pot smelling strongly of sage to her master and his guests in the downstairs parlor. Alice followed the woman as far as the door, listening to the rise and fall of Otis's nervous, fiery voice: *Sam steps wrong with this one. . . . Degrades the cause . . . Talks independency . . . The madness of it . . . Lawless rabble . . . Bedlam . . . I fear it, sir. . . . I fear it. . . .*

If Freeman got a word in, Alice couldn't pick it out. She returned to the table and the cup of tea the woman had left her; she hadn't dared hope for and, in fact, barely yet believed what her nose had told her: Bohea. Alice sat and sipped and attempted to make some sense of what she'd heard. Here she was, at James Otis's kitchen table, the man she had heard so much talk of, the man who had stood up before the legislature and challenged the laws of Parliament, and what did he talk of now? Fear! Of a Pope's Day gang! A little parade of boyish mischief makers, or so they had always been at Dedham.

But now Alice could hear the low, steady rumble of Freeman's voice, almost like a lullaby, as if he were attempting to settle his friend to sleep. Otis's voice came back, softer now, and once or twice Alice heard the widow's clear note. Once she heard Otis's voice rise in wild laughter, break, and fade.

It seemed a long time before the servant reappeared and fetched Alice to the front hall, where the two men and the widow now stood before the door. Alice peered at Otis; the whale had disappeared, and so had the eagle. Alice had once seen a weasel suck the innards out of a hen's egg, and that was what Otis resembled now: not the weasel but the hollowed-out egg. He kissed the widow's hand again, mumbling an amputated, "Pleasure . . . too long," but even that rang empty.

Once they were under way in the carriage the widow attempted some banter about the non-importation plan implemented by Otis's wife, but Freeman would accept no diversion. He leaned silently into the corner of the carriage, his face well shadowed. After a time he burst out, "Did you know the governor once called Otis 'as wicked a man as lives'? Did you know he once said that the troubles in this country take their rise from and owe their continuance to that one man? Well, he'd best look now and see the friend he has in him!"

The widow exchanged a look with Alice. "I might understand Mr. Otis better than you do, Mr. Freeman," she said. "He believed his reasoned argument over the sugar would prevail, and not only did it not prevail, the stamps came. Next here comes Adams, with his gangs and his talk of independency, and poor Mr. Otis, who was happy enough to twist the cord, now stands back aghast at the idea of cutting it completely. He thinks, surely he must think, What will happen if we cut it? Will we end with Mr. Adams and his mob ruling the province? Will it all end in havoc?' And so he grows cautious. He thinks again. He contemplates which is the lesser evil: King George or King Adams. And I for one think such contemplation, while perhaps serving ego as much as politics, is to his credit. And our benefit. My grandson's benefit. I would see Nate someday standing before the justices engaged in educated argument, not lying dead on some bloody Boston cobblestones."

Freeman said nothing. The carriage reversed its route past the Town House and continued no great distance before stopping in front of a flat-faced, two-story brick house with no kind of sign to identify it. The driver removed the trunk and deposited it in front of the building; Freeman got out, paid the driver, and lifted the knocker on the door. A woman dressed in homespun pulled open the door and greeted them with a curtsey; Mr. Freeman called her Mrs. Hatch; she didn't appear to know the widow. She pointed Alice to the kitchen and led Freeman and the widow up the stairs.

The kitchen was bustling, or so it appeared, for the room was small for the number of people within it. A girl as black as a charred stump sat dressing a fowl; a young man in a tradesman's apron stood unwrapping a collection of pewter spoons from a flannel cloth and laying them on the table; a boy who looked to be about five worked at filling a kettle from a water bucket he could barely lift off the floor. The black girl saw Alice, wiped her hands on her apron, and walked to a small door at the back of the room, where she stood waiting. Alice followed. The girl led Alice into a small, windowless shed attached to the kitchen, pointing to the pallet along the far wall. "That you," she said, the accent of Africa still on her. "Sleep there."

Alice didn't want to sleep there. The shape of the room reminded her of her room at Verley's; the lack of windows, the pallet on the floor, reminded her of the Barnstable gaol. Alice took one step, two, until she reached the bed; she dropped her sack on it and backed up again to stand near the door.

She heard the widow's voice behind her. "I want the girl who came with us. What have you done with the girl who came with us?" The widow appeared in the shed door, looked around, and said, "You're to sleep with me. Roll up your pallet and come." Alice did as she was ordered, wondering as she did so who had given the order—the widow herself or the man who had stood surety to deliver her safe to the Suffolk courtroom.

The widow's room was neat and well enough fitted with a bed, a chest, a chair. The widow pointed to the floor on the far side of the bed, and Alice laid the pallet down. She looked out the window and saw the Town House steeple, along with a large swath of King Street below.

The widow pulled off her cap, dropped it onto the chest, and sat heavily on the bed. "I dislike travel," she said. "More and more with each addition to my years. Floundering about someone else's house. Unable to get a simple cup of tea when I wish it. Attempting to beat some life into a worn-out bed tick. Lying awake all night listening for a strange step on the stairs."

"You'll find no worn-out bed tick here," Freeman said from the open door. "And if you wish a cup of tea, you need only appear in the parlor downstairs. As to a strange step on the stairs, it will likely be mine. I'd a message waiting for me that Mr. Verley's lawyer should like to meet me upon my earliest convenience; I think I'd best seek him out now."

An odd deafness settled over Alice's ears; either that or utter silence fell at that moment over the room and the street below. After a time she heard the widow say, "Would you consider this invitation to bode well or ill?"

"I think well," Freeman said, but at the same time he gave Alice a look so full of gentleness that the words brought her no comfort; why should he think her in need of such a look now?

Freeman left them. The widow said, "Shall we see if the Hatch kitchen can brew up something less foul for tea than Otis's, or should you prefer to rest?"

A belated cowl of guilt dropped over Alice, one she hadn't felt while sipping the fine Bohea at Otis's. She said, "I'd prefer a rest, madam."

The widow left, and Alice returned to the window. Pockets of men idled about in the street below. Alice spied Freeman among them, distinctly tall and purposeful, the neatness of his queue and the whiteness of his stock standing out against his surroundings. As Alice watched he appeared to slow his step and turn his head left and right, as if to listen to the rumblings of the men as he passed through; whatever he heard seemed to stall him, for which Alice was glad, for she discovered she was loath to have him pass from her view. At length he picked up his original speed and rounded the corner by the Town House; Alice retreated from the window. She lay down on the pallet and closed her eyes, feeling it a promise to the widow to do so, but with no thought of sleep. She listened to the town noise, so different from the noise of Satucket: a steady drone of voices broken by the occasional shout, the rattle of the cart wheels, the whoosh of the carriages, the stray toll of bells. *I think well.* Or ill. She thought of the words Otis had quoted, apparently from some book of laws, or rather she thought of one word Otis had quoted: *free.* Of late the word had meant being set loose from the gaol, not being hanged. This *free* that Otis spoke of was another thing.

Alice heard the widow return, but she didn't open her eyes. After a time she heard a heavier boot on the stairs. She leaped up. The widow sat perched on the edge of her bed; Freeman came into the room and folded himself into the chair in silence.

"Speak, sir!" the widow cried. "Well or ill?"

Freeman lifted his eyes to Alice. What was it there, the old sadness, or a new? He said, "We must leave it to Alice to decide well or ill. It would appear Mr. Verley grows a conscience; either that or he grows nervous as he nears the hand of justice. He's offered to release you from his service, Alice, his pair of conditions being that you be returned to Mr. Morton to serve out the remainder of your time there and that we file no countersuit against him. Apparently your first master has long repented letting you go, and Mr. Verley now wishes to repay his original kindness by returning you to him. While admitting no ill treatment of you he nonetheless forfeits any time penalties on account of your running away, and this is perhaps the greatest advantage to the offer. In addition to serving out the two years remaining on your contract you must make up the one year that transpired during your absence, but this is to be expected as a matter of course; in the ordinary way of things the court could, in law, order seven times that in penalty for running away. And I'm sure you see the further advantages to the offer. You need not go before the court; you need not run the slightest risk of a return to Mr. Verley; in fact, you need not distress yourself by seeing Mr. Verley at all."

"But what of Verley?" the widow cried. "What punishment for Verley in this scheme?"

"Mr. Verley loses Alice's time."

"He loses her time! He loses her *time?*"

"We must think of it in practical terms. Had Alice sought recourse within the terms of the law, notifying the constable of the alleged abuse—"

"A constable who is no doubt Verley's brother or uncle or cousin. And what is this talk of 'alleged abuse'? Do you forget what you saw?"

"I speak only to a point of law. The abuse has not been proven and, indeed, it would be near impossible to do so to such degree as might justify a countersuit. We give nothing away there. In addition, although I've every confidence of successfully making Alice's present defense, there is nevertheless the risk of events unforeseen. Here is an alternative to risk, and as such it must be presented to Alice; it must be left to her to choose."

Alice said, "Mr. Otis made mention—"

"Yes, he did. And perhaps an Otis might turn a hangnail into a disfigurement, but I've no such confidence in my skill. 'Tis the rare case indeed where a master is ever charged with the crime of physical abuse against a servant without a witness present. The abuse may be evident, but how to prove it occurred at the master's hand?"

"And you call this justice," the widow said. "You sit before this child and call it by that name."

"My dear widow, you mustn't obscure the advantages for Alice in this offer of Mr. Verley's. She serves out her time in a place where she was well treated, by her own admission, and for three years only. At the end of that time Mr. Morton will free her and she may go out and earn a wage. With this plan Alice may avoid returning to court—"

"An advantage which grows on me each minute. Very well, Alice, you've heard Mr. Freeman describe Verley's magnificent offer of nothing, and as I imagine you've more sense than I, you'll see how it serves you. Now, then, what say you?"

Alice did see how it served her, and yet she sat blinking at the widow and Freeman, full of barely captive tears. She could wonder at her misery, at her foolishness. Little more than a year ago she'd wanted nothing better than to return to Mr. Morton. He hadn't helped her when she'd run to him, it was true, but neither had he harmed her, and if she thought back over the years she'd spent with him she could summon nothing but kind looks, honest care, attention beyond her deserts. In fact, her dream of a comfortable life for herself had never gone past finishing out her time and staying on with Mr. Morton at a wage. Where had that old idea of comfort gone? Had life with the widow taught her a better one? Had she been so great a fool as to take Freeman's words *The widow and I will take you home* as meaning they would keep her there? As she was naught but servant to Mr. Morton, so she was naught but servant to the widow and Freeman, with the added difference that her time wasn't theirs and never had been. Nor was it hers for three more years. And if she'd been so foolish as to spend a short minute taking Otis's fantasies as fact, Freeman had now made it clear she should no longer do so. So what were her choices? To work for a Morton or to face a Verley, to face a chance of being returned to Verley. What choice, then?

Alice turned to Freeman. "I'll go to Mr. Morton."

The widow stood up and walked out.

THIRTY-FOUR

The Negro girl served the widow and Freeman a good supper in the parlor below: pudding with berry sauce, toasted cheese and bread, pickles, and nuts. Alice saw the food as it left the kitchen where she sat at table, eating her bread and cheese alone; Mrs. Hatch and the boy had disappeared. As Alice ate and watched the Negro go back and forth she wondered about her; she wondered too about the Negro who had answered Otis's door. What might it feel like to be enslaved, not for a set number of years, but for life? If Otis's Negro had heard Otis use the word *free,* what could he possibly hope the word meant for him?

So intently was Alice's mind occupied that when Mrs. Hatch's Negro returned from one of her trips to the parlor and shouted, "You, there, what you do?" Alice started in her chair. But the Negro's eye was fixed on the back door. Alice whirled around. A mulatto boy stood hanging on to the back door latch and scowling, first at the Negro girl, then at Alice.

"You Alice Cole?"

Alice nodded, too surprised to give proper thought to whether she should admit to the name or no. The boy wouldn't come into the room but stood as he was and held out a paper toward her. Alice got up, took the paper, and unfolded it. She had expected it to be from Nate, but it wasn't his hand. That was Alice's first thought—that it wasn't Nate's hand—but her second thought took all else away as she realized whose hand it was. How odd, she thought, that she should know the hand she looked at better, despite the changes to it since she'd seen it scratched across a tablet at Mr. Morton's table.

Alice,
I must speak to you go with the boy I beg you don't doubt my intention it is for your good only.

A. Verley

Alice lifted her head to look at the boy, but he only waited to catch her eye before slipping back through the door. Alice read the note through once more. *A. Verley.* No longer the Nabby Morton of the brook, but the Abigail Verley of the poker, and yet there sat the hand of Nabby.

Go with the boy. Why should Alice go with him? What might Nabby want with her? Alice could think of nothing to her benefit. She could think only of the poker. But why such a note? Why now? For a minute Alice wondered if Nabby had made her own escape from Verley, and if she had, what she could want with Alice, how it could be for Alice's good only. Alice could think of no reason to go with the boy. And yet, however many times she might picture Nabby turning away from her, striking her, raising the poker to her, she couldn't lose the other pictures: the shared tears, the shared brook, the shared horse-chase, the shared pie.

And the poker.

Alice got up, dropped the note into the fire, and followed the boy's route out the door. The Negro girl watched her with little curiosity. What could it matter to her? Outside the door Alice saw no sign of the boy and felt something she might have counted as relief until she spied him stepping out of the shadow of the next building. Again without waiting for Alice he slipped into the alley beyond. Alice followed him. It seemed an ordinary alley, with the usual puddle of stinking water and heap of refuse; nothing could have belonged to it less than Nabby Verley, standing alone in a fine, plum-colored gown that had come from no one's house loom. She stepped forward.

Alice stepped back.

"You've no call to fear me, Alice," Nabby said. "I come only to give you warning."

"You come late, then."

Nabby took another step forward.

Alice took another back.

"You stupid girl," Nabby said. "You stupid, stupid girl! Do you think I snuck away from my husband's rooms just to give you a slap? Stand where you are, then, and make me scream across at you, but listen to what I say or suffer for it as your own chosen consequence."

Alice stayed as she was.

"All right, then. Hear what I tell you, Alice. My father isn't well. 'Tis a mortal ill laid on him. He'll not live the month."

"I'll pray for him, then."

Nabby stared at her. "My father deserves your prayers. Yours above all. But if you choose to take that tone you may keep them. I don't come for your prayers. I understand my husband has made an offer to keep your case out of the courtroom. This is why I come, to warn you not to accept this offer. Are you such a fool indeed that you don't understand what my father's illness means to your life circumstance?"

Alice considered. She said, "When your father dies my time will pass to your brother Elisha, at the westward."

Nabby blinked at her. "But, of course, you don't know about that, either. My brother and his wife and children were murdered in their beds by a pack of Indians unwilling to call the war over. 'Twas this news sent my father to his own bed, where the lung fever overtook him. Now do you see what my father's death means for you?"

Alice didn't. And then she did. "It means I shall be returned to your husband."

"So you're not stupid after all. In fact, I never thought you were, and certainly my father didn't. 'What a clever child! See how quick she smiles! See how bright her eye!' Yes, my husband is my father's heir, and if your lawyer agrees to my husband's proposal, you'll end up returned to him. You see how well he plans? This way he need not risk exposing himself to any embarrassing counterclaims you wish to lay on him in the courtroom. But don't think my husband forms this plan because you continue to bewitch him; he wants you back only to make you pay for running off from him. You may trust me in this, Alice; you see, I've come to know him better than I used to do. He will make you pay for running off from him."

Yes, Alice could believe that Nabby knew her husband something better now. She looked her over for signs of the kind of wear the man had given Alice but found nothing beyond a certain pinched look around the mouth, a hunch in her shoulders that hadn't been there before.

Nabby reached into her pocket and withdrew a small, rectangular pouch, lumpily rounded at the bottom. She extended her hand to Alice. "Take this. 'Tis a letter to my father's cousin, Mrs. Story, in New York, a mantua maker; she'll take you into her house and put you to work in her shop. The ship *Boston* is tied up at the long wharf; you'll find more than enough money in there for your passage and a bribe to the captain to ignore your lack of paper, but you must go now; they sail this tide." When Alice didn't reach for the pouch, Nabby shook it at her. "Take it! Now! Be gone! I must get back before I'm missed."

Be gone. Those same words, thrust at Alice a second time. What could it be but a sign? Alice stepped forward and opened her hand under the pouch; Nabby let go, and a pleasant weight dropped into Alice's palm. But despite Nabby's desire to be gone, she stood as she was, and Alice stood as she was, the silence expanding between them, as if in an effort to push them apart where their feet wouldn't. Alice didn't know what held Nabby there, but for her it seemed more words were owed. What words, though? Did a bag of money cancel a blow? Did an absent thanks cancel an absent apology? Did they indeed stand now with nothing owed?

Nabby stirred herself first. "You've aged in your year gone, I see it in you, Alice, and yet it only lights you more. I wonder if you even now understand the power of that light. I, who cannot love you; I who must go at once or risk all peace; here I stand, gazing at you as if at the last ember in the fire."

Alice said again, "I shall pray for your father," but not as she'd said it before, and Nabby dipped her head in quiet acknowledgment. She stepped around Alice and set off up the alley with the same quickness of step that Alice remembered, if not the same life; as Alice watched she tried to imagine what might come next for her. Surely the money in Alice's palm had been stolen somehow from Verley; just as surely he would miss it, but would he believe his wife possessed of enough courage to have stolen it herself? If he remembered the old Nabby, the one who had lain with him in her father's front room before their marriage contract had been signed and laughed about it later, perhaps he would believe it. Then what would he do?

Nabby disappeared around the corner. Alice loosed the strings that tied the pouch and upended it over her palm. Four pounds spilled into it. She closed her hands around the coins, unfolded the letter. It began *Honored Madam* and went on to describe Alice as honest and hard-working; it asked the woman to take Alice in as "a favor to the writer and a favor to yourself, for the girl will serve you well."

Mrs. Story. High Street. Alice took the happy-sounding names as a sign. She tried to picture New York, but she could see only the Pownalborough Nate had described: a new courthouse, a fort, mills. She thought of Nate and what it might mean that she'd not heard from him, whether he had changed his mind about urging Alice to come along. It didn't matter, of course; Alice couldn't risk a Pownalborough with a runaway sixteen-year-old boy; but what of a New York, another mistress, another job, another home far, far away from Verley?

Alice tried again to picture the streets of New York, but this time the streets of Boston thwarted her, or rather one particular street, the one she'd been knocked into on her arrival a year earlier. She saw the street as if she stood in it, and the man with the white handkerchief who had picked her up out of the mud, the woman with the scarred hands who had returned her basket to her. She thought back to what she had wondered about them when she'd first seen them and what she knew about them now; she pictured them discovering her absence and what they would say, how they would look. The widow angry. This face she knew. But what of Freeman? She saw Freeman's face filled with something worse than anger, something akin to the old hurt he'd shown over Otis's defection, or Parliament's ignoring all their carefully reasoned petitions.

Alice blinked hard to erase the image of Freeman's face, but the only thing that seemed to blot it was Verley—Verley beside her as they stood before the justices—which was what lay ahead of Alice, now that the Morton plan had gone awry. Alice clutched the hard, comforting edges of the coins, gripped the paper till it crumpled.

Mrs. Story. High Street. In New York she need not worry over Verley; in New York she need never see Verley again.

Alice walked to the end of the alley and stood, looking down King Street toward the wharf. She closed her eyes and gave her head a little shake to loose the image of Verley, but the image had stuck hard. As it would stick in New York. As it would stick in Satucket. But who had offered her Satucket? No one. New York was the offer now. She would be safe in New York. And yet thinking the word *safe,* Alice found herself looking the other way on King Street, toward the inn, toward the people waiting there. Toward one person waiting there. *You may trust me with Suffolk as you trusted me with Barnstable.*

Alice pushed Nabby's coins and letters back inside the pouch and pushed the pouch deep into her pocket. She turned right, toward the inn.

SHE FOUND THEM in the parlor, Freeman frowning over the newspaper, the widow turning the pages of an almanac, too fast, surely, to have caught more than the advertisements. Freeman's legs were so long that they canted up toward his knees before sloping down to the ground; a child could slide from his knee in either direction: to lap or floor. He looked up and saw Alice, but his frown barely eased; Alice was part of his troubles just now.

She stepped into the room. "I must speak with you, sir."

The widow looked up and set down her almanac; something about the gesture disturbed Alice. Did the widow think herself included in that 'sir'? Did she think herself entitled to share all with the man, including Alice's private conversation? A violent rush of emotion came at Alice unaware, streaking through her heart and out the other side, imbedding itself in her spleen. She wanted to be left alone with Freeman as she'd been left alone with him at Barnstable. She wanted the widow gone from there.

Alice turned her back to the widow and faced Freeman. She told Freeman most of it just as it had been: the Negro boy's message, the meeting with Nabby, Mr. Morton's illness, Verley's plan to get her back again. She didn't mention the money, or the letter, or the *Boston*, perhaps tied up at the long wharf yet, perhaps already sailed on the tide.

When she'd finished, Freeman peered at her in some puzzlement. "I looked into Morton's situation back in May. It appears I must do so again. We might consider Mrs. Verley to hold her own reasons for wishing you gone. We mustn't take her word as sworn."

There Alice experienced a second, surprising, violent surge in her emotions. She didn't care whether Nabby told the truth. She didn't care whether Mr. Morton was well or ill. She was tired of carrying Verley around inside her head through all her life. She looked at Freeman, making note of another small shift in his features that had turned puzzlement back to frown. Oh, how she knew that face now! *You may trust me with Suffolk as you trusted me with Barnstable.* She may. She could. She would. She said, "I'd prefer to go to court as we'd planned, sir. To settle it. For good and all."

Alice stood and waited for the shakes to come, but nothing happened. Something in the gaze Freeman fixed on her, as if he'd begun to form a new idea of her, made her feel wildly brave. Strong. Why, she had just made Verley do something against his will, and not the other way around! Verley hadn't wanted to go to court and now he must, because of something she had just said! She, Alice Cole!

Freeman continued to study Alice. After a time he gave her a brief nod. Alice didn't know that she could call it a nod of admiration, or even approval, but it was a regard of a new kind, and it was all. *All.*

She turned away to keep it frozen in her mind just as it was and climbed the stairs, leaving the pair to talk of her as they would below.

Once in the widow's room Alice went to the trunk and pulled out the sewing kit she'd packed in it the week before. She went to the window to capture the last of the light, pulled up the hem of her bodice, and picked it apart at the seam. She lay in the four pounds Nabby had given her, and sewed it closed. When she let the hem fall the thick seam concealed the coins well, but if she ran her hand down the cloth she could feel their shape, and that too made her feel strong. Four pounds. Her own.

THIRTY-FIVE

Alice woke on the morning of her second trial thinking an odd thought: how strange that a life such as hers should hold two such days in it. She tried to comfort herself with the thought of the next day, when all courts should be behind her, but as she couldn't settle into any certainty of where that day might find her, it didn't ease her. All the ease she could muster came from this odd, new strength in her, but in truth it ebbed and flowed as the morning crept on.

Freeman and the widow spent a good deal of that time in muted discussion behind Freeman's closed door. Alice didn't dare venture too far into the hall, and from where she stood she heard only the occasional heated rise in tone. From the widow: "Contingency!" as if repeating Freeman's word; from Freeman: "Practical—" and from the widow again: "Practical! Hah!" but then a falling-off. Alice gave it up and went back to her room.

When the door finally opened, Freeman went directly to the stairs, the widow to her room. She looked Alice over, brushed down the back of Alice's skirt, retied the ribbon that held her hair. She said, "Come," and herded Alice ahead of her down the stairs. Freeman stood outside the door, beside the carriage. He handed Alice in, squeezing her hand before releasing it. Alice took the squeeze as the same kind of sign the old look of gentleness had been. The widow climbed in beside Alice. The carriage had so short a trip to take that Alice held out little hope of any kind of disruption to the journey, and indeed, they arrived at the courthouse with such great speed that Freeman hadn't managed to complete his sentence to the widow about their plans to sail for Satucket on the morrow, assuming completion of his business.

His business: Alice.

They pulled up in front of the courthouse. Freeman helped Alice out and kept his hand on her elbow as he steered her through a high, wide door into a room that she didn't see, because Verley stood inside it. Alice had fixed it in her mind that she wouldn't look at Verley, and in that way she might pretend that he wasn't within reach of her, but in fact she did look, and what she saw amazed her: this man who had loomed as high and wide as a barn in her dreams didn't come up past Freeman's shoulder. Verley saw Alice and began the old smile, but before it had reached its limits it faltered. *She* made it falter. She, Alice, who hadn't been able to meet Verley's eye since their initial encounter at Medfield. And how could she not stare? So small he seemed! So coreless! And how could he not seem so, next to Freeman?

Soon enough Verley got his smile back, his brash eye back, his pushed-out chin back, but none of it worked the same on Alice, now that she had seen underneath; she could look at Verley now and see nothing but painted surface. So dazzling was this new idea for Alice that she could take in only the general shapes and colors of that second courtroom, making note of its differences—no jury, no crowd of spectators—sure proof of how dull the crime of running away must stand next to the crime of murder.

The charge was read, and Alice could not refute it: she had, indeed, run off from her lawful master, Emery Verley, with three years' time remaining on her contract. When the judge asked for Alice's plea Freeman could only answer, "Guilty, but with cause."

So Alice's second trial began. Verley's attorney stepped forth, a man as different from the Barnstable king's attorney as Verley was from Freeman, or so it seemed to Alice. The first part of his speech, describing Alice's crime of running away while under debt to a master who had "lawfully fed and clothed her and attended to her health in the most conscientious manner," could not have moved the justices greatly, but from there he grew warmer.

"I must now give you some idea of the character of this man, this Emery Verley, Your Honors; I must explain to you that he only took on this girl's indenture as an act of the purest love and kindness. The girl had reached an age—indeed, her old master, Mr. Verley's father-in-law, had reached an age—where the girl had proved too difficult for him to handle. And as Mr. Verley's wife still held an unreasonable attachment to the girl, fostered during her motherless childhood, Mr. Verley succumbed to her wishes and took over the girl's indenture. Her former unruliness was soon brought under control with the kind of firm and consistent treatment that had been missing at her previous master's, or so Mr. Verley was led to believe by what now appears to have been a most devious, deceitful plan to lull him to sleep in order to effect her escape at the first opportunity. Mr. Verley now asks only what the law allows him in such circumstance, and this is the return of the girl, with the addition of seven days for each day absent appended to her contract."

No witnesses were called. Verley's attorney rested there, as if in wait for the simple matter of the justices working the arithmetic. Alice hadn't been taught in the subject of mathematics, but she knew how to multiply one year absent into seven additional years on her contract. She knew the eternity of another kind of hell when she saw it.

Freeman stood up and addressed the justices, but in a different voice than he had used before the jury at Barnstable. He spoke quietly. Sadly. "Your Honors, we do not argue the fact before the court that Alice Cole unlawfully left her master. We argue that she left out of the greatest necessity, that necessity being the securing of her safety, and that only a fifteen-year-old girl's natural ignorance of the law sent her outside the purview of the legal process." There he began, again, to outline the abuses Alice had suffered at the hands of the Verleys. Freeman included in it the birth and death of Alice's infant, and at first this shocked Alice, that he would expose her to a second judgment on that count, but after a time she reconsidered. Surely the news of the trial at Barnstable would have traveled with her to Suffolk, and any omission now might appear an attempt at concealment. Indeed, Alice looked at Verley and saw no surprise in him at the news that a child of his had been born and died in the year since he'd last seen her.

Freeman called but one witness, the widow, who testified that she had employed Alice Cole on her immediate arrival in Satucket and witnessed bruises about the neck, a burned hand, a cut cheek, a torn shoulder. Verley's attorney asked, as the king's attorney had asked, if she had witnessed Alice receiving such injuries and could attest to the fact that they indeed came from Emery Verley. The widow answered only *no,* a lesson she'd perhaps learned from Shipmaster Hopkins. Freeman had perhaps learned a lesson too: he'd not brought the shipmaster with him.

When Freeman had finished, the chief justice took up and examined several papers that lay before him. He addressed Freeman. "You have no witnesses to this abuse at the hand of Mr. Verley?"

"Mrs. Verley was witness, Your Honor, although she declines to admit it. But although the law does not allow Alice Cole to speak in her own defense, you might consider allowing a brief examination of her person. It bears its own evidence."

The chief justice nodded. The sheriff drew open the gate on Alice's box and led her to the bench. Freeman picked up Alice's hand and first flexed then extended it, comparing it to the other, as Otis had done; he took her by the chin and turned her cheek for better viewing of the now-pale crescent. But as Freeman turned Alice's face his eye met hers, and it seemed to her that something changed in him. Or was she looking only at her own changed reflection?

Freeman dropped his hand from her chin. He said, "If I may quote to you from our colony's Body of Liberties, Your Honors: 'If a man smite out the eye or tooth of his manservant, or maid servants, or otherwise maim or disfigure him, unless it be by mere casualty, he shall let them go free from his service.' I respectfully request that the court consider the physical evidence before you, making note of the disfigurement as well as the reduced function, and declare Alice Cole a free person."

Alice stared at Freeman. He would free her! He would try this! She stood fixed in her spot as he continued to speak his piece, much like the one he gave at Barnstable in its content, but spoken in such quiet conviction it allowed no doubt of it. Oh, how could her trust in him have faltered? He would free her from Verley! He would free her altogether! *The widow and I will take you home.*

Alice was sent back to her box. The chief justice called on Verley's lawyer to rise. "What have you to say in answer to this countercharge, sir?"

"I say, Your Honor, that from the first word my colleague has spoken to his last, it is a fiction of the highest caliber. I must salute him. Why, I might even believe him! But my client of course refutes every claim. You have before you a deposition from Andrew Sherbourne, the Medfield smith's apprentice, although he was not at such leisure to travel as some others here, but you may read there that he lay with Alice Cole from soon after the time that she arrived at Medfield until the very night she convinced him to run off with her. He saw the error of his ways and returned at the first opportunity, but the girl wouldn't be persuaded. In fact, she attacked him so violently he was forced to cause some slight injury to her person to get free of her. 'Tis all in the paper, Your Honor."

And so the smith's apprentice was brought back to life. Another circle closed, like a shackle. Alice didn't know the smith's apprentice, but she couldn't imagine him possessing any interest in returning her to Verley; she could, however, imagine what threat might have been brought against him to coerce such a statement. Alice stared at Verley's lawyer as he lied in all his calmness, then looked up at the justices to see by their faces what they might make of it; she was surprised to discover that even as Verley's lawyer talked, the five pairs of eyes were fixed, not on Verley's lawyer, but on *her*, as if they would see what *she* made of it.

Alice must have lost track of some minutes, for the next thing she took in was the fact that Verley's lawyer had returned to his seat, and that the justices were filing out of the courtroom to a small chamber adjoining. In their absence no one spoke. If anyone looked at Alice she didn't know it, because she had fixed her eye on the homespun cloth that covered her legs. Her armor.

The justices didn't stay out long. When they had regained their seats the chief justice said, "Lydia Berry, will you approach the bar?"

The widow stood up and stepped forward.

The chief justice said, "You took this girl, Alice Cole, in your employ, once she'd run off from her master?"

"I didn't know her to be run off. I thought her time served. In truth, there was some trouble about a reference—"

"The court has not called you to the bar to account for your harboring of a fugitive. The court has called you to give testimony to the fact that she came to you direct from her previous employment."

"She did, Your Honor."

"And what account do you give of the girl since she came into your employ?"

"Why, she's worked for me at spinning and some weaving, doing various other domestic chores as I've needed them, all with industry and without complaint; I may say without reservation I'd not find a better girl if I looked over the continent."

"You paid her for this work?"

"Her keep and care and sixpence a day."

"For what period of time?"

"Just over a year."

The chief justice turned to Alice. "Has any harm been done to your person while under this woman's roof?"

"None, sir."

The chief justice said, "It is the judgment of the court that the defendant's plea of maiming and disfigurement is insufficient. Freedom is denied."

Freeman leaped up. "If you please, Your Honor—"

"Desist, sir. You do not prove your case. The girl shall serve out her remaining time. The court does not, however, grant Mr. Verley's claim that the act of running away extends her time to the additional seven years. She will serve the remaining three years on her contract and no longer."

Alice looked at the chief justice. A strange thing seemed to have happened: he had turned to Verley sitting there. Like Verley, he could do as he liked with her. Alice felt a hard, bitter anger sweep through her, that for a minute she could have put her faith in such a man, but with the anger came another thing, sprung from the wild courage she'd uncovered in herself the day before: the certainty that no matter what the court ordered she would not go back to Verley. She'd run away before and she would do so again. She'd find Nate and go with him to Pownalborough; she'd find another ship to New York and go to Mrs. Story; she'd set off on a new, strange road if she had to. And this time she had four pounds in the hem of her bodice to aid her.

But the chief justice had continued to speak. "Although the court does not find Alice Cole maimed or disfigured to the degree the law requires to award her her freedom, it does give considerable weight to the testimony presented here and the physical evidence of her person. If her present employer, Lydia Berry, wishes to pay Mr. Verley a sum of eight pounds against future time lost on his contract, the court will award her the remaining three years of Alice Cole's indenture."

"Eight pounds!" the widow cried.

The chief justice's head came up in surprise. "You will confine your remarks to a negative or affirmative, madam."

"You would give that man eight pounds for what he's done to her?"

"Madam, I issue you one more warning only. You will answer the court as you are directed, or you will be brought before it on your own charge."

Freeman said, "Your Honor, if I may speak with the witness."

The chief justice nodded. Freeman joined the widow at the bar and began to whisper. The widow whispered back, or attempted to whisper, but Alice could hear her plainly. *Not a bent pin.* Freeman whispered again, something louder, with a hint of impatience in it, out of which Alice could pick out her name, the word *value*, the word *save*, and near the end, the word *loan*. Out of the widow's answering whisper Alice heard only the word *crime*.

Freeman returned to his table.

The widow said, "Your Honors, I shall pay Emery Verley eight pounds in the interest of removing Alice Cole from such hell as she has suffered in his home. But I wish it marked down by your clerk that I would otherwise not compensate this man for his sins any more than I would compensate you for your own."

The chief justice leaned forward and spoke to the clerk, no doubt forbidding him to mark down any such thing. Verley turned and smiled at Alice, even said something to her, but Alice didn't trouble to listen. His words were nothing. He was nothing.

The widow and I will take you home.

THIRTY-SIX

By the time they exited the courthouse the late-day shadows had begun to descend; only then did Alice realize it was stifling and must have been, no doubt, since morning. She'd never in her life felt so run out of everything: strength, breath, understanding. If the carriage hadn't pulled up at once she might have sat down on the steps and slept the night there; she didn't know anymore how to work her feet or lungs or mouth or ears. She got into the carriage somehow; the widow climbed in and slumped across from her; Alice attempted to say the words *thank you*, but either said them twenty times or none. The widow babbled a string of words back at her, half enraged, half exuberant; the name Verley ran through them, but Alice no longer cared to give the subject of Verley any more of her than he'd already claimed; he might haunt her nights yet, but in daylight he was now erased from her slate like a misspelled word.

After a time Alice surfaced from her stupor to realize that the carriage hadn't moved and, in fact, Freeman wasn't in it; he stood on the courthouse steps, talking to a man who flung his arms about in agitation, first pointing in a southerly direction, then at the sky, and then to his neck. At length Freeman broke free and slid onto the seat next to Alice; Alice prepared another attempt at *thank you*, but before she could push it out Freeman called to the driver, "Hanover Square!"

"Hanover Square!" the widow cried.

"Did you not hear the man? They've got Oliver in effigy, hanging from a limb at Hanover. They've closed the shops, and a mob's gathered."

"Oliver?"

"Andrew Oliver, the new stamp agent. Our lieutenant governor's brother-in-law."

He turned to Alice, smiled. "Well, child—"

Alice opened her mouth to say her thanks and burst into tears. Laughter. Tears. She threw her arms around Freeman and laughed and cried, soaking his coat; he put an arm around her and patted her back, fumbling out his handkerchief, his white handkerchief; he wiped her face and his coat in turns.

"Now, now. Here, now. I did nothing, you know. You did it all by standing there. You and the widow. I only wish I'd been able to secure your freedom. . . . Here. Here, now." He removed his arm and plucked her hands from his neck as he'd done once before, but gentler now. He poked his handkerchief into her palm. He turned to the widow and began to talk of stamp agents. Effigies. Mobs.

Alice sank back against the seat, abruptly alone. She was so very tired, and yet she felt she might leap out of the carriage, run all the way to the wharf, and fly from the wharf to Satucket with only a lift of her arms. Oh, she understood well enough that she wasn't free as Otis and Freeman would call her free, but that had been their dream; her dream had been to get shed of Verley and return to Satucket, indentured or no. She wondered how the widow could afford eight pounds to give to Verley and then remembered one of the words Freeman had whispered to the widow: *loan*. He would loan the eight pounds, and the widow would pay it back out of the saved wage she no longer had to pay Alice. Alice did the sum and determined it shouldn't take more than a year for the widow to repay the loan; after that she wouldn't have to pay Alice until the remaining two years of her contract had run down. It would work to the widow's advantage; it could even be said to repay some of the debt Alice owed for her care and kindness. It could even be said that Alice could count herself freed twofold.

But oh, the slowness of the carriage! Oh, this Hanover Square, this effigy, this dawdling mob! Alice could see them as the carriage funneled from Marlborough Street into Newbury, pressing forward as they pressed forward, until they reached the crossing with Essex and Frog where the crowd spread out like a spilled pitcher of cream. The widow and Freeman leaned out of the carriage to get a better look; Alice stayed as she was until the widow pointed and cried, "There!"

Alice looked out. Ahead of them sat an enclosed green, sheltered by a pair of huge elms; from the branches of the largest tree hung a pair of grotesque forms, one in the shape of a man, the other in the shape of a boot with the figure of the devil rising from it.

"So they blame Lord Bute too," Freeman said.

The crowd shifted, closed in, tightened around the figures in the tree. Alice was forced to acknowledge that she'd never seen such a mob, two thousand at least, and being fed yet from all four corners of the crossroads: mariners, tradesmen, and some that looked more like gentlemen but with workmen's long breeches and leather aprons thrown on. This was no Dedham Pope's Day gang.

As Alice watched, the blade of a knife flashed in the sun above the effigy of Oliver, and the figure came tumbling down. A ready-made funeral bier was raised, the effigy laid on, the bier hoisted onto thick shoulders, and a procession began, the crowd falling in behind the bier in neat, solemn rows. Freeman ordered the carriage to follow.

"Where on earth do they plan to go?" the widow asked.

"The Town House, or so Griffin told me. The governor's council sits there now, discussing what action to take over these effigies, this mob."

The carriage crept along, the street ahead full of men and shadows of men, stretching too far now for Alice to see them all. As they neared King Street the procession slowed to a near standstill, and the carriage with it.

"Best to walk from here," Freeman said. He paid the driver, and they disembarked, Freeman taking each woman by an elbow and guiding them down Water Street onto Pudding Lane and so around to King. They stepped into King Street and moved toward the inn, but Freeman kept turning his head, looking behind, and so Alice looked too. The procession had come into King Street and now surrounded the Town House. The bier was lifted up before the windows of the council chamber, and three great *huzzahs* arose from the crowd; Alice felt it rumble in the ground under her feet like the pulse of a great beast with four thousand legs; she looked at the pale faces now lining the council chamber's windows and wondered if they felt it as she felt it, as if the power had drained from the building above into the street below.

Someone cried out "Oliver's stamp house!" And the cry moved through the mob. It surged down King Street toward them, no longer solemn, no longer in neat rows. Freeman stepped back into Pudding Lane, the widow with him, but Alice slipped her arm loose, stepping farther into King Street. She thought she'd seen Nate Clarke's brightly pale hair near the front of the crowd. She heard Freeman call behind her, "Alice!" She heard an answering call from up ahead, "Alice! Alice!" She looked back, but already the edges of the crowd had obscured her view of Freeman. She looked ahead and caught sight of Nate again, the pink face topped by damp hair, but there the crowd was on her, sucking her in like quicksand, dragging her away from Freeman. She watched Nate's shoulders beating back and forth like wings as he worked his way through the bodies toward her; Alice tried to stand her ground, ignoring the elbow here, the hip there, until Nate washed into her like a drift log on the crest of a wave—up in the air, down. He gripped her by both arms.

"Alice! What are you doing out here?"

"We've just come from the court!" she cried. "I'm free of him!" And so it seemed at that minute exactly why she was out there, why she'd loosed herself from Freeman and stepped into the street to find Nate, why Nate was there, why the whole crowd was there: Alice was free of him. Indeed, Nate grinned as if his cheeks would split. He picked her up into the air but set her down at once as the crowd surged. He caught her by the hand. "Keep fast!"

The crowd swept them down King Street, shrinking or growing at each crossroads as some of the better-dressed men drifted home and rougher ones joined in, men with axes, brickbats, clubs. The cry went round and round: "To Oliver's wharf! To the stamp house!"

The great beast moved into Kilby Street and onto the dock, surrounding a half-built brick warehouse. The axes and brickbats came out; the crowd surged again and began to attack the building. Once the first timbers came loose others picked them up and began to swing them; Alice felt the cool breeze against her sweaty palm as Nate dropped her hand and thrust himself into the mob to swing a timber of his own. Alice stood in amazement as within five minutes the warehouse was taken down to the ground.

The air lay thick with brick dust and the whoops of hot, sweat-slicked men. They swarmed over the pile of bricks, scavenging what pieces of wood they could find. Another cry went up: "To the fort hill!" The crowd surged again, the men shouldering as many timbers as they could carry.

Nate returned to Alice, collected her hand, and pulled her with him after the mob. The flush on him wasn't just from the heat, and there Alice understood that Nate hadn't been pulled into this scene by accident, that he was part of it, and unless Alice chose to fight her way through the strange streets alone she had no choice but to follow along.

The crowd streamed down the road and onto another whose sign proclaimed it Oliver Street; Alice didn't like the look of that name. The mob still carried the effigy of the stamp agent, lying on his funeral bier; did they hope to exchange the stuffed man for the real one? They rolled up to a fine, big house, neatly fenced, with well-laid-out gardens, and soon a play began, the effigy removed from the bier and beheaded while others picked up stones and hurled them through the house windows. Nate dropped Alice's hand a second time, picked up a stone, and hurled it; glass exploded and fell; he picked up another stone.

The crowd swarmed again, this time toward the top of the fort hill, and another pantomime began: the effigy stomped on, or "stamped" as the cry made it, the wood from the warehouse stomped on, a fire kindled out of the confiscated timbers, and the effigy tossed on. Torches sprang up against the growing darkness, and it seemed to Alice that with the dark the little order that remained now disappeared. The more respectable in the crowd had most all drifted away, but Nate did not; Alice dared not.

The mob swung back again in the direction of Oliver's house, looking for something more to burn; they tried to enter through the door, but it was bolted. Stones, brickbats, axes, came out a second time; any windows that had survived the stones didn't survive these weapons, nor did the doors, or the fence surrounding the garden. Some of the crowd began to chant for Oliver, but even the greatest fool on earth would have had fair warning to flee before now; all they managed to capture were chairs, tables, looking glasses, wainscoting, everything handed along a line of chanting men and fed into the fire on the hill. As the flames stabbed higher into the night sky it seemed to Alice that the power the crowd had captured at the Town House burned away with the flames. Who would heed the authors of such rashness, such violence, now? Nate had carried his own share of wood to the bonfire, but when he returned to Alice's side the flame in him seemed to have died down, as if a like thought struck him. Or was it the law that cooled him? He pointed. "The governor. With the sheriff."

As Nate recognized them so did the crowd, but unlike Nate, the sight of the law didn't give them pause. The stones still flew, but in a new direction now. Nate held a broken chair-back in his hands, but he loosed his fingers and let it slide to the ground. The governor made a brief attempt at speech but no doubt saw the futility of words against stones; he scrabbled away into the darkness with the sheriff behind.

Nate seemed in an instant run out, exhausted. He said, "Come," and took up her hand, led her down the hill. He smelled of sweat, smoke, rum—a different boy than the one she'd touched at Satucket. He cut into a narrow street without a street sign, and then another, and another. The houses thinned. They came to a low stone wall surrounding nothing but black space, and Nate helped Alice over it. Against the black Alice made out a distant house and barn, and nearer, what appeared to be an old carriage, sloping down in back over a broken axle.

Alice said, "I must get back. They'll be worried," but Nate had already climbed into the carriage, collapsing against the musty cushions. He said, "We have to talk, Alice. To plan for Pownalborough."

Alice hesitated. She had no idea of going to Pownalborough, but neither had she any idea where she was; nor did she care to face the dregs of the mob straggling homeward all across town; she needed the boy to take her back to the inn. She stepped up into the carriage and sat down.

Sweat. Smoke. Rum.

After a time Nate said, "I wonder what they would have done if they'd found him home."

Alice said, "I don't like to think. Nor do I like to think how I worry Mr. Freeman. He set me loose from Verley this day, and this is how I pay him. I must go."

Nate jerked around. "Oh, Alice! I forget! You're free now!"

"Not free altogether. The widow bought my time. I go back with them on the morrow."

"The ship for the Kennebec leaves on the morrow!"

"I must serve out the widow's time."

"You 'must'? There is no such 'must' now, Alice. A law, an indenture, none of it requires your obedience unless it speaks to a natural justice. When did you agree to slave your life away to fill another's pocket? What right has anyone to lay claim to what's yours unless you consent to it? It isn't the widow's time, it's your time. Come with me. You must come with me!"

He had worked himself back into the fire. Alice could feel his body heating up and dampening with sweat, and then a most strange thing happened. *He* began to tremble. He twisted toward her and put his arms around her, drawing her tight against him, as if, contrary to the evidence in his skin, he were cold and needed to draw some heat from her. Oh, Alice could know that need! She could know that trembling! She let her arms circle him, pressing her hands flat against his back, that back she had wondered about in Satucket, and found it just the perplexing mix of hard and smooth she had imagined. He stopped shivering. He found her face, turned it, kissed her. She smelled the rum and drew back. She didn't know this boy. She attempted to pull away, and after a brief tightening of his grip he released her without a struggle. He said, "Never in my life would I hurt you, Alice. You must know this."

I wonder what they would have done if they'd found him home. Very well, perhaps Alice did know this. He wouldn't have hurt that man, Andrew Oliver, and he wouldn't hurt her. She'd asked him not to touch her and he hadn't. She'd asked to be let go and he'd let her go. Which was all very fine, but it didn't erase the fact that she *must* go. Now. So Alice thought, but even as she thought it she was settling back against the cushion, Nate's arm was coming around her. She could feel his cheek against her forehead, his other arm coming around. She thought *How good this feels.*

Slowly, muscle by knotted muscle, her body gave over, her mind gave over; she let go of the long, long day and closed her eyes.

SHE WOKE THINKING herself behind the woodpile at Dedham, waiting for Mr. Morton's household to waken. She opened her eyes, saw her knees poking up under her skirt, and a pair of man's knees beside them. She leaped up and was out of the carriage before Nate had gotten his limbs in order, but he scrambled after her.

"I must go."

"No, Alice. *No.* Please. You see how the sky lightens? 'Tis so near morning now. If we go to my rooms and pack up my bag it will be time to go to the wharf. We can't risk going back to the inn for your things; we'll buy new when we get there. I'll have ten and six after our passage."

Ten shillings sixpence. To start a life on. Alice reached up and touched Nate's face, the whiskers a whole night older than the last time she'd touched them, rougher now. She said, "I don't go back because I 'must.' I consent to go back. He saved me from hanging. He freed me from Verley. If you knew how he took care of me at Barnstable—"

Nate drew back, looked at her. "*He?* Why is it always *he* you talk of?"

"And the widow. Of course I mean the widow too."

"No, Alice, I don't think you do. I think you mean him alone, and I think I know why you mean it. You said it to me that night I woke you at my grandmother's. You said to me, 'Mr. Freeman knows about night meetings.' It *was* Freeman, wasn't it? Freeman and you! Freeman's child! My father said so, all the town said so, they said why else would he work so hard for you for no pay? But I said no. And then I came to see you in gaol and there you were alone with him, and such looks as you gave him! But after the trial, after what he said happened to you, after what the widow said, I thought . . . why, I believed them! And now look at you!" He stepped close to her, gripped her face, turned it to the gaining light. It flamed, she knew it. He said, "Look at you! I knew it when he tried to chase me off that night; I knew it when I gave him the letter for you. I could see it in him as I see it in you now! All this 'I must go back'! You go back to Freeman is what you do!"

Alice thought to stop Nate, to tell him how wrong he'd got it, but instead she stopped herself. How wrong had he got it? The part about the child. This she must deny, for Freeman's sake if not her own, but after that . . . oh, after that! What wasn't true? The fact that Nate had said it out loud before Alice had even said it to herself made it no less true.

But Alice couldn't say that to Nate. She could only say what she owed.

"My master got my child on me before I came here. Mr. Freeman hasn't touched me."

Nate said, "You may trust in it, he will. Come, I'll take you back to him."

THIRTY-SEVEN

T he waterfront came awake as they walked, shutters creaking wide, cartwheels grinding over the stones, gulls starting up their disagreements over pilings. The town seemed altered since the events of the night before—sharper, more dangerous. *I wonder what they would have done if they'd found him home.*

Nate walked just ahead of Alice, not fast enough to lose her, not slow enough for her to catch him up. They turned onto King Street; Alice took an extra skip and caught him by the sleeve. "The inn's just there. You'd best go back now."

He didn't stop or speak; he swung around and broke off down the street at a run—the boy who'd torn to bits a stranger's warehouse and home, then held her in perfect stillness the whole night through. She watched him as far as the turn, thinking of the night of the frolick, of how she'd understood then that she might call him back or let him go as she willed; she wondered if she could call him back now. But to what purpose? He was bound for Pownalborough, Alice for Satucket. And yet she was taken by surprise at the lurch in her gut the minute she lost sight of him, as if he'd been erased from the earth; as if the earth had already shrunk in his absence.

Alice turned around and stepped into King Street. She thought of what Freeman might say when he saw her returned, what his face might look like. She thought of what might happen next. *The widow and I will take you home.* But what then? Freeman hadn't touched her, that was true. But was the thing Nate had said also true? *You may trust in it, he will.* Alice had roused Freeman's flesh once; she knew this because she'd felt it with her own fingers. And she suspected he might have removed his hands from her swollen breasts something faster than he'd managed to. There was that on the one side, and on the other side a shameless, stubborn woman, who, if she loved him at all, loved him less than she loved her house. And, even Freeman must admit this, she was growing old.

These were the thoughts that comforted Alice as she walked along King Street. She passed the Customs House, the Exchange Tavern, a pair of flat-front houses, a row of shops just opening. The inn sat ahead. The door swung open, and Freeman stepped out as if she'd willed him, but the widow came after him and stood in the open door. The widow, always! Alice stopped where she was and slid into the long morning shadow of the building next to her to watch and listen, as she'd done so many times before.

The widow said, "What time was it you checked Nate's lodging?"

"Midnight, or near to. The rioters had just disbanded."

"Best go back there first, then. We last saw her with him; he's our best clue. I'll wait here and send someone after you if she comes."

Freeman turned to check his watch with the aid of the new-slanting sun. The widow lifted a hand and rested it on the back of his coat, a gesture Alice recognized, or something like, as the one Freeman had used against the widow's closed bedroom door. Undesired, one of the marked passages out of Freeman's book of Shakespeare came back at her: *By my troth, my lord, I cannot tell what to think of it but she loves him with an enraged affection.*

Alice turned away, not thinking where to go as much as where not to go; she didn't want to go into the inn; she didn't want to see the widow so fresh from such a scene. *Could* the widow love him? No. *No.* Not as Alice could. Not as Alice did. Alice would never put a dower right above such a man. The widow didn't know how to love; she knew only how to humiliate and shame.

Alice had begun to walk, and without realizing it she had walked, again, toward the water; having no better plan at hand she continued all the way to the wharf and walked out onto it. She passed the *Betsey,* in the early stages of preparing for its departure for Satucket; she passed another ship, the *Anne,* with all the bustle on deck of a ship just arriving; she passed another ship, the *Doyle,* undergoing a similar but more advanced procedure to the one on the *Betsey.* She saw no ship called the *Boston,* although she hadn't expected to see it; according to Nabby it had sailed the day before. As Alice passed the *Doyle* she heard one of the crew make mention of Maine; was this the ship Nate would take to the Kennebec? He wouldn't have had time to get all the way to his rooms, pack his bag, and return to the wharf; if she lingered there she would no doubt meet up with him as he arrived. Would he argue again that she come with him, or was he done with her, having returned her, as he believed, to Freeman?

The passengers on the *Anne* began to disembark; Alice stood and watched them with no other purpose in mind than to see if she might find her seven-year-old self among them. A pair of aged men, a youthful couple, a middle-aged man alone, an older couple, another couple with two near-grown boys, all passed Alice without causing her to turn her head, but when a large family surged down the gangway toward her, making the usual kind of family clamor, it drew her attention.

Each parent held a small child in its arms, despite the woman's being heavily gone with another one; the two next smallest children were held fast in the whitened fingers of a pair of older siblings. As Alice watched, a sturdy, red-haired boy just into his men's pants broke loose of his sister and careened drunkenly down the ramp toward a seagull alighting on a piling. The bird saw its danger and left its perch, madly beating its wings to lift itself over the water out of the boy's reach; the boy's eyes followed it up and up, but his feet still pumped along below, unmindful of the dock's edge approaching.

Alice leaped. She scooped the boy into her arms and backed away from the dangerous edge, holding him as fast as she'd ever held a goose while plucking; the boy reared back to see who had captured him, and at the shock of the strange face he set in to bellow. Alice put him down but kept tight hold of his wrist until the mother could come up, the jouncing babe in the mother's arms already joined in the wailing. The mother thrust the babe at Alice and grabbed up the boy. "Thank you, thank you! Oh, Tully, you bad boy!" She smacked the seat of his breeches, which curiously made Tully leave off his wailing. The rest of the family circled around, the father taking his turn to chastise Tully and the sister who'd unleashed him.

Alice walked away from the commotion, jiggling the babe; she began to sing the old song of the bird on the cradle. To her amazement, the babe quieted. She turned toward the group and saw that the father had set the child he'd carried into the same little hands that had just let loose of Tully. Alice counted six children in all, not finely dressed but not poorly either, and as neat and clean as any sea voyage could leave them, which meant they all stood in need of some attention to their person.

The man came up and held out his arms for the babe. Alice handed it over. The child wasn't above a year, she guessed, but whether girl or boy she couldn't determine. The man said, "Thank you, indeed, miss.

I am indebted." He reached into his pocket, but his eye flew back to his wife and the boy she struggled to pin against her big belly, causing him to fumble the coin out of his pocket and into Alice's hand without looking. A sixpence, and no doubt more than he intended, but when he was able to glance down and see what he'd done he made no correction. Some coin to spare, then. He walked back to his family, his hand cupping the child's head in what appeared to be an oft-used gesture, so naturally did his fingers take the curve of the child's skull. As he neared the group he raised his voice in a more cheerful version of an ox driver's gee-haw. "Come along, now, come along! Only four blocks to home!"

Home.

Alice tried to imagine such a family's home but could only make out the widow's all over again. *The widow and I will take you home.* Again Alice pictured her return to Satucket and settling back into the widow's house, but again, she had some trouble with the image: the smiles that wouldn't meet all three together. The widow's and Freeman's, yes. Alice's and Freeman's, yes. The widow's and Alice's, yes. But all three together? Why wouldn't they go back as they'd been?

Because they weren't as they'd been.

Alice pictured herself at her wheel, watching more secret looks, watching more touches like the one she'd just walked away from outside the inn. She pictured herself watching and waiting and wishing for . . . what? For what Nate had promised would happen if she returned to them. For a man to do a thing that would make him no longer what she wished him. For misery to descend on a woman whose courage and kindness had brought Alice out of the greatest, blackest hole. For of course the widow loved Freeman. How could she not love such a one?

The father had tapped and prodded his children into formation. He drew back alongside his wife and took Tully from her arms, exchanging the burdensome boy for the lighter child, but even with that lessening of her load the woman needed a minute to steady herself before she set off.

There would be other Verleys in the world; Alice knew this. But surely there must be other Freemans, other Widow Berrys. The family set off down the wharf, past the *Betsey*, past the *Doyle*, toward King Street, where the gold unicorn and lion, the symbols of the English crown, gleamed atop the Town House. They reached King Street and turned left, into Kilby Street, past the red and gray pile that had once been stamp agent Oliver's warehouse. Alice followed them.

THIRTY-EIGHT

October 19, 1765

M r. Rufus Dolbeare and his brother Joseph blew into the keeping room with the wind, talking as they came. Mr. Rufus Dolbeare brushed the wet leaves off his boots and into the fire, making the fire hiss and sizzle; his brother dropped into the chair with a brief nod at Alice; neither gesture slowed their gabble. Alice handed her apple peeler to the oldest Dolbeare girl, Sukey, and got up to look into the cradle, thinking she'd heard the babe begin to fuss, but if it had, it had done so while it slept. Alice left the cradle, turned to the cupboard, took down a pair of mugs, and filled them from the beer barrel. October had come in cold and wet and stayed so; Alice might have preferred a cup of tea, but for the Dolbeare men it would be beer and nothing other.

Mr. Joseph Dolbeare accepted his mug from Alice and beamed at her like Tully when she soothed him with a piece of apple dipped in honey. Mr. Rufus Dolbeare came up to the cradle and leaned over. He had a soft, sad face that only lightened when he gazed at his wife, or, as now, when he looked on one of his children. He said, "How does it today?"

"Quite well, sir," which was to say the babe had got over its colick and slept so long that Alice had woken it twice to make sure it breathed yet.

Mr. Joseph Dolbeare had paused long enough for his brother to make his familial inquiry, but now he took up as he'd left it; all politics of course, as it was every evening. The August fourteenth actions of the Boston mob had been imitated up and down the coast, Rhode Island being the quickest to ignite with the hanging of effigies of its own, but New York, New Jersey, Connecticut, and New Hampshire had since followed the Boston example, not of the fourteenth of August but of the fifteenth, when they brought the stamp agent to the same tree where his effigy had hung, now called the Liberty Tree, and forced him to resign his office. The royal governor in the Massachusetts colony, along with the governors in the other colonies, had attempted to find other stamp agents willing to accept what now looked a most dangerous position, and failed in each instance.

The debate had now turned, as Otis had predicted, from points of law to points of battle; around the Dolbeares' fire Alice heard the talk of armed resistance, of independency. She also heard talk of Otis. He had been chosen to represent the colony in a Stamp Act congress, soon to meet in New York, the first such assembly of representatives from all the colonies. The significance of such a gathering was not taken lightly by the Dolbeares, nor, Alice imagined, would it be taken lightly by king or Parliament. Alice wondered if Otis feared it as much as he'd feared the mob; if so, he would have a fine dance to perform as one of its representatives.

The second oldest Dolbeare girl, Keziah, came rushing in from out-of-doors carrying a bird-spattered sheet that had been left out on the grass to dry, with a howling Tully stumbling behind her. Alice listened to Keziah's story of the troublesome boy and what appeared to be a justifiably angry goose, put a salve on Tully's pecked cheek, and collected the sheet for rewashing; there the babe did wake and needed changing of a dirty napkin. Next Mrs. Dolbeare came in with the two remaining boys, who were captured by their uncle and tossed in the air until the smallest puked up his dinner sausage. Alice mopped the floor and put the little boys to filling the kindling box, which meant as many sticks on the floor as in the box; when Alice finished sweeping up, Mrs. Dolbeare asked her to run to Dock Square for some honey for their supper.

The Dolbeares didn't live far from the square, but whenever Alice was sent on such an errand she took the slightly longer route past the water; despite the wind and chill the sight of it thrilled her as ever. As she walked she took in sea and sky and wharf and shops together; she wouldn't have said she looked with any particular purpose, or that she looked for one thing over another, until she spied the *Betsey.*

Alice had lived in Boston with the Dolbeares for two months and had walked at least six times to the market square and back as her employers requested; never had she seen a ship from Satucket village or a passenger who might have recognized her. The *Betsey* sat tied up along one of the smaller wharves used for long-term berthing; Alice recognized the neat box of its stern, the sweet lift of its bow, the bright trim; she might almost have said she recognized the smell of Satucket on her. She walked slowly toward the wharf and past, but she saw no one about the ship at all, its sails tightly furled and the deck cleared of any cargo. She turned and walked back the other way toward the Dock Square, stopping again as she came even with the *Betsey.*

Alice had thought often of the people she had left behind at Satucket; in truth, her sleep was chopped to bits with them. It had happened so fast, her decision to follow the Dolbeares, and from there it had happened even faster. Mrs. Dolbeare had stopped and started more than once in her walk down the wharf, the burden of even the smallest child too much for her in her condition; Alice had caught up and offered to carry the child until they reached their destination. To the natural inquiry of her own destination Alice had been able to answer in honesty that she looked for work, and there removed Nabby's letter from her pocket, adding the smallest of white lies about the sudden death of the Mrs. Story mentioned in the letter. Before they'd completed a block Sukey had managed to pick up a nail in her shoe, and John to lose his hat; Alice removed the nail and recovered the hat, all with the babe on her hip; somewhere over the next few blocks it became understood that Alice would keep with them until Mrs. Dolbeare had come through her travail. A few days later Mrs. Dolbeare delivered the colicky infant, but then spent two weeks in her bed with afterpains and delirium. By the time Mrs. Dolbeare returned to her kitchen Alice had fitted herself so essentially into the household that no one had yet raised the subject of her leaving.

Soon after settling in at the Dolbeares' Alice had begged pen and paper of Mr. Dolbeare and written the widow a letter. She told the widow she was safe and that she would remain until her death ever grateful for all the many kindnesses the widow and Freeman had bestowed. She began the next sentence: *The reasons for my leaving,* but cross-hatched over the words, incapable of sorting her thoughts and laying them down; she would have liked to write the letter over but didn't want to ask Mr. Dolbeare for another costly piece of paper. She ended by wishing the widow well, and promising to send her the eight pounds as soon as she could save it. She'd contemplated sending the four pounds she'd received from Nabby, which still hung safe and heavy in the hem of her bodice, but felt too little confidence in the security of her position to risk it. Alice signed the letter, *With the greatest esteem and the humblest yet most whole-hearted affection, Alice Cole.* She put no return address on it.

Mr. Dolbeare had reported to Alice that he'd put the letter safe on a ship bound for Barnstable; Alice asked the name of the ship and was told it was the *Hannah*, a name Alice didn't know.

But here, two months later, sat the *Betsey*. Alice continued to stand, staring at the ship, and after a time she saw life: the old, familiar, square-built shape of the shipmaster, moving with steadiness but no great nimbleness along the rail to the bow, where he began to knock at something with a mallet. Alice remembered her first sight of him on the same deck more than a year ago; she remembered his kindness in overlooking her stolen passage, his willingness to testify at her first trial. She remembered too his question to the widow on her return from the trial at Barnstable. *Girl's come through all right, has she?* Who else in all the village had asked such a question? She wouldn't count it against him that he'd never waited for an answer.

Alice stepped onto the dock, approached the *Betsey*. No welcoming gangway stretched from wharf to deck, but the tide had dropped and the ship's rail sat near level with the dock's surface. Alice made no effort to step down onto the ship uninvited; she waited, and after a time the shipmaster straightened his bent back, swung wide, and saw her. Oh, all the things Alice had learned by now to read in faces! Or was it just this particular face, opening and emptying all its secrets in its first glance at her? Alice could read them off as she could read the ads in Mr. Dolbeare's almanac: surprise, confusion, amazement, concern, and then, yes, gladness. Over it all he was glad to see her.

"Why, 'tis Alice!"

"Good day, sir."

He took a long study of her, from hair ribbon to shoes, then held out a hand to help her across the gap of water, over the rail, down onto the deck of the *Betsey*.

"Why, I must say you're looking well! So well indeed! And I daresay there's some I know who'll be happy to hear it!"

Would they? Alice didn't think she'd said it out loud, but it was all she wished to know on this earth: *would they?* She must have spoken, of course, or else Shubael wasn't the man of little perception she'd once believed him.

But there his face changed into something more like a shipmaster's. "You've caused unhappiness, young lady," he said, "and a good deal of worry, to those I hold dear to me. To those who don't deserve it, I might add, and from you especially."

"I'm greatly sorry for—"

"You needn't say it to me."

Alice stood silent.

"And you owe someone some time, as I understand it."

Alice nodded.

"So here lies the question: should I or should I not truss you up, toss you back in that locker, and haul you home to Satucket?"

That quickly Alice smelled it, not just the imagined whiff off the sails but the real thing, as if she stood that minute in the widow's dooryard: salt flats, pine pitch, fresh-cut hay, the juice off the cider presses. But so too could she smell something more cloying, almost rank: all the bad will she must surely have left there.

Alice turned her back on the shipmaster, picked up the hem of her bodice, and opened the seam with her teeth. She drew out Nabby's four pounds, whirled around, and held them out to the shipmaster. "If you would give this to the widow, sir. 'Tis but half I owe, but if you would tell her, please, the rest will come as I earn it."

The shipmaster stared at her in amazement. "You stole eight pounds from her on top of it?"

"No! Oh, no! Mr. Freeman loaned it to her, so she could buy my time from my old master."

Which meant, of course, that she had stolen it.

The shipmaster said, " 'Tis my brother's eight pounds, then?"

Alice nodded.

The shipmaster stood looking down at the money, no doubt thinking how many more pounds it could be said Alice owed his brother. But when he looked at Alice again something seemed to have amused him. He said, "Might as well pay himself, then," and funneled the coins into his pocket. He studied Alice some more. "I must say, you look in health."

"I am, sir. And yourself?"

"No worse, no better."

"And the widow and Mr. Freeman. Are they well?"

"The widow! Hah! Never better! And my brother a year younger each time I see him!" He stood looking at Alice some more. "Which brings me to the question of whether or no I should shut you up in that locker. Considering all things together, I might let you go, on one condition only. You must tell me where you reside and something of your situation; while you're about it you might throw in where you came by four pounds sterling to toss about like bread crumbs."

Alice told him. He made no remark about her shortened version of the four pounds but said, "This Dolbeare doesn't mind your lack of paper?"

"He believes me to be free." But there Alice thought: Did he? Or had he, like Freeman, sensed her status, and unlike Freeman, felt free to take advantage? Mr. Dolbeare paid her two pence a day beyond her keep and care, something far short of her wage at the widow's.

There the shipmaster seemed to run out of questions and no doubt stood waiting for Alice to go, so he could return to his mallet, but Alice couldn't bear to leave without asking the rest of her questions. She said, "Would you tell me, sir, if the widow continues with her textile manufacture?"

The shipmaster snorted. "She does. Her changed circumstance

doesn't change her. Her granddaughter Bethiah does her spinning now."

The granddaughter Bethiah. The impish girl who had hung so on her brother.

Her brother.

Dared she ask it? "I wonder, sir, if anyone hears news of Nate Clarke."

"Why, yes indeed. I delivered his grandmother a letter from the college not a week ago."

"From the college?"

"He sent a letter for his father too, but that one wasn't quite so well received. A slight overrun in the matter of expenses."

"At the college?"

"He'd damaged one of my brother's books and wished to replace it. The choice of book didn't please his father overmuch, either."

No, thought Alice, it wouldn't—a book that no doubt preached a higher law than that of a father. Or a parliament.

But Nate, at the college!

The shipmaster shifted his weight and looked at the sky; Alice realized she'd stood there dumb for too long. She said her good-bye and left the wharf with her mind in a storm, returning to the square to make her purchase, or she must have done, for when she arrived at the Dolbeares' she carried the pot of honey.

Mr. Dolbeare stood alone in the yard, peering up at the rolling gray clouds. "The wind shifts," he said. "I believe we'll have some fine weather on the morrow. They've been cooped up too long; I've a mind to hook up the cart and take them appling at my brother's orchard. What say you to that, Alice?"

Alice could remember only another day of appling, the sudden feel of life in her womb, her crumbling under the weight of it. Ever since that day the sight of apples had brought her stomach to her throat and her pulse to her temples. Perhaps she could claim an even greater illness and stay home. That course settled in her mind, she said, "I think it a fine idea, sir."

"A fine idea, if I do say. We must take advantage of the last of the weather. I'll propose it at once to Mrs. Dolbeare."

They went inside together. Mrs. Dolbeare was in her room, standing before an overstuffed workbasket, sorting piles of children's clothes by greatest need of repair. Mr. Dolbeare went in to speak with her, and Alice returned to the kitchen. She lined up Sukey to help prepare the supper and left Keziah in charge of the others, so the next Tully crisis, a shoe dropped "somehow" into the soap barrel, didn't surprise her.

The Dolbeares reappeared, and supper was laid down; then came the clearing up and the putting to bed of six children, not counting the infant in its cradle, who slept yet with its mother. Alice herded them up the stairs and helped those who needed it out of their shoes, stockings, dresses, and breeches; she settled them under their blankets in their shifts, two to a bed, dealt with a scuffle over a bolster, and left them to their children's dreams.

When Alice got back downstairs Freeman sat before the fire, talking with Mr. Dolbeare.

He sat just as he'd always sat at the widow's, back reclined, hips forward, knees up, wrists dangling from the chair arms; he wore the crimson coat the widow had made from the yarn Alice had spun, and the shoe buckles Alice had polished many times over; sitting there in the Dolbeares' chair he looked a stranger.

Mr. Dolbeare got up. He said, "A pleasure to meet you, sir. I hope we shall continue this acquaintance." Freeman stood and shook Mr. Dolbeare's hand; Mr. Dolbeare disappeared into the front room; Freeman turned to Alice. He pointed to the opposite chair, and Alice sank into it. Freeman returned to his seat and studied Alice; she felt as nervous as she'd felt standing before ten judges in two courtrooms.

He said, "Well. Here you are."

"I'm greatly sorry, sir, for—"

He closed his eyes, lifted a hand, waved it in the air. With his eyes closed Alice noticed the line of his jaw: clamped down hard. He opened his eyes. "I might understand why you ran off better than you think, Alice. I might also understand why Mr. Dolbeare would be most sorry to lose you, as he's just declared. But I would hear it from you, if you don't mind. Are you content here?"

Alice nodded.

"Treated well? Unharmed?"

"Yes, sir."

He studied her. "You understand I'm within the law if I take you back to Satucket?"

Alice's heart began to leap randomly about, as if it weren't sure where it belonged. "I do, sir."

"You needn't worry, Alice, I've no intention of carting you back there. I've made inquiry of this Dolbeare and I find him to be a man of good repute. I spent some time in converse with both him and his wife; I think you well enough situated here. In fact, I prepared the necessary paper this afternoon, in case things should prove out to my satisfaction." He reached in his pocket and removed a folded paper: a new indenture, taking her away from the widow and putting her to Dolbeare. Alice unfolded it, glanced at her name at the top and Freeman's signature below without troubling to read in between; she'd memorized three indentures by now and well knew the wording. But as she looked at Freeman's signature on the bottom she grew puzzled.

She said, "Mustn't the widow sign it, sir?"

"The widow? No."

"But the Suffolk judge bound me out to her."

"Indeed so, but your time passed to me at our marriage, in accordance with the law."

Alice didn't understand. She didn't understand at all. And then, of course, she understood it very well.

The widow and Freeman were married.

Alice looked away from Freeman, and back, and away, blushing like Nate. Worse than Nate.

Freeman said quietly, "I thought my brother Shubael to have told you. No doubt he's not used to it himself. It was done in something of a hurry, trying to get it in before the Act came down."

Alice was only too glad to be offered another subject to fix on. She said, "The Act, sir?"

"After the Stamp Act takes effect the first of November no contract will be legal without the king's stamp, which makes for an odd problem, as there are no stamp agents to sell them. The widow and I joined in the great rush with the rest of the village; we've been at wedding parties this past week from sunup to sundown." Freeman smiled. The smile sprang across his face like a jackrabbit, except that once a jackrabbit springs, it's gone. So this was the strangeness in him: not Dolbeare's chair but his new marriage, and this springy smile that he'd been at pains to tamp down.

Alice said, "God's blessing on you both, sir."

"Thank you, Alice." Even quieter now. As if he knew. He stood. "As my name has been put up for the legislature I'll be in town a good deal now; you may reach me through Mrs. Hatch if you find yourself in need in any way."

"Thank you, sir."

"And a letter to Barnstable or Satucket will always find us."

Satucket.

Alice said, "Will you tell me, sir, what happens to the widow's house now?"

"I bought it from her son-in-law. She retains her dower right, with title in trust to her grandson Nate."

Trust. Alice knew the meaning of the word only as she'd come to understand it thus far. She said, "But she travels back and forth to Barnstable with you now?"

"She travels as she pleases."

Yes, thought Alice, she would do.

They fell silent. It seemed to Alice that Freeman peered at her long, straining against the fire shadows, as if he would memorize her face. Or was that how Alice looked at him? After a time he took a step forward, lifted a hand, touched her under her chin. "Good-bye, child. I wish you well." He turned for the door.

Alice cried, "Sir!"

He paused, turned again.

She said, "I wish to say—" But what did she wish to say? Oh, how much she wished to say! She lifted the paper, but again he waved a hand, dismissing her words. " 'Tis as it should be." He continued to the door, his hand brushing the corner of the table as he went, leaving a flash of something behind.

He bowed.

Gone.

Alice stood and stared at the door he'd slipped through, the floor he'd trod, the paper she held yet in her hand. A drop of water fell on the parchment and she shook it off, slapping the wet off her cheeks. She pushed the paper into her pocket, banked the fire, crossed to the table to collect a candle, and looked down at the shining lump Freeman had left behind: the four pounds she'd given the shipmaster for the widow. Who was now Mrs. Freeman. Which made it Freeman's money now, loan or no. *Might as well pay himself, then.*

Alice put the coins in her pocket and retreated with the candle to her little room off the keeping room. She set the candle on the table along with the paper and stood staring at the black panes of glass, trying to sort out all the things she felt: stricken, heartsore, alone. But after a time Alice was forced to add another word to the list: curious.

What had changed the widow's mind about marrying Freeman? Had it been Alice, her talk of shame, repeated to the widow by Freeman? No. Without the face to examine, the words to overhear, Alice could only guess at the cause of so great a change, but somehow she couldn't think the cause the widow's sudden awakening to shame. Nor could she credit the rush to get in ahead of the Stamp Act alone, unless, in fact, the widow had intended to marry Freeman all along and had just been waiting for him to "argue the same point" for some time now. But no, Alice couldn't picture the widow sitting in wait either. She could picture her sitting and weighing, however, the scale finally tipping to the other side. But what would tip it? The promise of a dower right returned? The promise of a trust in her grandson's name?

There Alice thought of the other news Freeman had dropped on her in so offhand a way: his name being put up for legislature. A man thinking of serving as representative couldn't afford rumor of a whore at Satucket. *Who chooseth me must give and hazard all he hath* sounded fine enough on the pages of a book, but who gave what? Who hazarded what? Perhaps the widow weighed the value of Freeman's voice in the legislature over the importance of her own independence. Perhaps she thought of all those who might end up dead on some bloody Boston cobblestones, as she'd put it. Perhaps she thought of her grandson Nate.

Nate. Not at Pownalborough as she'd imagined him, but at Harvard College. Was he too like Otis, ready to twist the cord but not to cut it? Had he thought another thing about those "lawyers' tricks" and made his peace with the profession? Or did he plan to study the law in order to alter it?

The law. What a changing thing it was! One day it made Alice answer to a Morton, the next a Verley, the next a Widow Berry, and the next, unbeknownst to her, a Freeman. The thought that she had belonged to Freeman for even a few days unsettled her, that he, like the others, could have bought and sold her. Had, indeed, sold her. And for how much? Had he gained back his eight pounds? Was that why he'd left her four on the table?

Alice dropped her eyes to the paper Freeman had given her and tipped it to the candle.

In the fifth year of His Majesty King George III's reign this nineteenth day of October: Be it known that Alice Cole formerly of Satucket in the county of Barnstable and now of Boston County of Suffolk has served in full the terms of her indenture and is as of this date a free person entitled to travel and engage in commerce and make contract in the manner of any other free person. Signed this date by: Ebenezer Freeman, Esq.

In the presence of:

Shubael Hopkins
Clarke Winslow

Alice read the paper four times. After the fourth reading she folded it, rose from the table, and picked up her workbasket. Under the bodice she needed to rehem and the cap she was knitting for the new infant lay the cloth pouch, which now held the money she had earned at the Dolbeares'. She opened the pouch, and dropped Nabby's four pounds in, listening to the sweet click, feeling the happy weight of it. She laid her freedom paper in the bottom of the basket, put the money pouch on top, next her sewing kit, and last the cap and bodice. She snuffed the candle, hung up her skirt, took off her shoes and stockings, and slid between the linens.

A free person. Alice couldn't take the meaning of it. Could it be true that she was bound to no one now? That she might be ruled, as the judge had told the jury at her first trial, by her own good sense and understanding? Or, as Freeman had said to Nate, by her own conscience? *'Tis as it should be.* But oh, how strange it felt! How frightening!

The rain began to spit hard against the panes of glass beside Alice's bedstead. She thought of the family's trip to Mr. Joseph Dolbeare's orchard. She considered what illness she might give herself that would convince the Dolbeares to leave her to her bed, and then a new thought struck her: she didn't need to feign sickness if she didn't wish to go to the orchard. She was free now. She might do as she wished. She might quit the Dolbeares without fear and go to New York, or Philadelphia, or even Pownalborough if she chose it!

Alice tried to loosen her mind, to let it choose its own path, but it flew around willy-nilly among all the new things she'd learned that day from the shipmaster and Freeman. She imagined the widow and Freeman coming out of the one room in the morning, their faces open and secret together, like children with a new toy, not yet willing to share it. *The widow! Hah! Never better!* Yes, Alice might imagine it. And she could speak for Freeman's state herself, having seen that jackrabbit smile in him and something beyond the smile, a new air of peace in him. Yes, she could imagine them. So too could she imagine the granddaughter Bethiah at Alice's place in the corner, the widow's marriage no doubt removing the father's objection to his children's presence there. Nate might also visit as he wished now, when he wasn't at Cambridge.

Alice imagined Nate at Cambridge, leaning over one of Freeman's books, nodding yes over this page, no over that. She imagined Freeman not far off, alongside Otis in the legislature, their voices doubling and quadrupling as they argued reason over riot, a peaceable resistance over a bloodletting, as Otis had put it. Would they win their argument? Yes, they would; Alice felt sure of it.

After a time, as Alice ran over the images in her mind, she came to feel a new thing in herself. Oh, she felt chewed yet, torn yet, but below the raw edges she could feel one smooth one that she hoped would grow in time into something like the peace that she'd witnessed in Freeman. For indeed, all of it was, as Freeman had said, as it should be. She had seen into the hearts and minds of these people and knew for herself it was how it should be.

But where was Alice in it?

Alice heard an odd thump above. She leaped to her feet, gripped the candle, and took to the stairs, her free hand pulling at the rail to hurry her upward. The six children lay much as she'd left them, hunched into odd question marks and parentheses under their blankets, all quiet, all asleep. Alice pushed in one rump that protruded over the bed frame and pulled up another's blanket. She stood a minute and listened for any more thumps; the wind, she decided, picking up and knocking a hemlock branch into the roof. She turned for the stairs but paused, turned back, reached out, and touched the nearest red head, which so happened to be Tully's. She thought of her dead infant. Had she smothered it? Suddenly, there in the Dolbeares' attics, it seemed an old, tired story. It seemed another girl. Another Alice.

Alice went downstairs. Behind the Dolbeares' bedroom door she could hear the up-and-down of voices: Mr. Dolbeare telling Mrs. Dolbeare all about his meeting with Freeman. Alice began to cross the room to listen, but halfway there she stopped. It wasn't the workings of other people's hearts she needed to discover now; it was the workings of her own.

Alice returned to her room and climbed between the sheets. Her bed at the Dolbeares', so near the keeping room chimney, was much warmer than her bed in the widow's attics. Through the closed window she could hear the rain, the wind, the distant roar of the water;

in finer weather, with the window open, she could smell its salt, tainted with the other town smells, but salt yet.

Tomorrow, Alice thought, she might write the widow a letter, a better letter than the last had been. She knew some of what she might say but not all; the rest must come as she discovered it. Why, she might write to Nate too, if she wished it, now that she knew he was back at the college! She knew well enough what she would say there: That she'd been freed of her indenture. That her time *was* her own. That she was no one's slave. Perhaps the writing down of the words would make them feel real. Of course Nate might not wish to get any letter of hers, but if Alice wanted to write down the words she could write them; Nate could answer or not, as he wished it. Yes, Alice decided, tomorrow she would write to the widow. Perhaps to Nate. She would have the time, once the family left for the orchard, while she stayed behind with her feigned illness.

But there a curious thing happened; for a minute Alice couldn't remember why she'd planned to feign an illness. For a minute she forgot about that other day, that other orchard. She imagined the Dolbeare children spilling out of the cart into the fine day that Mr. Dolbeare had predicted; she imagined herself spilling out with them; she imagined the children running, laughing, Alice running after them, the sun warm on her skin, the grass cool on her ankles. Perhaps it was time for another orchard. Perhaps it was time for Alice to make another story for herself.

Alice rolled away from the slashing rain, pulling the blanket over her ears. Would it clear? Yes, it would; she was sure of it. She closed her eyes. She slept.

HISTORICAL NOTE

The first "slaves" brought to America were in fact white indentured servants; when chattel slaves from Africa arrived, they worked side by side with white indentured servants in similar working conditions. The first indentured servants arrived in Massachusetts in 1620 aboard the *Mayflower*; soon afterward Massachusetts legalized chattel slavery, the first colony to do so, and the word *servant* was frequently used to describe both chattel slave and indentured servant, but the distinction was a significant one. The master of an indentured servant owned that servant's labor for a restricted period of time, usually in exchange for payment of a debt or in exchange for training or education; the master of a chattel slave owned the slave's person for life. Within the period of an indentured servant's bondage, however, his "time" could be freely bought, sold, or traded.

The indentured servant held certain advantages over the chattel slave, including the limited time of service, the right to own property, and, because an actual contract existed, better protection via the courts. But to the indentured servant's disadvantage was the fact that his master often worked him harder and fed him less than he did a slave, especially near the end of the indenture, having no long-term investment in keeping his "property" in working order.

In the case of the indentured servant who voluntarily immigrated to America, his debt was usually incurred in exchange for his passage money, sometimes fraudulently inflated with extra charges to insure that on his arrival in America he carried a hefty financial obligation that would require extended years of work. Some indentured servants were forcibly immigrated to America: convicts, prisoners of war, or poor or orphaned children spirited off the city streets and essentially sold into a slavery that would not terminate until their adulthood.

But not all indentured servants were immigrants. An American-born young male might be put under contract to a tradesman by his parents in order to learn that trade or receive an education; on Cape Cod where Christian missionaries had a marked effect, an Indian or mulatto girl might be bound out by her parents "to learn the English Bible" in exchange for her labor. In fact, children could be bound out by their parents, or by the town fathers if they deemed their care inadequate at home. In the latter case, Massachusetts law declared that the selectmen or overseers of the poor, with the assent of two justices of the peace, could bind out any child seven years of age whose parents should be thought "unable to maintain them," males until the age of twenty-one, females until the age of eighteen. Provision was made for the education of such children: males were to be taught to read and write; females were to be taught to read as they "may be capable." The selectmen were themselves bound by law to inquire from time to time after the welfare of any child they bound out and to "endeavor to defend them from any Wrongs or Injuries." The law further stated that any "servants that have served diligently and faithfully to the benefit of their masters seven years, shall not be sent away empty." In Massachusetts, the standard for not being sent away empty was a gift of two suits of clothes.

An indentured servant could not marry without his or her master's permission; any misbehavior on the part of an indentured servant, such as running away, fornicating, or bearing a child, legitimate or otherwise, would allow the master to add to the servant's contract for the time missed. A runaway might receive an additional seven days for each day absent. A pregnant woman might receive an additional year to make up for her diminished productivity during pregnancy and child care, as well as a "fine" of added time for the act of fornication.

Estimates indicate that through the middle of the eighteenth century between 150 and 250 foreign-born indentured servants arrived in the port of Boston each year. During the revolution the influx of immigrants fell off and the practice began to die out, at least for a time; according to twenty-first-century reports, the recruitment and exploitation of indentured workers is now on the rise. In fact, according to John Berger, CEO of The Emancipation Network, an organization whose mission is to end human trafficking by promoting economic self-sufficiency for survivors and at-risk groups, there are more people living today in indentured servitude, or debt bondage, than in any time in history, it being one of the most common forms of slavery worldwide, including in the United States. Currently, there are an estimated twenty-seven million people living in slavery.